I0556112

THE COUNTERFEIT LADY

SONS OF THE SPY LORD
BOOK FOUR

ALINA K. FIELD

HAVENLOCK PRESS

Copyright © 2018 Mary J. Kozlowski

ISBN No. 978-1-944-063122

Havenlock Press

PO Box 1891

La Mirada, CA 90637-1891

Cover Design by Dar Albert of Wicked Smart Designs

Image Credits: Period Images

For Jim

Vowing she'll never submit to an arranged marriage, an earl's daughter bolts for the remote seaside cottage that should be hers upon marriage.

But instead of a quiet respite from her controlling family, she finds her refuge occupied by the last man she ever wants to see again—an American artist, who's also a thief.

And quite possibly one of her father's spies.

1

GORSE COTTAGE

THE YORKSHIRE COAST, 1821

*L*ady Perpetua Everly rattled the latch in frustration, and sat back on her heels.

Given the state of her half boots, that was probably a mistake. She shifted herself upright, fought her tight stays for a breath, and rolled the picks between her fingers.

By all the stars, she *would* conquer this lock. She would get this door opened and then she would close it again on the world outside. No one would know she was here. Not the people in the nearby village, nor the Riding Officer and the free-traders he chased, not even the local squire, Sir Richard Fenwick.

The cold flagstone soaked through her layers of skirts, crimping her knees and sending a moist chill into her marrow. When her grasp on the narrow picks slipped yet again, she tore off her wet kid gloves and willed her fingers to cease their trembling.

Jenny had laced her far too tightly that morning for any sort of calming breath.

Blast it. She could do this. She had learned how to manage a lock the same way she'd done everything—carefully, while no one was looking, using her intellect. During one of her brother's construction sprees to make the country estate and the London townhouse secure against yet another of Father's enemies, she'd stolen a new lock from a pile of them. It had been a day and a night of faked ague before she'd conquered that mechanism and returned it, to the relief of the servant charged with the inventory.

Jenny bent for the discarded gloves and hovered nearer. "It's a shame your spectacles broke. Shall I have a go at it, my lady?"

Perry squeezed her eyes shut. The rough road had rattled her glasses right off her face, but no matter. Only a few people knew she didn't truly need the spectacles, and Jenny wasn't one of them. Wearing them was her small act of defiance, and here, in her own home, she wouldn't need them. There'd be no one here to defend herself against. She could be her true self.

If she could but work the dratted lock. "You're in my light, Jenny."

The maid shuffled aside. "Such as it is on this gloomy day, miss."

This lock was not the newest sort, but neither was it ancient. Someone—her brother, Viscount Bakeley, her father, the Earl of Shaldon, or the family steward, someone —had included this unused, unknown property on the Shaldon maintenance list. The deed called this a cottage, yet it sprawled on the side of a cliff and had a plethora of windows and at least two outbuildings.

With a few more delicate jiggles and careful clicks, the

lock shifted, sending a warm elation that made her want to whoop. She tilted her chin and beamed at the maid.

"Good on, my lady." Jenny still whispered. "I couldn't have done it as well meself." She grinned. "*My*self."

Jenny had learned many skills in her rookery years, proper English not being one of them, nor proper limits on lacing a corset.

Never mind. Her other abilities made her a perfect companion for this journey.

The drops of comfortable drizzle that had beset them on the trip turned fat and impossibly wetter. Jenny's bonnet was limp and her gown clinging, as must be her own.

A cascade of louder crashes on the other side of the house made the girl tense.

"That's only the waves," Perry said. "Don't worry. You saw when we came up the cliff road how high we are."

High. Very high. As the plodding horse had struggled pulling their cart, the mist below had shimmied and shifted, revealing the sharp points below, Neptune's daggers, welcoming errant travelers.

At the narrowest point of the cliff road, she'd had to stop the cart and get out just to be able to take a proper breath. Whether the cause of her inability to breathe was the height or the tight lacing, she couldn't be sure.

Had that been the spot of her mother's accident? The road was so treacherous that every bend and every tight corner might lure a carriage over the side, perhaps even a rider.

Jenny had discovered a fear of heights. After that, there was no returning to their seats in the cart. The remaining few furlongs of slick coastal road, the only access to the cottage that dodged the village of Clampton, had stretched impossibly high, interminably long. Perry had taken the

3

halter of the hired plodder pulling the cart and untied Chestnut for Jenny to lead, warning her against showing fear to the horses, reminding her that the surefooted mare would not take her over the side.

Now Jenny was shivering again. Afraid of heights, and horses, and the sea, was this saucy girl.

"Stop shaking, Jenny, and don't be a nodcock. The waves can't reach us up here." Perry got to her feet. "We should get inside and light a fire. There's a storm coming in."

"Storm's here already, my lady." The words rattled through chattering teeth. "I wonder, will there be coal?"

Coal? She hadn't thought of fuel. Whether the estate's steward kept this house fully provisioned was an open question. Perhaps along with their soggy basket of food and the feed for the horses, she should have hauled up some wood on the cart she'd obtained from the inn where they'd stopped for the night.

She certainly didn't wish to visit Clampton and make her presence here known.

She shook off the worry and tried to sound cheery. "We'll throw a chair on the grate if we must." The latch opened easily and the slightest of nudges swung the door wide. No squeaking, no creaking. Well-oiled and well-maintained, like everything in the Earl of Shaldon's empire.

The air inside wafted to her, her corset cutting off her sharp intake of breath.

She glanced at Jenny and put a finger to her lips. All was dark inside, and no movement caught her eye.

Perry squeezed her eyes and inhaled again, ignoring the stabbing at her chest. No odors of cooking.

Lamp oil, she decided, and a burned-out fire, smells that might have lingered from a recent visit by the maids who

4

serviced this property. Bakeley had such arrangements for all of the family estates.

She eased in another breath and another odor came to her. Her eyes shot open and anxiety rushed in.

She stood perfectly still and beat the alarm down to a rumble of unease. She had lived around men all her life—her brothers, her footmen, her grooms, her father's spies and soldiers, all of them mostly well-washed and well-laundered. But even so...

Very likely, a man was here, or had been here recently. And there was another scent, one that poked deeper than the damned stays. She squeezed her eyes tight.

Turpentine.

Fox yielded his watching place to the rain and, out of sheer force of habit, closed the kitchen door noiselessly. No boat would come close to these rocks in this weather, especially not the curricle that had been dodging in and out of the cloud cover in his scope.

He set the instrument on the rough kitchen table, tore off his neck cloth and wet coats, and pulled at the shirt sticking like a second layer of skin. Then he went to stir the embers in the wide hearth.

This hearth would accommodate the angles of a Benjamin Thompson design, but the lady had failed to install the Massachusetts-born inventor's modern cooking stove. Still, the room otherwise bore her stamp—fine pots and dishes graced well-built shelves, and a collection of ornamental rolling pins decorated all the walls. It was a fine place for a cook to work, and for a man to think.

And in his case, a fire, a strong drink, and some thinking time were in order. This waiting while his wound healed had been fruitless and boring. He was no closer to finding his quarry than on his arrival weeks earlier.

His fine brushes, however, had acquired their own frenzied life. One he couldn't control. Like the stack of canvas in his rented rooms in town, his work here was more evidence of a pointless obsession; pointless and mad. He found last night's bottle, raised it to his lips, and drained the last swallow of brandy.

He swirled the bottle. Never mind. His room on the top floor held a case of full bottles next to the spare canvases and paints he'd hauled up and stashed near the yawning windows. The brandy was partial payment; the brushes and paints were his cover from his real task. Both were also his escape from the tedium of this mission.

God's blood, when this job was over he was going home to New England to take up the land his brother had promised him. The English could find a new artist to paint their lords and ladies.

Cool air touched his cheek, sending a prickle through him. He set the bottle down carefully.

There were no leaks or cracks in this tight seaside cottage, not on any of the four floors, and certainly not on this servants' floor, walled as it was on one side by the hard rock of the cliff. *She* would not have allowed it. Nor would she have returned for a visit. The only spirits he believed in came out of a bottle.

At the open door that led to the stairway, he paused to listen. The quietest of footfalls. The swishing of skirts. A hushed feminine voice.

He ground his teeth as irritation spiked through him. A woman was here, and no lady would be out in this weather to visit a single man.

There was however that damned Scruggs' girl at the inn.

She'd pillowed her big breasts into his shoulder whilst serving his dinner there his first night in the neighborhood, and blast it, every time he stopped in for a pint, she flirted without shame. Scruggs always sent one of his boys with bread and supplies. If the fool girl was here, she'd come on her own, likely expecting a few coins for a tumble.

Unless...He had no specific reason to think Scruggs was spying on him, no reason to distrust Scruggs—nor any reason to trust him. Scruggs had been the innkeeper here on his last visit, ten years past, and *she'd* trusted him.

And then she'd died. Something to think about—loyalties could be bought.

Muffled, furtive steps crossed the front hall to the tall windows that looked out on the sea.

He'd locked all the doors, and none of the locals had a key. His presence here was known to the villagers in Clampton, purposefully known.

If this was someone else, he'd not be snatched up like a worm on a hook. No matter that, as far as he knew, the fish he was after had not come close to shore yet.

Whoever this was had picked her way in.

He patted his sleeve over the sheathed blade strapped to his arm.

PERRY STOOD AT THE MULLIONED FRENCH DOORS LOOKING out over a narrow-tiled terrace. In the distance, a boat, as tiny as a beetle on the top of a pond, bobbed on a sea that roiled like her heart. Next to her, Jenny's mouth had dropped open.

"Are you wondering what you've got yourself into?" Perry whispered.

"You did promise an adventure, miss." She put the tip of

one gloved finger on the pristine window. "But I'll not go out there on any boat, no matter."

Perry grinned through trembling lips. Nor would she, if she could help it.

"No? In for a penny, in for a pound." She took a breath and another fragrance came to her, the scent of her mother's preserved rooms at Cransdall. Her father had not bothered looking for a new countess to occupy them, thank God.

"It's spotless. They must have a girl come up from the village to clean," Jenny whispered and pointed. "Except for the mess over there."

Empty dishes and a glass rested on a pretty oval table. Nearby, a dark shawl, much like the ones her mother had favored, draped over the back of a sofa.

Perry stood taller. "The house is not let. No one should be here but me. I have a right."

"But no key, miss?" Jenny arched a brow.

The sound of a footstep drew their gaze to the drawing room door. A man stood in the shadow, tall, with dark hair longer than what was fashionable. Dim light caught the white of his linens. He was naked of coats.

The clacking in her chest beat all the way to her ears. Inside her pocket was a pistol, not primed, not cocked, and no doubt far too wet to fire.

He stepped through the door, into the gray light from the windows, and her heart all but stopped.

Fox was here. Fox, the artist. Fox, the scoundrel. Fox, the thief.

2

A FOX IN THE HOUSE

"*L*ady Perpetua." The patiently condescending tone might have come from Bakeley. That tone had dogged her through all of her growing up years.

Fox's hands went to his hips. He had a laborer's hands, too wide and too strong for a man wielding a dainty paint brush. The movement stretched the almost sheer cloth of his shirt over a chest equally too wide and too strong, while damp, dark locks dangled over his forehead and dripped over the scruff on his cheek,

Warmth uncurled in her chest, as if she were fourteen again.

She fought down the madness and dipped her head slightly. "Mr. Fox."

The curl of his lip sent a quiver through her.

Damn. Damn, damn, damn. Years ago, she had followed him around like a bird-witted puppy—no, a foal, he had called her, on account of her height and her long skinny legs.

He'd seen them, when she'd fallen out of a tree spying on him.

Her face glowed hotly. The memory had mustered a blush.

She lifted her chin. "What the devil are you doing in my house?"

He blinked and went still. "Your house?"

"Yes."

Fox stirred and moved closer.

She crossed her arms over her chest. He matched the move, looking her up and down and glancing at Jenny. His mouth quirked at one corner and his eyes softened.

A smile being pushed down—she'd seen that look so many times. He was holding back from laughing. One didn't laugh at the daughter of the countess who was one's patroness.

He'd actually said those words to her once.

"I repeat—"

"There's no need to repeat yourself, Lady Perpetua. I heard you the first time. I'm painting."

That familiar accent, so flat and American, still jarred her.

He'd been painting in London when she'd stumbled across a landscape in a stationer's window. Surprised to find him in London, still painting, still alive, she'd discovered his lodgings and commissioned a chalk design for the ballroom floor at Bakeley's wedding celebration.

And then he'd appeared at that ball and danced with her, more than once.

She shook off the memory. Why was he here? Was he here at Father's behest? Or...was he spying on the Earl of Shaldon?

"Since I am here, Mr. Fox, you must leave." He must, mustn't he?

Or…if she sent him away, would he go straight to Father and report her?

He waved a hand. "In this weather?"

"You are already wet."

"As are you." His gaze moved to her bosom in a way that made her hot again.

Irritating man. He was just like all the rest. "You must go back to your room at the inn, or wherever you are staying."

A smile lit his face and her annoyance spiked. Most assuredly he was not taking her seriously. Which no one ever did.

"I expect this rain will go through the night." He moved closer, extending a hand. "Come, Lady Perpetua. I assume you've brought a carriage? I'll help you unload, we'll get the horses to shelter, and then we can talk. Why should the animals suffer?"

The horses.

Heat rushed her again. Of course, there were no grooms here to dash out and see to the horses. He'd poked her in a sensitive spot.

She ignored his hand and brushed past him. "Come Jenny, Chestnut needs you again."

Fox toweled himself down, pulled on a dry shirt, and walked to the window. The lugger that had been out at sea was gone.

And no wonder. The sea was enraged, battering against the cliff that supported this cottage, gray fog blending with the sharper swirls of the water, spongy foam tipping to white. He committed the shades to his memory and found his spare waistcoat.

His only coat and his freshest neck cloth were in the

kitchen drying, along with Perry and her maid and their clothing. He'd built the fire high for them to change out of their wet things and warm up, and left them there, the maid shivering, Perry fussing at him to leave.

In spite of the miserable weather, it was the first complaining Perry had done. While the storm unfurled sheets of rain, she threw herself into the unloading and unharnessing. Mud up to her ankles hadn't deterred her. Her dress, not a particularly delicate weave, drat it, had still managed to cling to her form, confirming all the measurements he'd taken at Bakeley's ball. The little foal was still taller than all the women and many of the men, and she'd filled out quite nicely with ample breasts and, below that small waist, hips that a man could hold onto.

His body stirred, and he cursed it, looking around at his notebooks and canvases. He'd need to keep her out of here until he could burn these.

He took the stairs down one level. The carved door of the suite of rooms belonging to the mistress of the house was closed, but not locked, he knew. He'd peeked in upon his arrival, inspecting the house, but he'd not crossed that threshold, not on this visit, not on the one ten years earlier. This was Felicity Everly's bedchamber and it was fitting that Lady Perry should sleep here.

The Holland cloths came off the furniture easily. Stripping the counterpane exposed bare ticking, so he pushed through the door to the dressing room and rummaged through cabinets, throwing one set of bedding on a cot for the maid. Clutching the other linens, he went back to the main chamber and began laying out sheets.

His damned artist's mind reared, seeing her here, imagining her wheat-colored hair spread upon the pillows, envisioning her stretched between the four posts, long legs extending under a rucked-up, sheer cotton nightdress.

He stood tall and took a deep breath. Hell, that wasn't the artist in him—that was the man.

Yes, Fox, and you might as well torture yourself dreaming it because you'll never get closer than this.

Hopeless colonial. He laughed, finished the bed-making, and went to pull the board off the fireplace. This close to the sea, the nights were chilly, and she'd been shivering today. She'd be needing a regular fire. He would have to haul up some wood.

Downstairs, at the door to the kitchen, he knocked, heard a muffled "Come in," and pushed the door open. Damp warm air, scented with woman, made him take a step back.

"For heaven's sake, come in and close the door. You're letting in a draft."

Chuckling, he obeyed.

YE GODS, THE SIGHT OF HIM SENT A TREMBLE THROUGH HER that had nothing to do with the air. He'd changed out of the clinging shirt that had plastered him, but he was still only partially dressed. His shirt front flapped at the neck, revealing tanned skin, scattered dark hair, and a neck corded with muscles. He was as sinfully handsome as one of the sculptures of the blasted gods gracing the British Museum.

He'd never been one for painting such myths, though. She'd discovered him that year eking out a living selling landscapes. But years ago when he came to Cransdall, he was known for his paintings of horses—that skill had caught Mama's interest—and his portraits.

13

Oh, yes. She'd learned more of his subjects much later: rich Cits, well-kept mistresses, and one very rich widow who'd kept him for months as a *guest*.

An unladylike growl rumbled out of her.

Truly, it had been the horses that brought him to Cransdall. After painting Godolphin's progeny, Fox had stayed to do all of the human portraits—her mother's, Bakeley's, Charley's, and hers. It had taken him months. He'd left behind four portraits—five counting the horse.

And he'd left with one priceless masterpiece he'd lifted from the wall in her mother's rooms, just before Mama's death.

Bakeley said it wasn't so. He'd said it when Mother died, and he'd said it again a few months ago, before the ball held to celebrate his and Sirena's marriage.

Perry had seen no proof of innocence. She'd so wanted to question Fox about the subject on the night of the ball, but he'd slipped away quietly, and when she'd had a chance to sneak off and visit his rooms, he'd left London entirely.

Fox tugged at his loose collar. "You're warm enough, I see."

She swallowed against the tickle in her throat. "And you are half-dressed. Where is your coat? Your neck cloth?"

He waved a hand in the general direction of clothing-draped chairs. "Are they dry yet?"

He'd found a fresh shirt and waistcoat in *this* house. "Have you more clothes at the inn?" she asked.

"No, Lady Perpetua." He smiled, his eyes crinkling.

Irritating man.

Jenny bustled at the rough-finished, old-fashioned kitchen dresser.

At least she assumed it was old-fashioned. Bakeley made sure Cransdall had the newest of everything, but she

14

had no idea how other houses compared. In truth, her social calls and house parties did not include visits to the kitchens.

"The bread is a bit soggy, my lady, but the cheese is good," Jenny said.

So soggy bread and cheese for dinner.

Jenny opened another parcel and whooped. "None of the eggs broke neither. And we've got ham here, a fresh joint, and some carrots and turnips. T'would make a good hot stew, those last bits, and these apples for a dessert." She looked up at Fox. "Sir, does the woman who cleans for you also cook?"

He blinked.

Taking his time to answer. If he'd been one of the lordlings she met at house parties and fêtes, she'd chalk his silence up to the shock of being addressed by a servant. But this was Fox. He'd always measured out his words in dribs and drabs.

"The woman who cleans for me," he said, finally.

Jenny lifted a shoulder. "Well, the house, sir, it does seem very clean, excepting where you've left some dishes and such."

His dark eyes glimmered. The corners crinkled again. "I wasn't expecting company. No one's been in to clean during my stay. The house was closed up so tight no dust was allowed in." He lounged back against a worktable. "I expect someone comes in now and then. I don't expect a visit any time soon."

She blinked. He didn't expect a visit? He had no plans to leave?

She turned away. "Bread and cheese and a bit of the ham tonight, Jenny," Perry said. "There's a knife on the board behind you."

15

"Saints, I hope it will keep. I hate seeing a good joint be spoilt."

Fox readjusted his leaning, pulling Perry's gaze to his long-muscled legs. His head all but touched the low ceiling. "Just cook it up, Miss Jenny."

He shot Perry a look that said to hell with your aristocracy. Oh yes, Fox was thoroughly a republican, even though he'd been born too late for the American revolt, and out of the country for the last war with the colonials. If not for horses, he'd never have come into the Earl of Shaldon's sphere.

But...a memory jolted through her. Bakeley's wife, Lady Sirena, had whispered that Father and Bakeley had actually approved Fox's attendance at Bakeley's wedding ball.

And had she not herself seen Father at the ball, speaking to Fox in that way that meant he was not just an arrow in Father's quiver, but might be something more?

The man who had stolen a priceless painting?

She clenched her fists on the back of a chair. No one would tell her anything, not even Charley.

"Grab a pot from the pantry, Miss Jenny. I'll haul in fresh water."

Jenny pressed her lips together. "I'm just Jenny, sir. Not Miss Jenny. And I'm a maid, not a cook."

Under his steady gaze, she squirmed. "I mean, I don't know how."

"You don't know how to cook?" The words burst from Perry's mouth. She had assumed—but then why had she assumed? They hadn't discussed this. Jenny grew up on the streets, probably stealing pies when she was overwhelmed with hunger.

"And *you* don't know how to cook." Fox was looking directly at her, that gleam still lighting his eyes.

16

He'd turned the tables on her, damn him. She needed him out of this house. This was her house—would be her house, someday, when she married. *If* she married. If she could not get that ridiculous clause out of her mother's will.

Never mind, she intended to go on as if she had. She intended to claim this as her very own house for as long as she wished. Bakeley would have to come himself and haul her out.

She pushed herself up from her chair and looked around for the door to the pantry. "I've seen bread made, and bread toasted, but otherwise I've not had occasion to learn." As he well knew. The family had always had excellent cooks. "But I shall muddle through. And you will help me, Jenny."

Fox crossed to her and took both of her hands in his large ones, sending her nerves rattling.

3

VERTIGO

*H*is stubble had tones of red, and under the short scruff, a seamed scar ran down his jaw.
"You're both fair exhausted," he said. "I'll cook. You watch and learn. This..." He put a finger to the center of her forehead— "very deft mind needs only one lesson, Jenny. Keep up or you'll risk being sacked."

The touch of his finger sent a spark through her, like a small strike of lightning she'd read about in one of Mr. Faraday's experiments, rippling warmth like the rings in a pool where a rock has dropped, and she was in the pool, not breathing. Behind Fox's back, Jenny covered her mouth.

With that, her breath and her brain returned. Before she could push him away, he'd disentangled himself and stalked to a door. Her hand went to her chest but she quickly dropped it.

Jenny's lips twisted and quivered.

"Stop smirking," Perry hissed, "or I'll send you back on your own to London."

Jenny shook her head. "Yes, miss. But you know they'll be searching for you, and if you send me back alone, your father's man Kincaid will lock me up and put me on bread and water until I spill."

"Kincaid would do no such thing." Fox returned with his pots, his face bland.

But he'd heard every word, calculating that she had escaped, that she also didn't belong here. He would use it against her in the battle to come.

THEY ATE IN THE KITCHEN, ALL THREE OF THEM TOGETHER. It was novel and cozy, and strangely liberating. Fox had not asked her dining preferences, he'd simply taken three plates from the matched set of crockery and set them upon the servants' table. When Jenny opened her mouth to protest, it took but a look from him to quell her. The girl had fussed nervously with her food the whole meal. Her discomfort left Perry with much to think about.

As had Fox. He'd spoken altogether more words that night than she'd heard in all his months at Cransdall. He'd explained all the steps of making a stew, and covered all that he knew about everything from skinning game to omelet-making. She had learned new skills in her plan for independence.

Once Father had her removed from the cottage, where would she go? Not back to London, and not to Cransdall, nor to any of her brothers' homes. She had money, but stretching it would mean more eating with servants, and she couldn't drag Jenny along for an extended adventure. It wouldn't be fair to the girl, who was rising in life on the only path open to her.

Jenny stood and began gathering dishes. Perry stood also and reached for a plate.

"No, miss," Jenny said. "I know how to wash dishes and

19

how to put up what's left of the food. Rest yourself and I'll get the kettle for your tea. It should be hot now."

She remained seated. Fox sprawled blandly, like a well-sated footman quite at his leisure. That is, he not so much sprawled as his considerably long legs had nowhere to go but far out in front of him, and his long torso fit awkwardly against the slatted chair. It was hard to be so tall, and didn't she know it. He must be terribly uncomfortable.

And they needed to talk, away from Jenny's ears.

The tea they'd brought had kept dry. She busied herself with the pretty pitcher Jenny found. "You've no brandy, Mr. Fox?"

"Not here."

"Will you have tea with me?"

He nodded tersely. She could see by the firmness around his mouth, he didn't want tea.

"You'd prefer coffee, wouldn't you?" she asked.

"Yes."

"Well, I'm sorry. I didn't bring any. Come along then. Jenny, you'll find us in that parlor."

Fox reached for the tray she was holding, and she pulled it away.

"If you would carry our bags instead?"

Fox watched the swish of her gown as she climbed the stairs. This one, a fine light blue lawn sprigged with pink flowers, would be sheer enough if it weren't too dry to cling. Juggling the tray in her hands, she clutched her skirts high enough that he could see her trim ankles and calves in the slippers she'd exchanged for her boots. They were dainty, heelless little things that would have made a smaller woman look like a child instead of a lithe opera dancer or

Aphrodite's apprentice. She navigated the stairs with that tray nimbly. Lady Perry had finally learned to manage those long lovely legs.

He paused on the step and juggled the maid's valise and Perpetua's larger bag. He'd best keep his wits in his head instead of his breeches.

At the top of the stairs, she rested the tray on the banister and let her skirts drop. Eyes downcast, pink touched her cheeks in the gray light. Aye, she'd seen his grinning. He took pity on her and led her into the parlor, lighting a lamp while she readied the tea.

For now, he would drink the polite swill out of courtesy. He had pushed her hard tonight and she deserved that much. Once she was tucked into her mother's room, he'd uncork a fresh bottle and begin burning those incriminating sketchbooks.

She poured, as stiff-backed as the Duchess who'd wanted him in her bed. Lady Shaldon's invitation had saved him from that awful commission. At Cransdall, he'd found himself in a home full of humor, great love, and one long-legged girl budding into womanhood. Perry had fancied herself in love with him, at least for the first week of his stay, until his jabs and irritations had set her at odds with him. It was better that way.

But she wasn't a fourteen-year-old anymore.

She bent to pass him the cup and her bodice pulled, squeezing her bosom.

He tore his gaze away and stared into the swirling liquid, the same glittering dark amber as Perry's eyes.

She cleared her throat and he smiled, watching the color rise over her frown.

She was still a rebel. He'd watched her at Cransdall thrashing herself, over and over against the walls put up by

21

her world. And the business of seeking him out in London for a commission—it just wasn't done. Bakeley had been furious.

She patted her mouth with a napkin and squinted at him. Where were the spectacles she'd worn in London?

He sipped the hot liquid and waited.

"Mr. Fox." She eyed him over the rim of her cup. "I was very surprised to see you here. You say you are painting, but are you not supposed to be at Cransdall? My brother said you are commissioned to do a portrait of my father."

"That is true."

"So why are you not there?"

"Your father will not come down from London until after the coronation."

She sighed, but her shoulders stayed rigid. "That doesn't explain why you're here."

He waited, watching her mouth tighten and move as she squelched the emotions wanting to play across her face. As a girl, she'd been as purposeful as a dog after a bone, constantly chided and hemmed in by her governess, her brothers, and even sometimes her mother. Apparently, she'd learned a bit of self-control.

He'd heard she wanted to enter her father's Game. She would be relentless and dangerous, most especially to herself.

"Fox," she snapped. "Cransdall still has that room with the very good light. Go there and paint."

"Cransdall doesn't have this." He waved a hand toward the high windows where the rain beat and the noise of the waves sounded.

Her cup clattered on the saucer. "I'm here. I'm not leaving. You must go."

"And I'm here also. By your father's permission."

That brought her up. "But this house is mine." Her mouth firmed.

It was grim determination, he decided.

"The house will be yours when you marry. Have you married, Perpetua?"

Her lips curled in. She could not keep her eyes from narrowing. So, Lady Shaldon had not changed her will.

"Is there a husband lurking about who I'm going to have to duel with?"

The pink creeping up her neck turned a brighter shade and his gut clenched.

Was she running away from a husband?

Or…what was more likely, a prospective husband? Shaldon was no doubt pressing her to marry his choice of lordling. It was the way of their class.

"Who told you the house would be mine when I marry?" The words came out in a rush of air, and she stood, towering over him, fists balled.

Heat shot to his groin. He took her hand, squelching the instinct to pull her on to his lap. "Your mother told me years ago. You haven't married, have you?"

She blinked. He saw the sheen there and slipped his fingers around her other hand, gentling them.

"This was your mother's house, Perry." Shaldon should have told her. It should not have been left to a lusting retainer like him.

Her mouth firmed again, her eyes widening, assessing. "You've been here before?" she whispered shakily.

He firmed his grip. She'd made a leap that he must set straight. "You didn't know about this cottage? No. Of course *you* wouldn't be told."

"Were you here…before?"

"Yes."

"With my mother?" She choked out the question.

"Yes." He shook his head. "Not in the way you're thinking." He stood, still grasping her hands. "Come. The rain has stopped." He pulled a knitted wrap from the sofa, draped it around her shoulders, and opened the French door to the damp terrace beyond.

PERRY TOOK BIG GULPS OF THE DAMP, SEA-DRENCHED AIR, struggling to keep the spinning at bay. Fox had trapped her hand again, skin to skin, and she shamefully held on. The shallow balcony's rail was waist high for a short person. The two of them could topple over far more easily. His grip on her hand, the view down the rocks, and the news, the awful mention of him being here with Mama—she was reeling.

He shifted hands and put an arm around her, tugging her into his warmth. "I won't let you fall."

Her insides rattled as if a war had been torched within. She, who stood eye to eye with men, the awkward, towering Long Meg...next to Fox she felt womanly. Hadn't his height always been one of his draws? Until he'd begun to tease her like an insufferable older brother, turning her feelings upside down. And then her mother's treasured painting went missing the same time as Fox. If she clung to those unpleasant memories...

She closed her eyes and all of her senses went to the places where his body touched hers, sending delicious warmth through her, tingles, shivers and a feeling of perilous safety. One strong hand fitted with hers, the other cradled her shoulder. She struggled to breathe.

"Perpetua." He gave her a gentle shake. "Perry."

She opened her eyes. Only the closest family and friends called her Perry.

24

There was real concern in his gaze, the teasing absent. As it had been when they'd danced together at her brother's ball.

In fact, other than a few lapses tonight, he'd been more serious than he'd been all those years ago at Cransdall.

But he'd never, ever touched her like this, not even when they were dancing, not even when as a girl, he'd helped her up after she'd fallen out of the tree right in front of him.

"I'm fine now," she said, only she wasn't. She'd never be fine again. "It's the elevation, and all this wild crashing." She made herself walk to the edge where the parapet hit her below her hips. He trailed along with her, still attached.

She forced her gaze to the wild waves below.

"Tell me…" She cleared her throat and spoke louder so he would hear over the tumult. "Tell me what you were doing here with my mother."

"At her request I escorted her here."

"*At her request?*"

He turned her to face him. "It was *not* what you're thinking. She came here to meet your father."

"My father?" She sounded stupid, even to her. She cleared the moisture from her throat again. "My father was in…Spain. Or France." She gazed out over the water. "Or somewhere." Always somewhere else, her father had been during those years of the war.

"Yes. She came here to meet him when he could get away. She was meeting him then."

"But she brought you along."

"She came here to meet your father. She asked me to escort her here, which I did. And then I left."

She shook her head. "She would have asked Bakeley to bring her."

"He wasn't around."

25

Of course, he was right, blast him. Bakeley had gone off to buy horses before Mother left, and Perry had been sent off to visit a distant cousin.

"Charley was there."

"He was too young then."

The kindness in his gaze angered her.

Her mind went to that time. Her mother had grown thinner with some worry. She'd been vague and distracted about it and once had even become angry when Perry had railed against being restricted to riding with at least two armed grooms.

She'd been a dreadful child during that time. She squeezed her eyes against that load of guilt.

His hand still warmed her. A shiver went through her. "What were you to her, Fox? Or maybe I should ask, what was she to you? Were you..." She sucked in a breath. "In love with her?"

"In love?"

She felt his body rise taller, never releasing her.

When she opened her eyes, the truth she saw in his gaze pressed all the air from her lungs. "*Oh, my God. You. My mother.*"

She was a fool. Fourteen or twenty-four, at any age she was a fool.

She tried to pull away, but he yanked her closer. "*No.* Not like that. She was like a...a mother, Perry."

"A mother."

He nodded, unconvincingly.

"You and she were not lovers?"

His gaze darkened, light from the glowing ocean making his eyes sparkle. He turned her to face him and tugged her tighter, pressing them together hip to shoulder, squeezing the air from her, forcing her chin up.

"Your mother and I were *never* lovers. Never. Never inclined to be either. *You* were fourteen. Far too young." One broad finger touched her lips. "Then."

Wild anticipation pulsed through her. He set her back from him. "Come. I'll show you to your room."

4

INTO THE FOX'S DEN

Fox refilled his glass and swirled the amber liquid. The light from the lamp lit through the brandy, the glints and highlights so like the color of Perry's hair in the afternoon sun. It had been a near thing on the balcony. It had taken all his resolve to set her back and even more to not follow her afterwards into her mother's bedchamber.

He tipped back the glass and let the liquid burn through him. Not a top-notch batch was this.

Scruggs had supplied it, but he'd been cagey about the source of this brandy. Smuggled, no doubt, and a man in this kind of business had to keep secrets.

He sensed something more to the man's reluctance though. Whether Scruggs had recognized the new tenant, Mr. Goodfellow, as the man he'd met briefly all those years ago, was uncertain. It seemed likely that whatever ties and obligations the innkeeper had to Lady Shaldon's grandfather—and his free trading connections—had died with her. He'd deemed it wise to not mention his true name or his connection to Shaldon.

The revenue officers, once they had the Kentish coast in hand, would throw more cutters this way. Scruggs had no reason to trust the new tenant at Gorse Cottage, and most certainly not this one. He had a fair handle on all the local ring's calendars and hideaways.

He would not be able to go out tonight, though, not with Perry abed and unprotected. If Scruggs knew she was here, so would the whole district. The foolish girl.

A door *snicked* shut on the floor below, just loud enough to hear over the ebb of the surf. He loosened his grip on the glass and set it down.

Locked doors wouldn't protect Perry. She needed to leave and go and find a lordling who would marry her and allow her to return to this cottage as the true owner. By that time his own job would be done, and he would be gone.

And by God, he'd finish this final commission for Lady Shaldon, if he could but bring his attention away from the girl on the floor below.

He pulled the sketchpad from the table and opened it, tracing a finger over the line his pencil had left. Putting pencil to paper had not cleared this obsession. It was his curse that he'd hold these images in his mind forever.

Sooner or later, Perry would come snooping in this room. It was a shame to destroy good work, but there it was. The sketches needed to go as well.

The hair on his neck rose. The staircase had creaked and then he heard them—footsteps, stealthy and soft, approaching his room.

His weapons lay over near the bed. There was no time to retrieve them.

The rap on his door was sharp and commanding. So, her snooping would be sooner.

He was too late in his purpose tonight. He flipped the

sketchbook closed, leaned back in the chair, and poured another finger of brandy.

"THE BED IS FRESH MADE," FOX HAD SAID AT THE DOOR OF Perry's bedchamber. Then she'd heard their bags touch the floor and when she'd turned, he'd disappeared.

He'd left her steaming and stewing in a hot and cold mix of emotions as tangled as the knots of her stays. It took Jenny, once she'd arrived from the kitchen, long, clucking minutes to undo the mess Perry had made of the laces.

She'd tried to breathe her way through it but every inhalation brought her mother's scent, a light touch of lilac, with it. This room with its green-papered walls and tester bed was so like her mother's room at Cransdall.

For years she'd shunned the countess's rooms at all of their family homes. All of them held too much of the spirit of the woman who'd left them so suddenly, so cruelly.

Nor could she here, tonight, dodge her mother's spirit. The pineapple carved into the mantelpiece would have made her mother smile. The apple green Bells of Ireland woven into the counterpane were so like the ones Mother had nurtured in the garden. And the painting—that was Mama's first pony. There'd been a similar one in Mama's dressing room at Cransdall. Mama had painted both pictures herself from memory.

And if that bed were freshly made, Fox had laid these sheets. Every part of her quaked, unsettled and restless and hot. She threw back the stifling bedclothes and paced the room barefoot. Not so much as a feather tickled her toes. The room had been kept as if waiting for Mama to return.

Mama had left Cransdall the same time as Fox.

She paced to the window and opened it. Damp fog

slicked her body. She found her dressing gown, shrugged into it, and went back to the window. Here and there, the layer of moisture shifted, the iron-gray sea dappling and cresting and holding its secrets.

At the inn where she and Jenny had stayed the night before, Perry had used a false name, to throw off whatever pursuers Father might set upon her. Surely her mother had stopped there also on her secret journey ten years earlier before the last grueling leg along those cliffs.

Pain stabbed at her chest. *Those cliffs.*

Her mother had perished in a carriage accident, one so violent it had taken her lady's maid and her coachman also. She'd heard whispers of a wheel falling off the carriage, not such a great catastrophe on a straight stretch of road. Yet no one had lived, not even the horses.

When word of the accident had reached Perry, she'd rushed back to Cransdall and met Bakeley and Charley escorting three coffins. Both her brothers were so closed-in with grief and grimness she'd been unable to break through. Mama and two of the servants she'd known all her life were dead, and there'd been no one to grieve with.

And then Perry had discovered that Mama's priceless masterpiece, a colonial Spanish artist's rendering of Saints Felicity and Perpetua before their martyrdom, had gone missing.

Fresh grief pushed her back to the edge of the bed. She wrapped her arms tightly and tried not to sob. Her mother's death had been no accident and somehow Fox was involved. Or if he was not involved, he knew something.

He'd distracted her earlier, touching, holding, almost kissing her. He'd cooked for her, readied her bed, and steered her away from her questions.

It was a kind of seduction. She'd observed Charley, her

31

brother, in his days as a rake bantering with widows, dodging straight answers, leading them up to the brink, luring them in. Some of the women were just as clever, if one could count such nonsense without purpose as cleverness. Perry didn't.

But of course, Fox had a purpose. He didn't truly care for her, he was just stirring the embers of the girlish attraction she'd felt all those years ago.

He'd had lovers among the women he'd painted. He was skilled at seduction, surely a liar, and likely knew more about her mother's death. She found her dagger and strapped it around her arm, under her sleeve. Without Jenny's help, it was awkward. She must get used to that awkwardness if she was to live as an independent woman.

She went up the stairs. Had he told her he was on the top floor, or was it just something she knew about him, that he would choose a high floor with the best afternoon light?

She gripped the banister. In their conversations so far, she'd let her attention jump around, let him lead her astray. She'd not paid attention to what he wasn't saying.

At the door, she knocked firmly and heard an equally firm order to enter.

5

SECRETS UNVEILED

*F*ox lolled in an armchair, coatless, his white shirt flopped open to a muscled, hairy, masculine chest.

Heat thundered through her and she tore her gaze away. The nearby grate was laid with unlit kindling and wood, freshly placed, she would guess from the shavings that littered the hearth.

No healthy, dry man would want a fire on a night this mild. Even if he'd gone out after delivering her to her room, he wouldn't have got himself wet. The rain had stopped.

He hadn't stood at her entry, as a gentleman would. Perhaps he was ill.

She forced her gaze further. A narrow bed had been pushed into a far corner, the linens spread out but rumpled. The tall windows on three walls, east, west, and north, were closed, the curtains pushed wide apart. Near the west window an easel stood, its canvas draped by a white cloth. Two pristine canvases leaned in an open space along the wall.

"You should not be here." His deep voice drew her gaze back.

That heat she'd felt earlier thrummed in her chest, threatening to make her quiver. Looking away hadn't helped. She steeled herself against her body's betrayal and spotted the half-empty bottle. "You're drinking," she said.

His smirking smile converted most of the burning inside her to ire. The insufferable ass.

Still, a drunk man might talk. She moved closer.

Fox uncurled from the chair and sat up.

Or, a drunk man might be dangerous.

Not Fox, though. Not to her. Unless he'd somehow been tied up in Mama's death.

She clasped her hands, bringing her knife nearer.

The bottle, a lamp, and a sketchpad sat on the table. "What are you drawing?" she asked, then silently cursed her distractibility.

Everything about this man was a distraction.

He rested his arm over the pad.

Well, well. They would come back to that. If he truly was here by Father's invitation, his drawings would have something to do with Father's work. Unlike many of his peers, Father did not have a passion for art. As far as she knew, he'd only ever personally bought one painting in his life, the stolen masterpiece he'd given her mother years and years ago, and it was completely unrelated to his business of spying.

She must remember her purpose. "Never mind the sketchpad." She infused her voice with congeniality, the way Bakeley's Irish wife, Sirena, might speak. "We didn't finish our discussion downstairs." How would Sirena say it? "I confess the sight of all those rocks and crashing waves below made me dizzy and distracted." *Not to mention the press of your hands.*

He watched her, his face expressionless.

There were no other chairs in the room. She looked again at the bed.

Fox shot to his feet. "Sit here. If you must."

"Very well." The seat held his warmth and his scent, brandy and musk and a tinge of the fine roan gelding she'd seen in the stable.

That fine horse was too rich for a portrait painter. It was likely from the stables at Cransdall. Her father was being excessively generous.

"Perhaps I might have a brandy also," she said.

He handed her his tumbler. "Here. I only have the one glass."

A tingle went through her at the uncomfortable intimacy. She raised the glass to her lips and sniffed.

"You won't like it."

Insufferable man. The glare she sent him made his lips curve, almost into a smile.

"What I mean is, it's not top quality. Not up to the standards of what your father keeps."

She took the barest sip and swallowed. The sharp, vinegary taste made her lips pucker and sent heat up her nose. She pinched it to suppress a sneeze.

His grin said, *I told you so.*

"Actually, my brother is the one in charge of searching out the best brandy. I believe Father prefers whisky. Perhaps it's Kincaid's influence. He doesn't much care for brandy."

She sloshed the liquid, threads of memory swirling. Mother's many lessons for Bakeley had included where and how to obtain the best brandy. She understood now—the veiled references had been to smugglers.

35

Were there smugglers around here? Was Fox involved with them at her father's behest? Nothing her father did was random.

"And neither do you."

His words pulled her from her train of thought. He was trying to befuddle her again.

She sighed, letting him have that point and lifted her chin.

Around her the air crackled. He towered over her, well over six feet of lean muscled man, his white shirt dangling open right over his heart.

Concentrate, Perry. If she must defend herself and pierce those firm muscles, there would be ribs there blocking her dagger. Her sister-in-law Paulette had shared the knife lessons she'd learned. That chest wasn't a good target.

His strong corded neck would be the place for a blade.

The thought sent the brandy sloshing. She set the glass down. She could never do it. And besides, he could take the dagger away and push it into her if he wished.

Warmth tugged at her insides. If he wished he could push something other than a dagger in her. She would resist, of course, as best she could.

Probably. At least for a while.

His hands went to his hips bringing her gaze along, sending her pulse into a brisk tattoo. He was aroused and not at all trying to hide it. Her thoughts tangled and twisted, the heat melting her insides from the top of her head to her very toes.

"Perry," he said softly, eyes dark, glittering. He saw her desire but how could he? She'd not moved. She'd not revealed anything. She felt as stupid as one of Charley's society marks.

No, stupid was not the right word here. She felt addled yet focused, numb yet alive, weak-kneed yet strangely powerful. She pushed back at the desire, trying to remember why she'd come here.

"Perry. Why are you here in your nightgown? You should be in bed."

He'd packed his questions with a sentiment more like brotherly frustration than a lover's teasing, helping to tame her wild heat.

"To talk." She flung a hand out. It landed on the sketchpad.

His gaze shot to the pad. He took a step closer. She flapped the cover open.

And lost her breath completely. The woman looking up from the page sparkled and smiled in a way she knew she never did in real life. She looked...beautiful. The face beamed a joy she'd rarely experienced in ten years. Only her horses, her nephew, and her new sisters could bring out this smile.

She could count on one hand the number of times she'd seen Fox since her mother's death, all of them last winter. When had he seen her smile like this?

Blood clanged in her ears bringing warmth to her cheeks. And why, of all subjects, had he drawn her? That could not be her father's commission, could it?

She flipped another page and there she was in the distinctive gown and headpiece she'd worn to Bakeley's wedding ball. Another page, and she was inclining her head in a country dance.

She felt suddenly foolish, naked here in her nightclothes with her hair tumbling around her shoulders.

Tame Fox? She was an idiot.

She jumped to her feet. "Never mind. Talking to you is like talking to Father or Bakeley or Charley. Keep your secrets and lies."

* * *

FOX SAW THE MOMENT SHE REALIZED THE DRAWINGS WERE OF her. Another woman might be flattered, might decide to climb into his bed and relieve this throbbing reaction.

Perry would never be that easy. As a girl, she'd always become churlish and defensive. There was more to her reaction now, though, a shakiness within her. The drawings had frightened her. The rod in his trousers had frightened her. Her desire—so palpable in this small room—that had frightened her the most.

"And this..." She clutched the pad close to her chest. "I'm keeping this."

That he couldn't allow. He reached for the pad, and his hand landed on her forearm, jolting him more. He peeled back her sleeve and saw the dagger, its grip cheap and worn in a tattered sheath.

In the quiet, the only noise was her shallow quick breathing and the pounding of his heart.

Shame washed through him. Damn Shaldon. Damn the villain he was pursuing for Shaldon, Gregory Carvelle. Damn Bonaparte and the Georges and all the others who drove the world into madness. He should not be here, in this house, with the girl he'd shamefully lusted after, the girl he'd frightened so much she'd come to him armed.

Her tension flooded into him. He held on to her for long moments until he could finally speak calmly.

"I won't hurt you, Lady Perpetua, but this is wild country and it's good that you're armed. I have a better blade in my trunk. I'll dig it out and give it to you tomorrow. Did you bring pistols also?"

"Yes."

"Do you know how to use them? No, wait, of course you do. Just please don't use them on me. I won't hurt you. I'm here with your father's permission, doing some sketching and painting." He dropped her arm and took a step back. "When you need a footman or groom, I can fill that role. Otherwise, I'll stay out of your way."

She brushed past him, leaving her scent, a floral mixed with a fear that shamed him. When the door clicked shut, he gripped the glass, tossed back the liquor, and stalked the few feet to the easel, throwing back the drape of the canvas.

Upon his arrival, he'd started the painting in a frenzy of work. It was incomplete, yet no one could mistake the model. She stood tall and defiant, her hair cascading over strong shoulders and delicate breasts, her nude body draped with the sheerest of veils.

This would have frightened her more. The shape of her breasts and her hips, he'd imagined, watching her move through the crowd at her brother's ball, watching her dance. Women's dresses now were not as blissfully revealing as they'd been a decade ago, but he'd seen enough women to guess at her nude shape.

He should destroy this. On the other hand, if she saw it, if he could cajole her past her fear...

Posing for an artist unleashed some women's inhibitions. But he wouldn't use Perry that way.

A movement outside caught his eye. He extinguished the lamp and stood to the side of the window, straining to see. A shadow moved through the fog below.

A figure steered his horse silently, slowly, stealthily up

the drive. Any clomps of the horse were swallowed by the relentless beating of the surf on the rocks below.

Fox pulled on his coats, sheathed his knife, and quickly loaded a pistol, his thoughts going to Perry. In all good conscience, he had to convince the girl to leave. She couldn't stay here.

6

THE SCOTTISH SPY

*P*erry turned up the lamp she'd left burning as a night light and carried it to the table.

She traced a finger over the first picture. The neckline of the gown was the same as the one she'd worn the day he'd brought her the designs she'd commissioned for the ballroom floor. Had she smiled like that? Not for him.

The second and third were from her brother's wedding ball, where Fox had danced with her, a waltz, holding her breathlessly close the entire time.

She turned the page. It was another sketch of her, on a street, her maid at her side, as if he'd spotted her through a window.

She stared into the lamp's flame. After she'd seen his painting in the shop window and discovered his direction, she'd escaped from her carriage one day, and hurried off to his street, looking for his lodging. The landlady had said he wasn't at home. Perry had scribbled a note and handed it over with a few coins to the happy woman, who had no doubt already extracted another coin from Fox for his lie.

The dressing room door squeaked.

"What's that, miss?" Jenny leaned over her shoulder. "Why that's you and Gladys!"

"Yes."

"It's Mr. Fox's work?" Her eyes were saucers.

"Yes. Did I wake you?"

Jenny bit her lip. "I heard you go up the stairs."

She flipped through more pages. They were all sketches of her. Some from several months ago, some of her as a young girl at Cransdall.

"And he gave you that?" Jenny's voice held awe. "They are very like."

"I took it. I don't think he wanted me to see it."

Jenny clasped her hands together. "He's sweet on you, miss."

Jenny's eyes held a look far too dreamy and romantic. "There is nothing sweet about Fox."

The girl pressed her lips together on a smile. "He's handsome, miss. And a good enough cook. But you would know best."

A door opened somewhere below.

Jenny straightened and glanced to the door. "I don't think I can sleep in this house."

They went to opposite windows.

"Over here, miss," Jenny hissed.

Perry turned down the lamp and hurried over. The stable door that she had latched so securely stood open.

Alarm bells rang in her head. Chestnut and the other horses might be in danger.

"Mr. Fox went down, do you think?" Jenny asked.

"Or he might be in the kitchen ready to spring out. I should join him."

Two men exited the stables, a tall one and a very tall one.

Her nerves jangled. There was no mistaking Fox. "Fox has a visitor."

Jenny drew in a sharp breath.

"What?" Perry whispered.

"That's Fergus MacEwen."

"Who?" She shook her head. "How could you possibly recognize the man from this distance?"

"You recognized Mr. Fox, miss, clear as a bell. On account of him being so tall. And Fergus—I mean, MacEwen—well, look at him. No one else walks with that swagger, as if he's God's gift."

She pressed her nose to the window. The second man *did* look familiar. Fergus MacEwen. "One of Kincaid's men."

"Yes. He and his cousin Boyd work for Mr. Kincaid. He brought them back from Scotland with Mr. and Mrs. Gibson after their wedding. Fergus has been gone from town for the last few months."

Kincaid's man. Who would also be her father's man, a rough and ready man, somewhere between a soldier and a spy.

Her head pounded. Fox and his guest were heading for the kitchen entrance.

"I'm sorry, miss. Looks as though we've been discovered by your father."

Found with Fox in a house with naught but a maid to shield her reputation. She would, if word got out, be ruined enough that Father would rush her and her substantial dowry into a marriage of his choosing.

Except, Father had sent one of his spies. It wasn't her brothers raging through the door.

Of course, not a one of them would force her to marry the man she was caught with: Fox.

A thought niggled at the back of her mind. Her father

43

had, somehow, manipulated all of her brothers into the marriages he wanted. He'd been most forthright with Bink Gibson, her eldest brother. But then, Bink, being a by-blow, was the one least under the forceful thumb of the Earl of Shaldon. Father had been devious with Bakeley, and manipulative with Charley.

Last month, he'd begun dropping the names of men he'd welcome into the family as her husband, and Fox's wasn't one of them.

Which, with Father, proved nothing. If she was contrary, like Bakeley, she might work directly into his plans. If he'd maneuvered her into visiting this house, as he'd set Charley on the mission that'd led him to his bride, she'd suspect Father wanted her to marry Fox. But he hadn't.

Except...it had been easier than she'd expected to find the papers naming the property that would come to her when she married. As well, he'd joined in on a discussion of the names of Yorkshire families with Sirena's dear friend, Lady Jane Monthorpe, and Charley's wife Gracie. And Father knew she planned to travel north with Charley and his new bride to their estate not much more than a long day's journey from here. And Fox claimed he was here by Father's instruction.

Could Shaldon want her to marry Fox?

Pure heat rippled through her again, and then she remembered Bakeley's hard stare when Fox had led her onto the dance floor the night of the ball. Fox was not good *ton*. Heavens, Fox had no place in London society—he was an American. And a mere painter of portraits and landscapes. As bad to some as a tradesman.

She, on the other hand, was the Earl of Shaldon's only daughter. No matter her age, her extravagant dowry would allow her to entice a peer to the altar—if she would but forfeit all prospects for happiness.

No. Father had sent this Fergus MacEwen to ferry her back to whatever lord he had in mind for her. And she was *not* going.

"He'll want a hot meal. They'll be in the kitchen."

Jenny pulled the ugly black shawl around herself. "Will we need the pistols, miss?"

A laugh bubbled up. She pictured Fergus MacEwen trying to carry her off into the dark night.

It wouldn't come to that. She would refuse to return, and if they tried to force her, well, she had a set of men's clothing packed in her bag and a very good horse. Just let them try to catch her.

"We'll forgo the pistols tonight. What do you know about this Fergus MacEwen, Jenny?"

"He's handsome as a devil and knows it, miss. Cocksure and full of himself."

Something in the girl's tone made her stop on the stairs. "A flirt?"

"Oh, yes, miss."

FOX STIRRED THE EMBERS OF THE FIRE AND STARTED A KETTLE. "There's a stew in that pot over there."

MacEwen lifted the lid, sniffed, and grunted. "'Twill do. Have you not got something stronger than tea?"

"Some rotgut brandy from the local smuggling ring. I'll have to fetch it from upstairs."

"Never mind." MacEwen pulled a bottle from one of his many pockets, took down two cups and poured. "Who made the stew, then?"

"I did."

"Good. I'd not trust one made by someone from this shire. His lordship sends his steward all the way from Cransdall to look over this wee house. Kincaid comes himself sometimes. Boyd and I have been here at times, checking for squatters."

They'd found loads of smuggled goods piled in the stables: casks of brandy, reams of silk cloth, and lace straight from Holland. Fox had heard the stories already when he'd first met Boyd and Fergus in Rotterdam.

MacEwen grinned at him, reading his mind, probably. Tough and strong, he'd be a good man in a fight. Shaldon trusted him, and Kincaid. He, on the other hand, was not well-acquainted, nor did he know why MacEwen was here.

Unless he'd come after Perry.

His protective instincts kicked in. Whether she realized it or not, the girl's lust for him had matched his own for her, which was probably why she hated him.

He watched MacEwen stirring the stew, belting back shots of whisky. Handsome, tough and tall, he was a bit taller than Perry. She would like that.

Blast it. Perry was having a moment of freedom. If anyone took her back to her father, it would be him, not some Scottish spy.

"I've information for you," MacEwen said, "Gregory Carvelle was spotted in Rotterdam two weeks ago, waiting for a boat."

"Two weeks ago? No boats other than fishermen arriving since then. The weather's been bad or the coastal patrol has been lingering. No words of any cargo arriving either. What news from Scarborough?"

"None. The coastal boys have been making their presence known there."

So, no news, more waiting. "I'll work on my report

tonight." He needed to do the blasted encryption. "You can take it back to London with you in the morning."

Without Perry. The girl would have a few more days of freedom.

But that left him alone to defend her, and this might be a very dangerous place very soon.

MacEwen raised one eyebrow. "I've not been in London these past months. My orders are to stay here with you, play the servant. Our man doesn't know you or me. When he shows up here, I'll take a message. We'll have some others along as soon as Fat George gets his crown."

It was Fox's turn to raise an eyebrow. "Such disrespect for your king."

The other man snorted. "We Scots warmed up his majesty's troops at Culloden. Got them good and comfortable and overconfident so you Americans could win your revolution a few years later."

"We are allies then?"

"Aye and both of us working for Fat—" MacEwen's gaze flew to the door and he shot to his feet. "What the—"

Fox took the kettle off the fire. "We have guests, MacEwen."

"My lady." MacEwen bowed, his face unreadable. Then Jenny walked in and his mouth went slack.

Holy hell, the man was about to drool over the maid. Fox swiped a hand on his face, squashing a smile. It just lacked this, it did.

"Jenny," Fox said, "Fetch two cups and the tea and whatever biscuits you brought."

7

AWAITING AN ARRIVAL

*P*erry saw the shift in Jenny and tried to fathom what about the girl revealed her attraction to Fergus MacEwen. Though she didn't smile, Jenny's face softened and brightened, her eyes went to MacEwen, then flitted away, then back again. Was that how she herself looked around Fox?

The heated looks were not all one way either. There would be mischief between these two.

She hadn't thought Jenny capable of more than lockpicking, perhaps some pocket picking, and some complicity in sneaking around. She'd never had a maid who showed interest in men, not in Perry's presence, anyway.

She glanced at Fox. He was fighting to hide a most irritating smirk.

Mischief, and that on top of the disturbing comments made by MacEwen. *When he shows up here, I'll take a message.* Drat that they'd not arrived sooner to hear who was supposed to arrive.

If he'd even mentioned it. Perhaps he was like Father, never giving anything away. Since Father's return a few years ago, she'd been observing his habits and techniques. Father never revealed anything he didn't have to, and he always pretended to know less than he did.

She lifted her chin. "What is your name, man?"

MacEwen was all polite deference introducing himself, but she'd heard his remark about the King. Never mind that she agreed with him, at least about George being a ridiculous figure, staging a ridiculously extravagant spectacle when some of his people were lacking in regular food. The undercurrent here of two rebels cooking up mischief under her roof made her uncomfortable.

"I've seen you with Mr. Kincaid."

"Aye, miss."

"You serve my brother, Mr. Gibson?"

"When your father or Mr. Kincaid tells me to do so. My cousin and I are distant kin of Kincaid and Mrs. Gibson."

She abstained from rolling her eyes. Weren't all the Scots distant kin of each other?

Jenny took the kettle from Fox and fussed with it, glancing over her shoulder at MacEwen. He didn't look back—the man's attention was focused squarely on Perry in a way that sent her skin wriggling, like a butterfly pinned to a mat.

She stood taller, bringing her eyes almost even with his. "Why are you here, Mr. MacEwen?"

Something shifted in his gaze. Fox drew closer, as if standing where he could come between them if they came to blows.

"I'm here on your father's business, my lady."

"And what is that business?"

A twitch started next to his eye. "I'm here to serve Mr. Fox."

Yes, she'd heard that part, and she'd also heard it was

49

pretense. Who was arriving? A smuggler? A spy bringing a report? Or...a traitor her father was hunting?

Her pulse quickened. There'd been much of that these last couple of years, her father seeking out the men and women who'd betrayed England during the long conflict with France. Why her father could not leave the war behind, she didn't truly understand.

"I see. My father sent you along to serve Mr. Fox, who's come here to paint. You're serving him, and yet he's cooking for you."

"As I made dinner for you and Jenny," Fox said. "I am, after all, one of those hardy republicans, throwing off the yoke of class and aristocracy." He went to the stew pot and lifted the lid. "Warming up nicely. Seat yourself, Lady Perpetua. You too, MacEwen."

The last was a terse command. MacEwen eyed him hotly and sat. She took her seat and glanced at Jenny, who nodded and brought her the teapot.

While she poured, Jenny went to the crockery cupboard, returned with a bowl and filled it with stew. Her breast brushed MacEwen's arm as she set the bowl in front of him, sending his dark eyes bulging.

The cheeky, clever girl. If MacEwen got her with child, she would make him marry her.

Or perhaps he had a wife in Scotland.

Perry took a careful sip of her tea. "As you're to be living in my home, tell me about yourself, Mr. MacEwen."

MacEwen gave a sketchy description of his roots and his history. He'd been in the army, as had many of Father's men. Both Jenny, and surprisingly Fox, listened attentively.

"What of your family?" Perry asked. "Have you a wife somewhere?"

"It's not wise for a soldier to marry, miss."

She infused patience into her smile. "That was a dodge, if ever I've heard one. A yes or a no, Mr. MacEwen."

He sighed. "No. No wife."

Jenny brushed Fergus again, setting down a plate of bread.

Fox's lips quivered.

"And do you know, Mr. Fox, I've never asked you that question. Have you a wife somewhere?"

His eyes narrowed on her, but he did not answer right away. She could see him struggling with what to say.

Perhaps he did have a wife. That would make him ineligible for marriage. It would increase the scandal if they were caught under the same roof, and if she actually dared to act on these unfamiliar feelings, the wickedness...

But no. She would not do that with another woman's husband.

HER QUESTION HAD THROWN HIM OFF BALANCE. HE SHOULD dodge as MacEwen had done, or lie and say yes. He might have married in America, which he'd left at the tender age of eighteen.

But here...nowhere in this old world was an impoverished painter a candidate for matrimony, and neither was a spy.

Her look was direct, but for once, shuttered. The sweep of her hair tied back loosely softened her narrow face and angular features, and the light from the lamp made her amber eyes luminous. Almost, almost, he could see her lips tremble.

He could lie, but he wouldn't.

"No."

She expelled a breath and her eyes softened.

51

No, Perry, not me. You cannot look that way at me.

"Nor do I wish to have one, which is why I hope that you will let me escort you back to the main coaching line so that you may return to London."

Her face paled and then colored deeply, the pink glow flowing into the lacy neckline of her night wear.

Shame smacked him like an invisible hand, but he had to go on, even with the maid and MacEwen listening. He reached for her elbow. "My lady, in spite of my handsome face, you could not wish to be forced into a marriage, not with the likes of me. Not that your father would consider me a suitable match. But to protect your reputation, he might insist you marry someone else."

Her face had gone stony. She tried to pull away, but he held on. "Or, he might *try* to insist and make your life a misery as long as you resist. Will you let me take you away?"

"No."

"I can escort you and your maid, my lady." MacEwen said.

"No," and "No," Perry and Fox said at the same time.

Her elegant chin lifted. "You both might as well tell me whose arrival you're expecting."

MacEwen opened his mouth, closed it, and looked at Fox. The silence stretched.

Fox nodded to MacEwen.

MacEwen cleared his throat. "A dangerous man."

She snorted. "Everyone who gathers about my father, friend or foe, is dangerous."

"He's a smuggler from these parts," Fox said. "And that's all that we'll say."

"Else your father would skin us alive," MacEwen said. "As he might do, did he but know you were here and we allowed you to stay."

She chewed on her lip, swinging her gaze from MacEwen to him. Finally, she pushed back her chair and stood and picked up a lamp. "Jenny, go back to bed. I'm going to check on Chestnut and then I'll come up."

And then she was gone.

The maid glared at MacEwen. "You," she said. She turned her accusing eyes on Fox. "I'll not go anywhere until Lady Perry returns safely to the house."

Fox snatched up the other lamp. "Suit yourself." And then he left.

8

A KISS

Outside, he spotted her lamp, bobbing along the stone path between pockets of gorse and wild berries. Perry would not stumble over that cliff, not if she stayed on the path to the stable. He waited until he saw the stable door open and close, then he turned his own lamp low, shuttered it, and set it down on the door stoop.

Out at sea, there were no lights. That didn't mean no one was out there watching, wondering who was lighting the path at Lady Shaldon's seaside cottage. And why they were there.

PERRY STARED THROUGH THE SLATS AT THE DARK GELDING confined there. A white diamond between his eyes reminded her of the foals borne by a spunky mare that Bakeley had purchased several years earlier. This one's eyes were slack from fatigue, yet he mustered the energy to lift his head and curl his lips revealing young sturdy teeth.

"Just like your surly master, aren't you?" she said.

MacEwen had ridden him hard and put him away quickly. He would need a good brushing down and a look at those feet tomorrow when she could see better.

She picked her way past the plodding inn horse and Fox's big gelding, down the row to Chestnut's stall. For a seaside cottage, this was a very fine stable. Fine enough for the Earl of Shaldon, though as she remembered, Father did not much give a rat's bum about the state of the stables. He'd left all of that to Mother and then, by necessity and birth, Bakeley.

As Perry drew closer, Chestnut turned in her stall and took two steps closer. Perry slipped inside.

The snuffing soft mouth tickled her hand and sent warmth through her. "I'm so sorry, my lady, I've not brought you anything." She chuckled. "And, anyway, we'd not have your insides twisting from eating soggy biscuits."

She smoothed her hand over the silky coat. "You did well on the journey today, my girl."

Chestnut's head lifted, and a current of air ruffled the straw, sending the hair on her neck dancing. She heard it then, the soft click of the latch closing.

"Lady Perpetua."

Her lungs froze. Fox had opened that door soundlessly.

Chestnut shuddered and shifted around, nostrils sucking in the air that Perry couldn't seem to find.

She sensed him moving through the dark and mustered a breath. "Go away. I'll not ride away in my nightclothes."

His dark form appeared next to her, silent and hulking.

Chestnut looked him over, remembering. She flicked her tail and nosed his hand.

"Traitor," Perry muttered.

Fox didn't laugh. His hand, that large hand with its long

fingers, slid over the horse, stroking and soothing, the action pulling the warmth through her own flesh, soothing the hair on her neck and the tension behind her eyes.

She straightened her shoulders. "You've no doubt come to tell me again how dangerous it is here. How I shouldn't be out in the stables at night."

"It *is* dangerous, my lady."

His lady. The words stirred her tension into a hot knot of unshed tears. She swallowed them back and made herself snort. "Ah, yes. Dangerous country. Smugglers and such."

"You shouldn't make light of it."

"I don't. I'm not unprotected. I have my knives and my pistols."

"Would you use them?"

"I've been tempted to use them on you several times this night."

His hand stopped. "Lady Perpetua, your government is cracking down on smugglers. Desperate men do desperate things. There is but one of you and many of them."

"There's a riding officer in these parts. There's a baronet justice of the peace down the road. I will look them up if there is trouble."

"And if they're part of the smuggling organization?"

Her mind froze around the idea.

But of course. She was not so naive that she shouldn't have realized—smuggling corrupted all of the locals. Though in all fairness, the smuggling in these parts had not been on her mind at all when she came here.

Fox pulled both of her hands into his. She dropped her gaze to them. "They won't bother me. I am the daughter of the powerful Earl of Shaldon."

He tensed at that and when he spoke his words were a

scold. "They could make you disappear and no one would know. You ran away, didn't you? You left London without telling anyone where you were going."

"I wasn't *in* London. Charley married. I was at his home in Yorkshire."

"He will be frantic."

She almost laughed. "You don't know Charley, do you? And even if he were the type to worry, he thinks I'm visiting a friend."

"So, you see. No one would know."

Anger rippled through her and tightened her chest. "You would know, Fox. *You* would know. Unless you're also part of it."

"What if they'd killed me?"

She pulled her hands away. "No. You're not going to muddle me again. I'm not leaving."

He moved closer, towering over her. "No matter whose daughter you are, it's not safe here for a beautiful young woman—"

"Stop." She slapped his hands away. Chestnut sidestepped, and Perry took a breath. "I am simply one woman. One spinster well on the shelf. Not young, and not beautiful."

"You *are* beautiful." He clipped out the words, harshly, but those strong, long fingers curled over her shoulders, working their artist's magic, sending tendrils of bright-colored feeling streaming into her, as if he could flick his brush and make her handsomer than God had made her.

She tried to swallow against a sudden dryness. She knew the truth. "Long Meg." She breathed deeply. "Horse Face. Bluestocking. Ape Lead—"

His lips pressed to hers and for a moment she couldn't

find air. He used that moment, pulled her closer, flattened all of her against hard muscles, wrapped her in his long arms. His hands cradled her, his fingers dancing and doing things to her neck and her back that sent her nerves spinning. She sobbed, caught a breath, opened her mouth against his, and surrendered.

Tender, long, moments of such melting bliss. Her head whirled with the feel of their lips moving together, their tongues probing with need melding them. Her hands slid under the silky hair at his neck, grasping the sinewy strength, holding him. She wanted him closer, deeper, and—

He pulled his mouth away and looked down at her, his eyes glistening like onyx. "Perry," he growled from a place deep in his center, "you *are* beautiful. And you must leave."

The sharp words cut her. He desired her. He wanted her gone. In the games her father's people played, both could be true. Especially for the men.

Not for a minute should she believe his words about beauty. Lord Baxter had taught her that.

"I'm staying. If I'm tossed in the ocean, well, I might as well be dead than be suffocated by men who think I'm stupid."

His jaw hardened. She tugged away, allowing a hair's breadth of air between them.

"You think you can kiss me senseless and I'll leave? I've been kissed before, Fox. I've had several proposals of marriage, and one nobleman tried to pull me into the mews where his carriage was waiting. I was able to get away because I am, as he said, a great lumbering beast." *A man must keep his eyes shut to swive a great lumbering beast like you.* She blinked tightly and inhaled.

Tension rolled off Fox. His hands tightened on her. "Who'd say such a thing? I'll kill him for you."

She shook her head. "He fled to France."

"Before your brothers could whip him."

"No. From his creditors."

She tried to lift her arms, but he'd tightened around her. "And anyway, you're not a killer. You can let me go now."

"Perry." Fox's voice rumbled close to her ear, the vibrations tickling her. "Those men are fools. They're simply intimidated by your height and your intelligence. Let me tell you what an artist sees. A woman of grace, tall and willowy, with a perfectly proportioned form. A square, determined jaw, an elegant nose, lips that are wide and plump. Eyes and hair the shade of caramel or creamed coffee laced with gold. Creamy skin—"

"Stop." He was doing it again. She wriggled and flattened her hands on the planes of his shoulders. "I had no idea you were a poet as well as an artist and spy, or whatever it is that you are. You wish to kiss me or flatter me into leaving. I'm not leaving. If you try to force me to leave, I'll shoot you. I'm not leaving."

THAT WAS BADLY DONE, FOX.

His time keeping her at bay with badgering and teasing and pecking at her had come home to roost. She couldn't see his heart when it spoke.

He slid a finger under her chin and lifted it. "The danger is real. If I can't keep you safe, you'll force me to die trying. And if I don't die then, your father will likely kill me later for not packing you back to your brother's." He pressed his lips to hers, claiming a quick kiss. He wanted to take so much more. If she stayed around too long, he undoubtedly would. She undoubtedly would let him.

The thought made his already pumped-up shaft jump.

59

"Finish your talk with the mare. I'll be outside."

He carried her heat out of the door with him. Outside, he took the short path to the edge of the outlook and pushed his fingers through his hair, sucking in the cold damp sea air.

And spotted the boat.

9

SMUGGLERS ON THE BEACH

Fox needed Perry in the house, locked up tight, her pistols ready.

He slipped behind a rocky outcrop. Through his spyglass he could see the oars going on each side of the tub boat, casks strung to the sides, bobbing in heavy surf. That would slow them down more than a bit. The lugger he'd spotted earlier before the storm was likely sitting around the rocky point to the north, and the local Riding Officer was tucked in the bed of Scruggs's maid, or drunk in the hearth room. Sex, drink, and money, they were all part of his payment.

He had time to get Perry inside and get himself down the cliff side.

Fox reached the stable door just as it opened, the lantern light flashing. He slipped in, slamming the door, grabbing her lantern and shuttering the light.

"What the devil are you doing?" she asked.

"We need to get back to the house."

He could feel her gaze on him. "Smugglers?"

"Yes."

She tried to push past, but he stopped her.

"I want to see."

Her nightclothes might shimmer against the high rocks.

"Wait." He found a dun-colored horse blanket and wrapped it around her. "You're entirely too bright." Entirely, completely, overwhelmingly too bright. And he could not deny her the excitement of seeing this.

With one hand she clutched the blanket in front, and the other slipped into his.

He led her to the outcrop where she pressed her hips against the boulder and looked through his spyglass. "Three men on board, two rowing."

As he'd seen. He needed to get down there.

"It looks to be heavy work. Are those casks of brandy?"

"Brandy or gin. Look to the beach under that outcrop. What do you see?"

"Nothing—or..." She drew in a sharp breath. "Shadows. The locals?"

"Most likely." He reached for her. "Come. I have to get down there."

She handed him the spyglass and followed along. "Is that the man, then?"

His Perry. So bright.

"I want to go with you, Fox. I have a dark pelisse."

"No."

She stiffened and stopped. Dug in her heels, the blanket slipping. He pulled it around her while she slapped at his hands.

"Perry." He jerked her close in her blanket. "Gregory Carvelle. That's who we're looking for."

Her sharp intake of breath told him she knew the name.

"*That's* the man?"

"Yes. You know him?"

"Yes. I saw him once at a ball."

If she had seen Carvelle, she would recognize him. He'd chased Carvelle's trail of snail slime across Holland without once seeing him.

"Charley's wife was once promised to him. Father was looking for him. His cousin was a traitor and so is he. He's a vile man."

"Come," he said. "Let's hurry."

MINUTES LATER, PERRY TURNED THE KEY IN THE LOCK ON THE grand entrance door and went to stand next to Jenny at the windows in the nearby parlor.

"Like shadows, they are," Jenny said approvingly.

"Yes." What they were truly up to, she couldn't be sure. Both men had donned the darkest of jumpers and trousers, black watch caps jammed tight over their already dark hair, and all done in minutes. Men's clothing was so freeing.

"Are we really in danger?" the girl asked.

"Of course not."

In the gloom, she couldn't see Jenny's expression, but her skepticism was palpable.

Her answer had been reflexive, unnecessary, almost disrespectful *noblesse oblige.* She was forgetting, this was Jenny, former urchin of the Seven Dials. Didn't she herself hate being treated like a child?

"Well, maybe."

Besides, Jenny might know more about this—didn't the servants always know more than they let on?

"Did you hear tell in the servant's hall of Gregory Carvelle?"

The girl stiffened. "Miss Gracie's fiancé, who beat her? The one they never found?"

63

She sighed. "Is there anything the servants don't talk about?"

"I only listened, my lady. Is Gregory Carvelle the one Mr. Fox and MacEwen are after?"

"So he told me."

"He told you? Then you got more out of him than I did MacEwen. You promised to teach me to load the pistols, miss."

"Indeed I did."

Upstairs in her bedchamber, they closed the curtains, turned up the lamp just enough to see, and she showed Jenny how to load and prime a fine pair of Mantons she'd filched from Shaldon House.

"Shall we wait in the kitchen?" Jenny asked. "I can make us another pot by the light of the fire."

Fox had warned them about keeping the house dark, so as not to draw interest out at sea. He'd issued a password, with instructions for them to keep the door closed to anyone who didn't know it.

Her gaze landed on the sketchpad she'd pushed to the side. What other secrets was Fox hiding? He would go down the cliff side, do whatever he had to do, and would have to climb back up. She had plenty of time to investigate.

"I'm going upstairs, Jenny."

The girl picked up a pistol and held it carefully pointed at the floor. "I'll go with you, miss."

JENNY WENT TO THE CURTAINS IN FOX'S ROOM.

"Wait," Perry said. "Don't close them. He'll notice they were disturbed."

She shuttered the lantern as much as she could. Surely, they were high enough not to be seen, but she would risk a dim light anyway. As her eyes adjusted, she saw Fox's coats and white shirt tossed carelessly on the bed.

"He's made his own bed," Jenny said.

Perry had noticed that before. "So he has."

His paints and brushes were also in neat order on a table near the draped canvas, rather too near the window for searching by lamplight. A travel trunk lay on the floor near the bed. They would start there.

Perry took the trunk and had Jenny look through the mattress and bedding.

"What are we looking for?" Jenny asked.

"Something hidden. Careful. His neatness perhaps has a purpose."

"Ah. Of course." Jenny patted the pillow back into place.

Perry went through the clothing, looking for filled pockets and finding nothing. She sat back on her heels and studied the trunk. She'd seen similar ones in the attic at Cransdall. She ran her hand over the leatherwork, feeling for notches or latches. Nothing. She tapped the bottom—quite solid.

"Under the lid?" Jenny knelt next to her. "That's a great deal of padding."

Perry slid her fingers along the seams and picked at the corners until she found a button buried there. The lining peeled away, revealing a notebook of superfine paper.

"Numbers. Letters. What do they say?"

She looked at the girl. "You can't read?"

"Yes, some." Jenny frowned trying to puzzle out the text.

"This is a code book. It says nothing on its own. And you must learn to read more than 'some'."

The girl's frown deepened. "Mr. Fox is a spy."

"So it seems. And don't ignore me about the business of

reading. You are far too bright to be ignorant. Let's put this back."

"Who does he spy for?"

Perry ran her fingers over the pages. Likely, he'd been spying for the Americans during the most recent war. Except, that war had started the year after his visit to Cransdall, and by that time, he'd disappeared.

There was no war now, but he claimed to be here at her father's behest, and MacEwen backed up the story.

"I think it's true that he's working for my father. Beyond that I cannot say." She flattened the book back into its hiding spot.

"You don't want to take it?"

"No. I'll know where to find it."

"Unless he moves it," Jenny said.

They shared a wry glance. Perry tucked the book in, secured the lining, and closed the trunk. "He'll know we were here, I suppose." She might as well try to keep a secret from Fox as travel to the moon. He'd see right into her heart and do his best to confound her. As a young artist newly arrived at Cransdall, he'd gone right to the business of punching holes in her puppy love. Because she was too young, too high in station above him, and too much the ugly duckling.

No one had told her that—she'd just known.

She'd stepped down from her high station for good, and she wasn't too young any more, nor did she have any illusions she'd transformed into loveliness. Let him come after her for searching his room.

"I might as well have a look at what he's working on."

"The light—"

"Be damned." She got to her feet and lifted the drape on the painting.

"Oh." Jenny breathed out the word.

A roomful of butterflies broke loose in her heart.

"It's you."

So it was. It was her, and not her. This woman looked like a goddess. She was no goddess.

"It's beautiful, miss, but, er—"

"Improper." The fluttering inside made her dizzy. "I didn't pose for this."

She wished she had. Her body tingled the way it had done when he'd kissed her.

She eased in a breath. "And look. In truth, there's more to me than he's painted here. He didn't allow for my stays squeezing me in tighter here." She touched the painting. It was dry.

Jenny giggled.

"Perhaps I should pose for him. You won't tell, will you, Jenny? And everyone who sees this will assume that I already did anyway. I'll remove all of Fox's illusions." And refute all of his lies to her. She was tired of lies. Tired of being an interesting specimen for the men in her world to poke at.

"Oh, my lady," Jenny's voice held a smile.

That the girl wasn't judging her eased some of her tension. She smiled back. "Oh, Jenny. What were you and MacEwen up to while we were outside?"

"Nothing," the girl said, too quickly. "That is, he's a terrible flirt."

And Jenny liked it. And she liked him. She and Jenny might both have a chance for a romantic adventure. "Will he talk to you? I need to know what's going on. I don't want you to do anything you're not willing to do, of course. You have a reputation to protect also." She pulled the drape over the painting. "There. I'm decent again. Jenny, I will work on learning things from Fox, and you can work on MacEwen. I promise, hand to my heart, no matter what happens, I will look after you."

"If you're not yourself exiled to an island somewhere like Napoleon, my lady." She laughed. "But, as you said, in for a penny, in for a pound. I'll work on MacEwen."

And enjoy doing it, her smile said.

IN THE SHADOWED COVE, THE FOUR NEW MEN LEANED against the rocks, all of them turned to the sea, watching the oars pushing against the surf.

"There," Davy whispered, pointing inland.

Gaz pushed the hand down and shushed him. He and his cousin Davy sat apart from the others, thank goodness. Blasted Davy and his ghosts.

"No such thing as ghosts." Gaz wrapped the other man's cold hand around the flask. "Take a swig. 'Twill wash out your brain."

Davy took a long hit and wiped his mouth. "I tell you, I saw her earlier, on the outcrop in front of the cottage. Come back to haunt us, she has. Scruggs—"

"Shut your face." The other four men he didn't know, not well anyway. They'd been brought in, part of a gang from somewheres further north. "The drink and your flappin' jaws'll get us both kilt."

Davy handed him back the flask and then froze next to him. "Look, Gaz. You've got to look."

He sighed and turned, tipping the bottle as he did.

10

A GHOST IN THE WINDOW

Gaz choked. The raw gin scalded his lungs and he had to muffle his wheezing. Two of the new men glanced over and then turned away.

"Bloody hell," Gaz croaked.

He glanced up again, and what he saw set his heart racing. In a top floor window, the white figure glowed like a selkie, tall, unmistakably feminine, shimmering hair streaming.

He'd seen her ladyship more than once, as a boy, delivering his mam's eggs. The lady used to come to the kitchen door herself when she was in residence, many a time. It *was* her. He dropped his gaze. Always kind, she'd been. "Bloody hell," he whispered.

"Bloody hell, 'tis where someone is going," Davy said, darkly. "We shouldn't—"

"Shush, man." He needed to think. He needed to get them through this night in one piece, and shutting Davy up was first. "'Tis the new tenant's woman, is all."

"Nay. He's but one man alone by hisself." Davy leaned close, blowing gin-breath at him. "Came alone, he did. An' he'll run, soon as she shows herself to him. That earl can't keep a tenant. *She* drives them all off."

Gaz didn't believe in ghosts. Not really.

Still…his jaw ached from the punch he'd caught earlier that day. Bloody Scruggs was on edge. The Dutchman was coming back. The town was too leery even to whisper.

If she'd come back for revenge, almost he'd be willing to help her.

"Oh, God." Air whooshed from Davy.

"What."

"The maid too. Oh, God, Gaz. She's back too."

"And I suppose all that's lacking is the bloody coachman," he said, trying to bring some humor. "I suppose he'll be lurking here somewhere, dressed all in black."

"'Tisn't funny."

The boat was nearing, and one of the new men was beckoning.

"Here." Gaz handed Davy the flask. "Pour this down your maw and stop talkin'."

PERRY AND JENNY MOVED DOWNSTAIRS, CHOOSING TO WAIT IN the dark in the house's main parlor with its tall French windows and view of the sea. If the village used this inlet for its smuggling, then the residents of this cottage had been able to see everything. Mother's grandfather had been in trade and then banking—likely his mercantile career had begun on this Yorkshire coast where he'd had strong connections.

Free trading, she realized, must have been part of it. Perhaps her grandfather had stood on that balcony observing the proper dispersal of goods.

Or—no. Like her own father, he would have been down

in the thick of it. Which was where she wanted to be, and it was fair enough since the blood of smugglers and spies ran in her veins.

She was still accommodating the idea that Fox was a spy. Yes, during his long months at Cransdall ten years ago, he had produced portraits of all the family but Bink and her father, who had both been, presumably, on the Peninsula in different capacities supporting Wellington.

Besides the portraits, why had Fox been at the Earl of Shaldon's home? Was he spying for France or America? Or was he somehow helping her father?

Mother had displayed a high regard for Fox, and if she'd asked him to accompany her here, she'd trusted him.

And then he'd disappeared until last winter, when she'd found his painting and recognized the scenery, the folly on the lake at Cransdall at sunset, streaks of light coloring the scene like a magical fairy world.

She'd run into him by that lake one boring evening, long ago, when she was angry and frustrated with Bakeley. Fox had teased her out of her foul mood.

"Where are they, do you think?" Jenny asked.

She shook off the memories. "Down there somewhere with the shadows." The smugglers had their lanterns turned to the dimmest of lights.

"Do you suppose someone else might be watching from high up like us?"

A pang of guilt went through her, and to be honest, jealousy. She should have thought of that. Jenny, a servant, was more astute, more practical, more level-headed than she. The daughter of a spy should have realized the free traders had lookout men, and yet, she'd stupidly exposed the light in the upper floor window.

"A very good point. That's entirely likely."

71

"Good that our two men have vanished into the night."

Fox was good at vanishing, as he'd done after Bakeley's wedding ball. No one knew to where. Except possibly her father, and if she'd asked him, he'd never have told her anyway.

The hair on her neck prickled. She'd found Fox again, even though she hadn't been looking for him, even though her father had not thrown them together.

He was here, she was here. He was, perhaps, the one for her, the one to help her launch her new life.

If he wanted to kiss her and lie to her, well, she might as well accept the dishonesty and see if it led to seduction.

Seduction...yes, she hadn't a clue how a woman went about seducing a man, but Fox certainly knew how to draw her out. Even when she'd hated him, it had been his teasing, goading, infuriating voice she'd wanted to hear. She'd stay to see where things led.

And then there was the matter of Carvelle. He'd mistreated Charley's wife, and he'd escaped Father's net. What he had done, besides acting with Father's enemies, she didn't know. But she would help Fox to capture him. And when Father came swooping in, she would try her own luck at vanishing. On the other side of that water lay the lowlands, and beyond that, France.

FOX TOOK THE SPYGLASS BACK FROM MACEWEN.

"Might be him," MacEwen barely whispered the words.

He'd moved noiselessly behind Fox, skirting the lookout the gang had placed on the crest of the cliff. Fox had found a snug spot to watch both the watcher and the action below.

The casks were offloaded, counted, and parceled off to the six men on shore. The oarsmen helped with the offloading, then climbed back into the boat. Their passenger came ashore and stood to the side talking to a seventh man who appeared, a burly man who fumbled his hat in his hands.

"Scruggs." Fox whispered.

"Aye."

The passenger had the advantage of height, but not bulk. Yet in spite of his wiry frame he commanded the other man's obeisance. Surely this was Carvelle.

He should send MacEwen back on the fresh gelding with a message, and himself follow the man to his destination. Likely, Scruggs would take him to the inn, and it was too late in these parts for a man to stop in for a tankard without arousing suspicion.

And he had Perry to think about. If he went to the inn, and MacEwen went with a message, Perry would be alone and unprotected.

Already she'd put a tall slender cog into her father's spy works.

The boat pulled away and the men started up the trail to the road, passing them not ten yards distant. Fox counted six men passing. Scruggs was one of them, as was the intimidating passenger. MacEwen took the glass and eyed the lookout man until he too had left.

When the others had cleared, he handed the glass back and whispered "Message?"

Fox shook his head. "Follow him," he said, breathing the words. He signaled that there were two men left below, and he would watch them.

MacEwen departed in utter silence. A skilled operative, he needed no more instruction than that. No matter the watchers or followers, MacEwen would find a way.

The two below were weighting and sinking the excess

casks in a tidal pool trapped by the rocks. Fox picked his way nearer.

They muttered and grunted as they worked and he heard snippets of words over the sound of the surf. "Shut up," the bigger one kept saying, but the other continued to mutter as they ran the casks down on lines. Though hidden from view of the sea or the shore, it was a shoddy job of concealment. A man could pull up those casks without so much as getting his boots wet.

So it was when a gang of smugglers had both the Riding Officer and the local Justice of the Peace in their pockets. The only reason they bothered with the sinking was to conceal the booty from the likes of him.

When the men finished their task, they hoisted their own casks, and headed straight for him. He slid into the shadows and held his breath.

"I tell you, Gaz, it was her. She's come back for revenge."

His nerves stood on edge, sharpening his hearing. They were almost upon him.

"Shush with it. No such thing as ghosts."

"You saw it."

"Will you shut it?"

They stopped right in front of him, voices so clear he could but whisper and join the conversation.

"I saw a woman, all in white. The tenant's got hisself a girl, is all. Snuck her in, he did when all the busybodies weren't looking."

"An' I says he'll be gone soon enough, just like the other tenants, and we be using that stable again." This one slurred his words. "Ain't no regular woman, Gaz. She's back to get the ones as threw her over that cliff, is she. I tell you—"

"Listen." A cask dropped. A shuffle. Someone gasped. The man called Gaz had resorted to force. "Listen. You yammer this to anyone else, it'll get to Scruggs. He'll know we know, and how long till he sets his man on us? Ya bleedin' idiot. You want to live, Davy?" More shuffling, grunting, and panting. "Then shut your trap. No more. No more to me, either, Davy, 'cause we don't know who's listening, and we don't know who to trust, 'ceptin' no one."

"We can leave."

"And how is Mam to live? What'll happen to the girls? What about yer boy?"

"I'll go and take Pip."

"And leave me with Scruggs asking why?" More shuffling. "C'mon."

Fox waited while they passed and their footsteps grew distant, and finally breathed again, blood pounding fiercely on every nerve.

In spite of all of his instructions, Perry had lit a lamp and stood in a window.

His skin rippled and a smile fought its way out. It was one of her acts of defiance and a damned brilliant mistake. Davy and Gaz believed her to be the ghost of Lady Shaldon, who it seemed had a history of driving tenants away from this cottage and limiting the smugglers' squatting to the stable and sheds.

More importantly, Davy and Gaz knew more about Lady Shaldon's death. Shaldon would want the particulars, and Fox would get them and to his lordship, all in good time. He tamped down his nerves and watched the retreating shadows.

Maybe Perry could make herself useful. She'd dug in her heels anyway to the point that a twenty-four pounder wouldn't blast her out of that cottage. To keep her safe, he'd have to stay close. Her presence now had a reason besides the obvious one banging around in his breeches, the one he could never give in to.

Once Davy and Gaz crested the road, he stowed the glass and picked his way down to the water.

Tap-tap-tap. Perry raised her head from the deal table in the kitchen.

Good God. She'd fallen asleep, and only the coals glowed in the oversized hearth. Across the table from her, Jenny was curled over two chairs, fast asleep.

Tap-tap-tap.

"Let me in," a man said gruffly.

She leaned against the door. That *was* Fox's voice, wasn't it?

"Who's there?"

He muttered the password and she slid the lock open.

Fox was a shadow wreathed in shadows. He was good at this business of being almost invisible. Perhaps that was another skill he could teach her.

His lip quirked up. "Let me in?"

She pulled the door wider, and wider still when she saw the tubs he had tucked under each arm.

"Smugglers' booty," she said. "Left behind? Or did you have to fight someone for it?"

His smirk grew into a full smile. "There's more of these submerged in that cove down below. Too much for the men to carry. Let's see what we have here." He went to the pantry, came back with a kitchen knife, and began to work the lid.

One did not use one's good stabbing dagger for such tasks, she guessed. "Will they be back tomorrow, do you think?"

"They won't want to wait long."

Jenny stirred, sat up, and rubbed her eyes. Her cap had slipped off and hair tumbled over her wary eyes. For but a moment she was that child again, waking up in a doorway, an eye out for the flesh peddlers.

Perry wished anew some happiness for the girl.

And that reminded her. "Where's MacEwen?"

The lid came off and Perry leaned closer to sniff. She turned away to sneeze, waving her hand in front of her nose.

Fox laughed. "It's gin."

"Dreadful gin." Though in truth, she had never smelled the stuff.

He dipped a finger in and tasted it. "It needs letting down. I wished for brandy." He walked away and came back with the bucket of water, a ladle and a cup.

Jenny was fully awake now, watching intently. "Is Mr. MacEwen coming back?"

"He'll be along in a bit." He dipped out spirits and added water.

Jenny moved closer. "You're watering the gin?"

"It's brought in over proof," Perry said. Years ago, her brothers had discussed the free trade practices over some badly mixed brandy. They'd discussed who of their peers with Kentish estates could fetch them a cask of pure spirits so they could add good water from Cransdall's well.

Fox glanced at her, his eyes warm with humor. "Know a bit about the free trade, do you?"

"More than a bit." Conversations came to her, talks between Bakeley and her mother. Charley had gone off to school about the time Bakeley's formal education ended and he came home to learn his life's work from Mother. The three of them were seldom in London during those long years of war. Quiet country nights had been filled with discussions of history and current affairs as well as farming and horses and commerce. Her education had not been as thorough as Bakeley's, but she would never need a husband to run an estate for her.

She smiled back at him watching him spoon spirits and water, stirring and sniffing.

"That should do it." He passed her the cup.

"I've never had gin. How will I know if it's right?" She sniffed. "It smells like…" She sniffed again. "It smells like the green glen near the lake at Cransdall."

She looked up into Fox's eyes, swimming in a darkness that sent tingles through her.

Perhaps he remembered the lake, and the night she'd run into him. He'd teased her without mercy that night.

The corner of his mouth quirked up again, in a way that made her grow very warm.

She cast her gaze down at the clear liquid and sipped. The zing of the alcohol burning the back of her throat was bearable, the taste was not. "I don't like it."

"I've tasted gin," Jenny said, not very subtly. "Used to have a nip now and then when Ma…" She stopped and bit her lip. Jenny had been one of the older girls taken off the streets by Perry's friend, Lady Hackwell, back when the lady was plain Miss Harris.

"Then you're our second expert." She handed Jenny the cup.

The girl drank and let the spirits sit on her tongue, like a lord they'd hosted at a dinner last spring. The high-in-the-instep fellow had taken the glass of wine, sniffed and swirled and smacked his lips until Charley had chortled and joked about wine connoisseurs loud enough for the fribble to be rattled.

Charley's fun-making had indeed rattled the man right off his high horse and into some parliamentary plot of Father's. God save her from her devious relations.

"What do you think?" Fox asked.

"It's good. A bit weak. You mixed it two parts to one?"

He took the cup back and drank it down. "More like three to one. Yes. Too weak."

He dipped out more, diluted it again, and shared it with Jenny.

"Better," she said. Is the barrel pure alcohol, do you think, sir?"

"I've heard sailors mix a bit with their gunpowder to test the proof," Perry said. "If the proof is too low, it takes the life out of the powder and it won't blow."

Oh, drat. She sounded like a pedantic bluestocking.

Jenny's face lit. "I've heard that, miss."

Her heart eased a bit. Like her, Jenny had picked up knowledge where she could.

"No need to fire up the cottage, though. We know it's pure." Perry went to get another cup and handed it to Fox. "You and Jenny have a nightcap and then up to bed. It's almost dawn. I'll have tea and wait up for MacEwen."

"Oh, no, miss—"

"You can take the next watch, Jenny. Do you think the gang will be looking for their missing tubs, Fox?"

He smiled up at her from his mixing. "I'm counting on it."

That smile started up a great buzzing inside her. She turned away and busied herself heating water and spooning tea leaves. Fox had a plan. And he hadn't said anything more about sending her away.

Every nerve in her body sprang to life, tingling warmth igniting a blaze in her like his smile was two hundred proof

79

spirits and she'd been packed with black powder. This was why her sisters-in-law went all moon-eyed around her brothers. This was why women did foolish things for men. This was it.

Please, God, before this was over, she would be very foolish.

11

A LETTER FROM GRACE

This far into the night, the free traders hurriedly stowed their booty in a cellar at Scruggs's Inn and took their leave of the place, breaking into pairs and heading back to their crofts and hovels.

It was a spot forsaken by all but the evil fairies. No overnight coaches plied this side road on regular runs, just the occasional lost traveler who'd missed the turning to Scarborough. The elderly ostler was part deaf. The young one would be asleep in the loft.

MacEwen saw the light in the window of Scruggs's one parlor, crept stealthily along the wall and stationed himself in the bracken below it. Scruggs kept enough rough weeds here that there'd be no tell-tale footprints left behind, and this spot had been tramped down by the dog MacEwen had seen wallowing here when he'd stopped earlier. Thank God, the lazy cur was gone now, probably asleep in the stables.

The window was open to the cool air and Scruggs's bellow was unmistakable. The other man's intonations—clipped and nasally, almost froggy—were a bit harder to discern. Mayhap he'd spent his life dodging men like MacEwen lurking outside his window.

"It's but one man in the cottage. Not *his* man. Some queer bookish gent, Goodfellow, took the place for the summer. Said summat about a death in the family and wanting to get out of the crush in London. That's all."

Scruggs's belligerent tones ended with a whimper. Sure, and this man was Carvelle. Shaldon had set MacEwen and the others tracking the scoundrel all over England and half the Continent.

"No," Scuggs said. "Don't worry about revenuers. The Riding Officer's green as spring corn, and Glenna's happy to be ploughed." He growled out a laugh. "Turned up his nose at her, did that Goodfellow."

Carvelle spoke quietly. MacEwen couldn't make out the words.

"As long as he gets his spirits and his cut, Sir Richard's happy to be locked up in that moldy manor. Don't bestir himself for nothing short of capital murder."

The hair rose on MacEwen's neck and a scent wafted his way. The high gorse rustled.

"Someone's out there." Carvelle voice came from above.

He melted back into the wall and slipped out his blade. Two golden eyes stared at him, teeth bared.

The window sash rattled. The fox jerked his head up and ran off through the yard.

"Bloody fox," Scruggs shouted. "*Boy*," he bellowed out the window.

The elderly servant stumbled from the stables, lantern in hand. Scruggs shouted oaths and instructions about his chickens and made quieter requests to his guest to let him show him his room.

By this time, the fox was long gone, and the inn's meager

staff would be stirring themselves. MacEwen would learn no more.

ONE DAY EARLIER

LADY SIRENA, THE VISCOUNTESS BAKELEY, WAS ALL LOVELY elegance in her fashionable morning gown as she took a bite of marmalade toast and unsealed the first letter on the stack next to her breakfast plate. No one would believe that only a year or so ago, Lady Jane Montfort had fished the girl out of a hedgerow on her family estate.

"I'm surprised to see you up so early, my dear." Lady Jane Montfort slipped into a chair across from Sirena. Sunlight streamed into the breakfast room of Lord Shaldon's huge home near Berkeley Square. In this quiet corner of the house, a few chirping birds in the garden added their sweet noise to the comforting sounds of distant traffic. "I am glad we left the party early, but even so it was very late. Perhaps you should have some more rest in your present condition."

"I'm fine, dear Jane. Bakeley has already left for some meeting regarding the coronation, and Shaldon is off to his study already. Kincaid came in early this morning bearing secrets." She grinned. "Will the torment to my curiosity never cease? In any case, we have this grand room all to ourselves. Have we not fallen into the pot of gold, my lady?" She set the letter aside and picked up another.

It was Lady Jane's turn to laugh. "You've done me a great kindness allowing this visit to your new home."

Lady Sirena glanced up and smiled. "Turnabout is fair play."

They both knew this "visit" had no fixed ending date.

Sirena's fortuitous marriage to Shaldon's heir had been a blessing for both the orphaned Sirena and for her benefactress. Jane's cousin, Lord Cheswick, would arrive in London any day and insist that she come stay with him and his petulant wife. She wasn't so sure she would go. She'd been invited to stay on at Shaldon House, and she could live very economically and peacefully here, as long as she kept a careful balance between saying too little and saying too much.

The thought stirred a sadness in her. Even a lady of a certain age liked to have her own home.

"Ah. A letter from Gracie." Sirena unfolded the paper and squinted at the lines. "Little Reina has had a belly ache from eating too many early berries. Their new estate continues to be lovely. Charley has been teaching Gracie how to ride and taking her around to meet the tenants."

"But I thought her last letter suggested...well, is that a good idea?"

Sirena waved a slim hand. "It's not certain. In any case, we are neither of us so far along." She flipped the paper over. "She says Perry has gone off to visit a friend in Yorkshire."

"By herself?"

"She's taken Jenny."

Lady Jane rested her fork on the plate. The maid, Jenny, had the makings of a wild little thing, as did Lady Perry, come to think of it. "What friend did she visit?"

"Hmm. She says here it is Cecilia Broadmoor."

Jane squinted at her cup. After so many years on the fringes of Britain's wide social scene, her memory of names was encyclopedic. "I know her. She's a bit older than Perry and...the last I'd heard, she'd married and gone off to India. She must be back visiting her family. I

84

attended a house party once many years ago at an estate near theirs and —"

She bit her lip. Before Charley and Gracie left for their new home, they'd had a lively discussion about Yorkshire families.

Lady Perry's interest then had been keen.

She felt Sirena's gaze on her. "The Broadmoors live in Lincolnshire," Jane said.

Sirena bit back a smile. "Perry has bolted."

Jane paced to the window and looked out, unseeing. Lady Sirena had done her own bolting a few months earlier and had been lucky to land in Lord Bakeley's noble arms, but it had been a near thing. Lord Shaldon was rounding up old enemies from the war, and at least one was still out there for whom Shaldon's only daughter would be a grand prize.

Shaldon was such a consummate actor his children thought he knew everything that went on. She knew better. They'd met many years before, when she had been not much more than a child.

She went back to the table, downed the rest of her tea, and wished Sirena a good day.

"Are you sure you want to go tell him?" Sirena asked. "Perry may never speak with you again."

"I'm afraid if I don't tell him, she won't survive to speak to me again." She sighed. "You of all people know the dangers, Sirena."

SHALDON HAD HOLED UP WITH KINCAID IN HIS SMALL STUDY, and both stood when she entered, two tall striking men of late middle years, and each seemingly unattached. Kincaid was the shorter of the two, a dark-haired Scot who had

85

served as Shaldon's second for so many years the men didn't need to talk to communicate.

Kincaid's personal history was something of a cipher. Not part of the *ton*, he'd appeared at his lordship's side sometime after Jane had met Shaldon, but nevertheless, many years ago. Where Shaldon went, he went, unless Shaldon sent him off on a tasking. He was related to Shaldon's eldest son's wife, Paulette.

Jane had exchanged no more than a few polite words with him, weighing his responses carefully. It had been enough to judge his character favorably. Whether he had a wife and family tucked away somewhere, she didn't know. She hadn't touched upon that topic with him.

Shaldon, on the other hand, was widowed. Either man was vital enough to take a much younger woman to wife. Or perhaps they preferred to pay for such *arrangements*. Men could be a fickle, dispassionate lot.

Shaldon invited her to sit, but she shook her head. They were obviously at their business, and she'd dispense with the niceties. "Sirena has received a letter from Grace. We believe Lady Perry may have departed their home using subterfuge."

12

A BARONET NEAR SCARBOROUGH

Shaldon sat down heavily.

"Bolted." Kincaid leaned a hand on the desk.

"She said she was visiting Cecilia Broadmoor in Yorkshire. But Cecilia married some time ago and the couple were posted to India. And the Broadmoors' estate is in—"

"Lincolnshire." Shaldon's dark gaze dropped to the sheaf of papers in front of him. "How careless of her."

Careless? Did he not mean thoughtless? Or reckless?

He sighed. "Well, we know where she's gone."

"I can leave in less than an hour," Kincaid said.

Shaldon shoved the papers into a file. "I'll go also."

Her heart accelerated. He had important obligations here. Perry must indeed be in danger. "You have the coronation, my lord."

His dark eyes gleamed. "Matters of state, Jane. The King will understand."

"Carriage or horseback?" Kincaid asked.

"Horseback, I think."

"I'll meet you in the stables." Kincaid left.

The rapid-fire arrangements made her head spin. She turned to follow Kincaid.

"Jane." Shaldon's voice stopped her.

"Tell me. You seem to know everyone. I recall that you mentioned the name of a baronet from near Scarborough?"

A baronet. Near Scarborough. She frowned and then immediately caught herself. Frowning only deepened the lines between her eyebrows.

She *did* recall a baronet with an estate near Scarborough. "Sir Richard Fenwick." A tall fellow with an ancient holding rumored to be falling down. A bit of a hermit, he was. She conjured up a face from a ball many, many years ago—dark hair, sullen eyes.

And she'd mentioned him when Lady Perry asked Jane to share all she knew about Charley and Graciela's prospective neighbors.

Oh dear. "Seldom in London, but I heard he was up from the country a few months ago."

His gaze held hers.

Fenwick. The Baronet was of an age with Shaldon, but as far as she knew he only moldered along on his estate near Scarborough and…

An old rumor came to her: Fenwick had offered for Lady Shaldon, back when she had been Felicity Landers. Felicity's grandfather had spotted him for a fortune hunter and sent him packing, and a short while later, the match with Shaldon's elder brother was announced. When the brother died before the wedding, the title and the fiancée passed to the current earl.

A fluttering started in her chest, just like the one she'd felt the morning Sirena had disappeared. She eased down into the chair. "How may I help, Shaldon? You might as well put your bothersome house guest to good use."

88

"You are not a bit bothersome, Jane. Would you fancy a trip to the coast? Or are you desperate to attend the coronation parties?"

The pomp and ceremony of the crowning had only been an excuse for her to come up to London last winter. She had business in London to settle, and soon.

And yet, and yet…Shaldon's hospitality had allowed her much needed economies, and she was in truth, grateful. Plus, in the past months she had grown fond of Lady Perry, and the young woman might truly be in danger.

"I fear I'm not up to travel by horseback. Might I take one of your traveling chaises, Shaldon?"

The smile lighting his face took years off him.

And, more worrisome, that smile sent a buzz of warmth through her. She'd not felt such buzzing in years, not in many, many, many years, not since Reginald.

And that memory was like a dash of cold water. She was no longer that foolish young girl.

"I'll send men with you," he said.

She put a hand to her heart. "I shall go pack. Safe travels, my lord. I will be close behind you."

WHEN HE FINALLY ACCEPTED THAT SLEEP WOULD NOT COME to him, Fox rose, dealt quickly with the mocking, incomplete canvas, dressed, and departed the cottage through the kitchen. All had been quiet on Perry's floor. She and her maid were both sleeping.

His fingers itched with the memory of curling around her shoulder and legs. She'd had a hard, worrisome journey from her brother's place. There was no telling when she'd last slept, for not even his manhandling her up the stairs to her bed last night had awakened her.

89

Lovely Perry. He needed it to be the last time he touched her. Touching her made him want her. Touching her made him rethink her ghostly usefulness.

All was quiet in the stable. MacEwen had either gone back out or was bedded down here after his late night.

Fox hurriedly saddled his horse. These locals were not stupid—they would see that Perry was flesh and blood, that she was a real woman, young and beautiful and very much alive, no ghost. He needed her to leave before danger found her. As soon as he could, he'd get a message to her brother Charles to come get her. She would despise him for it, but then, her dislike for him had always been his best defense—and hers.

For now, a bruising ride was what he needed, and then he'd pay a midday visit to the inn in Clampton.

It was well on in the morning when the tapping began in Perry's dream. Her mother was tapping at the door, and she had a pillow over her head. She was a great big girl, too old to throw herself onto a bed. Too old for tears. Too old to say what was wrong.

She sat up, heart pounding, and rubbed her eyes.

Charley had come down to her portrait sitting and said she must have legs under her skirts like the *girafe* pictured in one of Mama's French travel books. Fox had kicked him out. Fox hadn't laughed, nor even smiled, but she'd seen the effort it had taken him to resist. Even so, he'd coaxed her to stop frowning. He'd teased her about leaving him a great glowering subject, tried to make her smile, and finally, put away his brushes, disgusted with her.

Lady Perpetua, if you would but understand your brother is jealous that his sister is taller than him, you wouldn't be so missish. You're as sensitive as a raw egg. You'll grow up and take the ton by storm. For now, it's impossible to find your portrait in all of your frowning, and I am not going to waste another minute today trying.

And then he'd spent the evening flirting with one of the local squire's daughters who'd come to dinner. The hurt still stabbed at her.

"Miss." Jenny stuck her head in.

She pushed back the blanket, confused. Gray light streamed through the windows. Not a fine day, but she couldn't hear rain either. The green room was her mother's and—

She'd been in the kitchen. It was the last thing she remembered.

Jenny twisted her hands. "We've slept half the day away. Sure, and he must've carried you up, miss."

Up two flights of stairs.

She shoved back the covers and leapt from bed, searching her memories. "Did MacEwen come back?"

"Yes, miss. He carried me up. I remembered that, lessen I dreamt it."

"We don't know what MacEwen learned. What he did."

"No. We don't."

"I'm going to wake them." She searched for her robe.

"Do you not want to dress first? We'll hear them if they try to leave while you're dressing."

Jenny had thrown on her plain brown gown and tucked her hair under a cap, rather hurriedly from the way pieces stuck out. She had a pale morning gown draped over her arm, the stays in her other hand.

And she had a point.

"Yes. No stays though."

"None, miss? Well, I'm thinking you don't need them a bit."

The saucy girl tossed the stays aside, laid out the dress, and started helping Perry out of her gown, biting back a grin. "And also, there's the matter of that painting upstairs and getting your shape just so."

Heat crawled up her neck. Until her brothers married, she'd had no girls to share naughty jokes with. And she knew, such familiarity with a maid was not proper, but she couldn't help laughing. "You wicked girl," she said, and let Jenny settle the chemise over her head.

And wondered, not for the first time whether she would have survived a childhood in Seven Dials as well as Jenny had.

PERRY STEPPED INTO THE KITCHEN AND THE HOUSE RATTLED as the door slammed to.

The fragrance of bacon and toasting bread wafted to her, making her stomach rumble.

"His horse is gone." She went to look over Jenny's shoulder. "Eggs too? You're a fast learner. You've done a bang-up job."

The girl smiled. "And MacEwen?"

"In the stable, tending to *his* horse."

Expertly tending to it. There'd been no need for her to concern herself.

"He could use a bit of a grooming himself." She'd told him so herself in her best Lady Perpetua of the *ton* voice.

Jenny's face was tinged with more pink than the fire would induce. She'd noticed the man's scruffy beard. "Traveling, he was. Will you eat upstairs, my lady?"

"The kitchen is fine." The kitchen was wonderful. In fact,

in the mix of all of this freedom, she'd like to one day try her own hand at cookery.

Jenny set a plate of food on the table. "Shall I fetch him for breakfast when you've finished eating?"

"Fetch him now—or, better, take a plate to him. I doubt he'll come in. He's lingering in that stable to make sure I don't take Chestnut out."

Jenny pulled another plate and began filling it. "He'll need to wash and have a shave."

"Can you shave a man, Jenny?" she asked around a bite of bacon.

The girl laughed. "Fergus MacEwen wouldna let me near his neck with a razor, miss."

"You take him that plate. I'll pump out a fresh bucket and put it to heat."

A SHORT WHILE LATER, THE MARE SIDESTEPPED, NERVOUS about the extra stirrup hanging at her other side, and Perry shushed her. Chestnut had been trained to the sidesaddle, and the one Perry had brought along with her had mysteriously disappeared.

Never mind. There'd been tack and saddles enough in the stables—her mother's stables, she reminded herself, and she could saddle a horse as fast as any groom. She rucked up her skirts and swung her leg over the man's saddle, moving as softly as possible out of the yard, so as not to disturb MacEwen's shave.

She'd ridden this way many a time with a groom pacing behind, clucking, or Charley racing her, laughing. It was damn liberating. The next time she'd don the breeches she'd brought with her.

93

If Fox could steal her saddle, she could wear breeches. She could do dratted well anything she wished.

She reached the end of the short drive where the treacherous cliff road merged with the lane that led from Crampton and continued on south to Scarborough across the high moorland.

She pressed a knee to Chestnut and headed south.

The papers in Father's study showed that the path cut into the cliff had been the one to choose if she wished to dodge any neighbors, and that road was also on her property. It was hers.

Or would be hers when she married. She mentally kicked aside that small rock in her plans and followed the path through the gorse. Whether this wild parcel went with the house, she couldn't remember. The wild summer grasses stretched tall, this land unplanted and undeveloped. Perhaps it was too rocky to be under cultivation else her mother would have seen to it, like she'd seen to Cransdall.

But Mama had been dead for ten years. Enough time for wild plants to take hold of the earth again.

Perry brushed her eye and clucked at Chestnut to proceed. It was hard to believe that such a desolate landscape could be teeming with men and women sneaking about with goods brought in from the Continent.

Her nerves tingled and Chestnut's ears swiveled. She drew the horse up. There, in the brush, something or someone dark had moved.

13

PIP'S GHOST STORY

*P*erry touched her arm where the blade was tied. She was alone, and the pale green of her gown offered no disguise and her skirts rucked up were an invitation to a cur. Given the chance, a number of Charley's so-called gentlemen acquaintances wouldn't hesitate to pull her off her horse if they didn't recognize her as Shaldon's daughter.

How much less restraint could she expect from a rough free trader or a soldier cut loose from the wars, homeless and hungry.

Shoosh, Perry. She was scaring herself needlessly. Shaldon's daughter could be braver.

The dark spot held perfectly still, probably an animal, probably as startled as herself. She pressed the nervous mare nearer, not too close. With a proper start, Chestnut could outrun a two-legged pursuer, even on this unsteady ground.

"I say. Who is there?" she called.

The brush shivered.

She spotted a bit of brown drab, compact and curled in on itself. Her breath eased.

"Please come out. You're frightening my horse."

As if on cue, Chestnut snorted. The brown ball uncurled, crawled out and stood in the middle of the path, trembling, fists clenched, shoulders hunched.

It was a boy of about seven, if she was any judge of age. Light brown hair and pale skin peeked from under his cap.

"Good day to you." She scanned the moorland. He was alone.

Perry dismounted, and the boy shied away. She pulled out an apple she had taken and held it up to the mare, who eyed the boy, too nervous to take the offering.

She forced a laugh. "This is Chestnut. She is wary of you. Will you come close so she can see you mean her no harm?"

He shook his head.

"You do not speak? Are you a ghost then, wandering the moor all alone?"

His eyes widened and she could see they were a light shade of brown. His skin paled even more under the freckles sprinkling his nose.

She took a step. A soft cry escaped his lips.

"What is it, boy?"

"Y-you b-be the gh-ghost."

Another laugh bubbled up in her, this one real. "A ghost? Of course, I'm not a ghost. I'm but a lady, out for a ride. My name is…"

She should not give her true name. She did not want the locals to make note of her presence. The Justice of the Peace here, if he was in residence, would likely be an acquaintance of her father's.

"My name is Felicity." It was her middle name.

Too late, she remembered, it was also her mother's

name. The presence of a Felicity would be just as suspicious and ghost-invoking.

"But my friends call me...Lizzy, and you may also. What is your name?" She took another step.

He trembled more. She reached into her pocket and his little shoulders rose.

"Naught but another apple. You won't want the one that Chestnut has lipped." She dropped that into a different pocket. "Would you like this fresh one?"

He eyed it. Licked his lips. Shook his head. He had a mother or someone who had trained him not to take an apple from the stranger who might be the witch from the fairy tale.

"Truly, I am not a ghost. I'm but a woman. A mere woman, and the apples are good, brought from my brother's tree." She took a bite, chewed. Swallowed. "They're sweet. I have another as well as some biscuits."

His gaze went to her pocket and then darted back to her face. "They say you be she."

"She?" She took another bite.

His little chin went up and down. "The lady. A...a countess, she were. Thrown off the cliff and murdered."

Her blood surged. The bite of apple stuck in her throat and all around her the world stopped, only the crash of the distant waves and Chestnut's earthy breath breaking through her consciousness. She steadied herself against the horse and managed enough saliva to swallow. "Murdered?" Her voice sounded hollow, even to her.

"Aye. 'Afore I was born." The boy's tension seemed to ease. "You'd not heard? You're not from here."

"No."

"Everyone here knows. You didn't know?" A cocky note

had crept into his raspy voice, and all of his unease transferred to her.

Her mother had not died in a tragic accident. She'd been murdered.

Her pulse pounded in her ear. Who else knew of this? Surely her father did. And probably her brothers. And maybe Fox. And no one had bothered to tell *her*?

He cocked his head and eyed her speculatively. "Not going to keel over, are you?"

Keel over? This was a rude little man.

Well, she had weathered worse than this among the *ton*, and she needed information. "You've startled me, boy." She threw away her apple core and pulled out a cloth-wrapped stack of the biscuits that had dried out overnight. "Come along and have a biscuit with me, and tell me this ghost story, and then you may have my last apple, and perhaps Chestnut will feel comfortable enough to eat hers."

Still holding the reins, she unwrapped her package, took a biscuit, and offered him one.

He came close enough to accept one. A little thing, he was, thin, but not starved, with a face strained with too much worry for a child. She wondered if it was all due to the fright she'd given him.

"Now. You may call me Lizzy. What shall I call you?"

His chewing stopped. He frowned, chewed some more, swallowed, and shrugged. "Pip."

She handed him another biscuit. "Pip. Short for Phillip?"

The boy nodded solemnly.

"A lovely strong name. Tell me this ghost story."

"There once was a lady who lived there in Gorse Cottage —not allus, only sommat time she visited, see. But on one of her stays, late one night, someone came and threw her over the cliff and bashed her brains out all over the rocks."

Her stomach flipped again and a tingling started in her hands.

He finished his biscuit. "And not just her, her maid and her coachman too."

Fire roared through her, followed by rivers of ice, spots dancing in her vision.

Must not faint, Perry. Must not. She made her voice calm. "Who would do such a horrible thing?"

He lifted a shoulder and eyed the napkin. She gave him another biscuit. "No one ever says who, least not around me."

"But they know who?"

His brows drew together. "They're scared."

Her skin rippled. If they were scared, then the murderer was still alive and around. "I see. Do they know why she and her people were killed?"

"On account of the French, sommat said, but Gram says no Frenchies landed here and none ran around here without us knowing. No one comes through Clampton without us seeing."

"I did." But she'd taken a side road that skirted the town, and she'd made that stretch of the journey in early dawn.

He studied her. "Mayhap they thought you were her. She comes when there's a tenant at Gorse Cottage."

More astonishing revelations. Her mind reeled with them. "She comes here," she said woodenly. *She* was surely a living woman, and not a ghost.

Could Mama still be alive?

"Drives the tenants away. Will you be eatin' that last one?"

She handed him the biscuit. Her mother's ghost came here whenever there was a tenant.

"Is there often a tenant?"

"No. On account of her. And she keeps all the barrels out of her house. Don't bother with the other buildings though so they—

His mouth clamped shut. Only a child, but he knew the free traders' code.

"I see." She stopped and pressed her eyes closed. This was just like one of her father's schemes, resurrecting her mother to scare smugglers away. And did he know she'd been murdered, or was that merely the wild suspicion of unsophisticated rustics? The road was precarious enough that an accidental death was not out of the question.

"Where you be staying, Lizzy?"

When she opened her eyes, he was watching her, as savvy as any child of the London streets.

Unsophisticated rustics, indeed. The folk in these wild parts had engaged in the free trade for generations. They were cagey, and cool, and clever. Even this child was shrewd. And they were all good with secrets. She had merely frightened one out of him.

She could say she was a guest, at Scarborough perhaps, riding distance from here. And there was that baronet in the neighborhood who might host a guest.

"It is a secret," she said, buying time. "Come. I've given you all my biscuits. Now you must give Chestnut a scratch."

Distracted, he drew closer. The horse dipped its head, eyed the boy, and nosed him.

"It wants its apple," he said.

Perry pulled it from her pocket and handed it to him to present, a smile blooming on his lips at the tickle of the horse's mouth.

The smile warmed her. While Chestnut ate, he lifted a hand to stroke the horse, and Perry felt his delight all the way to her bones.

"I have an idea." She tossed the reins over the horse's head and took his hand. "Let's have a ride."

She tossed him up into the saddle, found a boulder to mount from, and hoisted herself up behind him. As Chestnut stepped out, the boy's stiff, startled little body relaxed against her. She nudged the mare into a trot and the boy's laugh sent a thrill through her.

WHEN FOX ENTERED THE INN, THE MURMURS FELL TO A HUSH and then resumed again, more subdued. The groggy-eyed locals had crawled out after a few hours of sleep, done whatever chores their women had forced upon them, and found their way here to get orders from Scruggs.

Nodding a greeting all around, he ordered a pint and looked around for a place to settle. The benches and stools held scattered groups of two or three men. Four other men sat apart at a table, hands gripping their tankards, gazes locked on him.

Outsiders, he'd guess from the glances the locals darted. Carvelle's reliable men, perhaps. Not likely to worry about a ghost, not likely to talk where locals or another outsider could hear.

No one invited him to join them. Not surprising, since last year a smuggler from this area named John Black had been transported based on the tales told by loose lips.

"May I?" He pulled a free chair from a table where two men sat and dragged it closer to the hearth, dead on this summer's afternoon. From this vantage point, he could watch the room and the doors, and dip into the conversations bubbling around him. Carvelle was not here, at least, not in this room.

The two men whose chair he'd lifted whispered. One, a

sandy-haired fellow, was already drunk. From the yellow tone of his skin, he'd been drunk since last night, or last week, or maybe even last month. The brown-haired friend made shushing noises.

His skin prickled. He recognized that shushing.

Fox nodded to them. "No rain today yet," he said in his best Eton accent. He was playing a bereaved secretary who'd just come into an inheritance.

The sandy-haired one's eyes widened. "Ye're the tenant up at Gorse Cottage?"

"I am."

Hair lifted along his neck, the ripple continuing down between his shoulder blades. For certain this was the ghost-believing Davy and his shushing friend, the men who knew who had killed Lady Shaldon.

Davy opened his mouth to say more, but the tap room door opened again and another man entered. Just like the others, Fox swung his gaze to him.

14

GOODFELLOW AT THE INN

A hale fellow this was, tall, well-fed, his gray hair tied into an old-fashioned queue under his old-fashioned tricorne. He was well-dressed and well-shod also, in the woolens and high boots of a hunting squire. The maid curtsied and ran to tap him a tankard, his order unspoken. The murmuring started up again.

He was a regular, and welcome, but not a mate to any of these men. Rheumy eyes under bushy dark brows scanned the room and landed on Fox.

His gut, so rarely wrong, matched a name to the beefy red face. This was the local squire, Sir Richard Fenwick.

Not, he decided, a mere tolerant recipient of bribes. He was a partner to Scruggs in the free trade. Was he also a partner to Carvelle?

The man headed straight for Fox, the strong ale sloshing onto his sleeves, splashing his boots and the poorly-swept floor.

"Goodfellow, is it?"

Fenwick cast a glance at Davy and his friend. They lifted their hats, drained their tankards, and cleared out.

"Ah, boys, thank you, thank you. How's your young Pip, Davy? Gaz, your mother? Join me, Goodfellow?" Without waiting for answers, he plopped on a chair.

Fox swallowed a frustrated sigh. Instead of asking questions, he'd be dodging them.

Fenwick got right to it. "How come you to take Shaldon's cottage, Goodfellow? Friends of the family, eh?" He chugged a drink. "Oh, beg your pardon. I'm Richard Fenwick. Sir Richard. Baronet." He grinned stiffly. "Minor, very minor compared to the Earl, isn't it? But I get on well enough. Friend of the family, are you?"

"Not at all. I'm a simple tenant. Happy to make your acquaintance, Sir Richard."

"Is that so? From these parts?"

"No. The Midlands and then elsewhere. My father was a factor for a large estate up north." True enough, though his father hadn't been in service—the estate was his own, and *north* was in *North America*.

"In the same line of work, were you?"

"No. I worked as a secretary." Also true; when he was sixteen.

"Indeed. For some great lord?"

The nosey lout. "No."

"Here on holiday, are you?"

"You might say. I lost my employer and gained a small inheritance. And with the spectacle of the coronation, it's a good time to be out of London."

"You worked there?"

"Some of the time."

Sir Richard considered that and grunted. "Detest the place, myself." He called for another tankard. "Lonely up there at Gorse Cottage, are you?" His gaze went to the fireplace.

"I enjoy the solitude."

Sir Richard did not immediately respond, caught up in some vision that made him frown more deeply.

Time for some probing of his own. "I understand from the estate agent it was a favorite haunt of the Earl's wife."

Sir Richard's gaze came up flashing in what looked to be anger, quickly masked. "Foolish rumors."

"I beg your pardon?"

"Rumors of hauntings."

"Ghosts? I only meant—"

"Felicity is dead. She's not coming back." Sir Richard swept a hand over his face.

"Do you mean Lady Shaldon?"

"Lady Shaldon." Eyes simmering with strong emotion, he took a quick swig, frowning.

"I heard that Lady Shaldon had died. Was her death tragic then? That's how most rumors of hauntings get started, I've found."

Sir Richard's mouth and fists tightened.

Fox leaned closer. "Not that I believe a bit in ghosts."

"Sir Richard." The voice calling was Scruggs', and none too subservient, as if the men were equals. Which perhaps they were—equals in crime.

"We'll speak again." The Baronet's chair squealed as he stood.

An hour and another pint later, having learned nothing more, Fox gave the gelding its head and dashed back on this well-trod path across the high Yorkshire moor. The villagers kept it up for the carts and donkeys they occasionally used for their hauls, and the footing was good.

Tomorrow, he'd send MacEwen to Charley. MacEwen

could make the trip in one day, arrange for a message to go on to London, and be back to Gorse Cottage in one more day. Shaldon might be busy with King George, but his son could come and help out. It would take one of Perry's brothers to blast her out of here, and if they could keep her visit secret, she wouldn't be forced to marry some titled fool for the sake of her reputation.

His fists tightened around the reins. The thought of her lying under some lout like Sir Richard...

No. He had to push that picture away. He was not the man for her, and she should not be here. More than her reputation was in danger. Under Sir Richard's fat, affable facade was a man he couldn't quite pin down. Involved with Scruggs, most certainly, if only to turn a blind eye. Was he also attached to Carvelle?

Charley might know more about the man. If Lady Shaldon had been from these parts, the families might have been acquainted. Though he had no idea whether Sir Richard kept a wife and children at home. He should have asked that question.

Nearing the cliffs and the turn-off to Gorse Cottage, he spotted a distant rider to the south, stark against the horizon. He pulled his spyglass from his pocket.

Two riders sat atop the one horse. A long leg stretched from under a skirt of the palest green. One leg. The body seated in front was much smaller, the jacket and trousers much darker.

He cursed. MacEwen had been tasked with keeping Perry at home. They'd even hidden her sidesaddle, so of course, she'd be riding astride. And where the hell had she found a boy child?

As he spurred his horse, Chestnut shied, and they

spotted him. The boy started to leap, and she caught him in time, handing him down to dart off through the brush toward town.

Perry turned her horse and cantered to him. Her bonnet had knocked back and loose curls framed her face. She looked windswept and fresh and astonishingly lovely. The perfect target for any man happening to wander by.

He slowed the gelding, trying to freeze the picture into his memory. He wouldn't paint it, not now, not until after he'd returned to America.

He stopped, tried to slow his heart, tried to beat back the urge to pull her down from the horse and onto the ground. Her skirts were already up. His gaze traced the lines of her lovely legs. Was she wearing pantalettes? They were in fashion now, but that hadn't always been the case.

She pulled her horse up alongside him.

The bounce of her breasts meant she had dispensed with her stays. Pulse pounding, blood flowing like liquid heat straight to his loins, he lifted his hat. "Out for a ride?"

She moved closer. "You owe me explanations."

"About the saddle—"

"No. No, Fox. Not the saddle. I am not wholly an idiot. I worked that one out easily enough." She spoke through tense lips, as if the words caused her pain. "And I'll have no more of your diversions and distractions." She raised her fist.

"Who *was* that boy?"

"No. No diversions. I will ask the questions, and you will answer them."

Dear Perry. He looked around. "If that boy was here, there could be others. Can we go back to the cottage to talk?"

She nodded, tersely, and edged out of his way. "After you."

He pulled up alongside her. "We'll go together."

15

A TERRIBLE SECRET REVEALED

Fox watched Perry pace the Turkish carpet of the drawing room, face locked into a mask of perfect aplomb. By the time they'd returned to the stables and seen to their horses, the afternoon had advanced into evening. Jenny was in the kitchen preparing dinner, with help from MacEwen, and neither would be underfoot for Perry's interrogation of him.

She'd come down from her high horse to this blandness. Someone had managed a bit of progress in molding her into a tractable woman suitable for marriage. The thought vaguely depressed him, but he comforted himself with the notion that they hadn't quite succeeded, else she wouldn't be here.

And her hands, gripped at her slim waist, showed the passionate woman inside, the woman he'd seen blossoming ten years earlier.

He unclenched his own fists. "Won't you take a seat?"

If she sat, he wouldn't be so tempted to go to her, to take her into his arms.

She nodded and seated herself like a queen, perching on

the edge of a wing chair, back as straight as the paneled wall. Her stony compliance was a deeper cut than any physical blow.

He deserved it, didn't he? Where Perry was concerned, he always deserved it. He turned the matching chair to face hers and sat down.

I will ask the questions, you will answer them, she'd said.

Or not. He lounged back in the chair and waited.

"What really happened to my mother, Fox?" she asked, her voice tense.

The question brought him up. Where the devil had it come from?

She's back to get the ones as threw her over the cliff...

"I don't truly know, Perry." That wasn't a lie. He couldn't say more based on the words of a drunken free trader. "I heard that her coach went off the road."

"Was it this road, the cliff road leading to Gorse Cottage?"

"Yes."

She put a hand to her heart and swallowed hard. "How? What happened?"

"I don't know."

"Fox, was she murdered?"

"I don't know that either."

"*Fox.*" Her face bloomed with color.

He hated this, hated the pain he was causing her. "I truly don't know, not for certain. What did the boy tell you?"

"That someone came, threw her over the cliff, and bashed her b-brains out." Her hands knotted together, and he felt the clenching in his own heart.

He couldn't leave her thinking her mother died so dreadfully. "Oh, Perry. I don't know that it happened like that. That might be a story the locals made up to keep outsiders away."

"Then how did it happen?"

He went onto his knees and took her knotted hands. "I wasn't here. I don't truly know. I'd guess your father doesn't either. I was told she was in the carriage returning to Cransdall, and..." He shook his head. "The wheel came off, or the axle broke. The carriage jumped that narrow road and fell onto the rocks below."

Was she thrown over? The picture was too terrible.

"How?" Her voice had gone small. "Mother always kept everything in prime order. And it wouldn't have been sabotage. She had guards around her, always. Father insisted. His work was so dangerous. He had so many enemies."

He released her and got to his feet, dragging a hand through his hair. "It's possible the coach was tampered with. The guards had left with your father."

Her eyes went wide and her mouth dropped open. The longing to kiss her astonishment away, to stop the questioning, was almost overpowering. She'd known nothing of this. How could her father and brothers not have told her?

How to tell the rest? How to say that Lady Shaldon's death had been in a way his fault?

She gripped the chair arms. "My father took her guards and went away?"

"Yes." His insides churned, nerves flaring with the memory of unbearable pain, inflicted by a noble barbarian who'd smelled like a Covent Garden whore.

He took a deep breath. That was all behind him. "He was supposed to accompany your mother to Cransdall. He should have been in that carriage also. Instead, he left with the others and went back to the Continent." Cold and heat came together on his skin. He clasped his hands behind his back to hide the shaking.

She pushed out of the chair and came nearer, within his reach, peering up at his face. "Go on."

"Your father had been captured and held for a ransom and not well-treated either. Your mother...organized...the payment and came here to make the arrangements for delivery, and to meet him when he was returned." He gripped her elbows. "You did not know any of this, Perry?"

"No. Go on."

"The ransom was delivered. Your father...arrived here."

And in between had been a whole world of events.

He took a deep breath. Beaten and bedraggled as Shaldon had been, his arrival must have left Lady Shaldon ready for a fight.

Perry had so much of her mother in her. He swept a thumb over her smooth skin. "Several days later, he returned to the Continent."

She frowned. "But why?"

And now they came to it. "To rescue the man who delivered the ransom."

"From the kidnapper?"

"No. From the French."

"It wasn't the French who held my father?"

His nerves roared with an unquenched need for revenge. He understood Shaldon and his quest. He knew what the man was about to his core. He knew why he'd not shared this with his children. All three—no, four including his by-blow—would have piled into his captor at the first opportunity and slashed him to bits.

He shook his head. "Not at first. It was a Spaniard. A French collaborator."

Her eyes lit and her mouth worked like she was tasting something foul. "The Duque de San Sebastian. He's in London for the coronation. I'm glad Charley cuckolded him."

He couldn't help laughing. His spunky girl had emerged.

No, not *his* spunky girl. He dropped his hands and took a step back. She wasn't his girl at all, and he must remember that.

"My brother Bink fought on the Peninsula and said the Spanish nobility were mostly spineless traitors. The Duque knew mother had stacks of money. How much was the ransom?"

"He didn't want just money."

"But the ransom—"

"He wanted the painting. Your mother's masterpiece. The painting of Perpetua and Felicity."

Her mouth dropped open and a wave of crimson lit her cheeks. "I thought you'd stolen it."

Sweat tickled his cheek. He wiped it away with the back of his hand. "In a way, Perry, I did."

He opened the French door to a sharp breeze. Outside, below them, the waves bashed themselves on those rocks, those bloody rocks that had taken Lady Shaldon's life. Fox sucked in a great lungful of air, remembering.

Through tense days and nights, he had painted, frantically, furiously. During the day, he brushed the contours of Lady Shaldon's strong face and elegant form, trying to smooth out the worry lines on the canvas, trying to remember the composure of her expression before the news of the capture had arrived.

At night—he must have started the copy a dozen times, frustrated and frantic to get all the subtleties of lighting right—and everything else, down to the back of the canvas

113

and the peculiar markings along the edge. An exact replica would be his gift to the woman who had shown him much kindness.

The pressure of Perry's fingers on his arm brought him back. She nudged him around facing her.

"Tell me."

"I copied it."

Her brows drew together. "You *forged* it?"

Not a pretty word and not apt for what he'd done. "Yes. I was there, working on your mother's portrait when the ransom demand came in. She...she lost her composure that day. The painting had been an early gift from your father and she treasured it." She had cried. Lady Shaldon had cried at her husband's peril and at the demand for the painting. He shook his head. "Why your father's captor wanted it wasn't clear. The painter, Lopez de Arteaga, had created the work in Mexico. As far as she knew, the painting had never been in San Sebastian's hands."

Perry's gaze held him, her eyes shining with an intensity and strength that was hers alone. She would be a formidable woman, if she didn't get herself killed first.

"Go on, Fox."

She would be as strong as her mother. She could handle the whole story, or at least as much as he knew of it. "Copying a great work is not unusual. I'd had commissions like that. And all art students copy the masters—it's how we learn. And I was good at it. So, I offered to copy it for her, in order that she would at least have that much."

"Oh, Fox." She swallowed and her eyes grew shiny. "Mother's was the last portrait, and you completed it so quickly—I had no idea." She shook her head. "I thought you were avoiding us. That you were anxious to get away. I had

114

no idea you were working on two paintings." She bit her lip. "But that space on Mother's wall holds a different painting. Where is the copy?"

He looked out the window. There'd be a few more hours of light, but the moonless night would draw out free traders. They needed to finish this talk so he could be about his business.

"I don't know. Maybe it washed out to sea when she died."

Her frown deepened, her confusion evident.

"She brought both paintings here. I believe she was dithering about whether to gamble."

"She loved that ragged old painting," Perry said sadly.

"Yes." And ragged it had been, darkened and cracked from rough care during its journey from New Spain to England. "Before the ransom demand, she'd asked me about sending it out for a careful restoration. But she told me the rough condition was part of the charm for her."

"As if it was as antiquated as the subjects depicted, she always said." Perry lifted her chin. "And was your copy cracked and darkened?"

"Not enough, I suppose, though I tried."

Perry inhaled sharply. "But...Mama was deciding whether to gamble? What do you mean?"

"She rolled up both paintings and then she waited until the very last minute to decide which to send. Whichever one she kept landed on the rocks with her and all of her baggage and was taken away by the tide." He waved a hand. "And if so, it's out there, somewhere, at the bottom of the sea, ruined."

"*No.*" Perry released him and pounded a fist on the wooden jamb. "How *could* she have risked that?"

She paced to the cold fireplace and back, stopping in front of him. "And the rest of the story? After Father's release, did the Duque discover a forgery and imprison my mother's courier?"

The shadowy light softened her strong features into the lines of an Athena. She'd shoved all the other women he'd known—lovers, models, even his first love, the woman who'd become his brother's wife—to the distant past. No matter where he went, or what he was painting, her face would be the one he remembered.

"I don't know that the Duque has ever investigated the painting's authenticity. But I'm quite sure he thought it was real when he unrolled it. And then, he locked the courier up with your father and turned both of them over to the French. He never meant to send your father home at all."

"How did Father—"

"He escaped."

Her gaze skittered across the room, hands knotting together again. She gave her head a little shake. "Escaped. And left Kincaid in a French jail?"

Kincaid?

She bit her lips. "Father wouldn't do that. Kincaid is his right-hand man."

He took a deep breath. She didn't know. Of course she didn't. Only Shaldon and Kincaid and a few others knew.

"Perry, it's understood that sometimes not everyone *can* escape. Your father's survival was the more important. He had great responsibilities to your country, and your mother was waiting for him here. And," He took a deep breath, "It wasn't Kincaid who brought the painting to the Continent."

Her eyes widened and then narrowed. Her mouth dropped open. So smart, his Perry. He knew the moment she saw the truth.

116

But he had to say it out loud anyway. He wanted her trust for what he must do next.

"I was the courier."

"You were?" The words *whooshed* out of her and she saw spots.

Fox was a bounder, a forger, and an American spy, and he'd saved her father's life. And Father had gone back to save Fox. And now he was here.

"Perry." He gripped her shoulders and shook them. "*Perry.*"

Fox had forged the painting. Not stolen it. He'd served her mother. He'd risked his life to save her father. He'd stayed in a French prison so her father could live.

She wanted to rest her head on his chest, but he'd locked his arms and held her away from him, looking into her eyes as if she would faint.

Well, and perhaps she might indeed swoon.

She straightened, managed a breath, and then another, and shook off his hands, searching his face. He looked... tired, wounded in some very deep place. He'd been held by the French, and French cruelty was legendary.

How long had they held him? Had they chained him? Beaten him? She scanned his body for visible scars.

There. The scar on his jaw, and evidence of another cut near his hairline. Had they known he was an American, not English? Her mind buzzed with questions.

"Perry, I'm going to send for your brother."

The words brought her up. Her brother—Charley, or Bakeley, or Bink, never mind which one—would carry her off. He wanted her gone. She'd be locked up, maybe married off. She took a step back. And another.

117

"It's too dangerous here."

Dangerous. The killer was still here.

"I can't...I know I said you could stay, but I want you safe, Perry." His fingers raked his hair. "I don't want you hurt."

He cared for her.

And she wanted him—he was her only hope for a chance at real passion in the cold, miserable life that society would allow for her. Her brothers could flout convention and marry the women they loved but...

Loved. She swallowed hard. Was this love she was feeling for Fox? Had she loved him while thinking she hated him, while trying to squash all her *feelings*?

And did he love her?

That painting in his room was evidence of feelings.

The painting.

She picked up her skirts and ran.

She soon heard his steps pounding behind, but she reached his room before him and closed the door, leaning against it, heart hammering, breaths coming in short spurts.

The long summer afternoon had passed into evening. Outside, the first shadows of evening cast a pall on the room. She looked around, one hand gripping the latch, her vision adjusting, while determined footsteps edged nearer.

He rattled the door latch and pushed, and she dug in the heels of her boots, scanning the room, finally able to focus. The easel—and the canvas on it—were gone.

A hot wave of anger swept through her. Had he hidden it away or destroyed it?

With one hard push, she was catapulted forward onto his bed. She reached out to brace herself and one hand struck an unlit lamp, the other pressed into the mattress. She struggled to right herself, to right the lamp.

"God, Perry." His voice shook. "This is why you must leave."

The lamp teetered and shattered, just like her heart.

16

A DAZZLING APHRODITE

*P*erry buried her face in the bed pillow. It smelled of citrus and Fox's own musk. She turned her head and rubbed her cheek against the linen. Today he'd left the bed rumpled and messy and—yes, he was right. By all that was holy and proper with the *ton*, finding herself plopped onto his bed was why she must leave.

She turned on her side and curled her legs, relaxing into the cloth-covered ticking. Fox's bed was considerably lumpier than hers.

"Get up." He spoke from next to the bed.

She waited for his touch.

"Get up."

"I'm not a performing dog."

"Of course you're not. You're Lady Perpetua, the daughter of the Earl of Shaldon."

She squeezed her eyes tight against his cold jabs. No tears. She would not cry. She would *not*. No matter how unfair he was, talking to her as if she was a spoiled miss.

She wasn't spoiled. She hadn't even been a spoiled child

all those years ago. She was dutiful, and kind, and a rule-follower.

And so tired of it. She'd grasped this chance to take charge of her life, and she was determined to stay the course.

She pushed herself upright on the edge of the bed, with Fox standing just within reach. The dimming light shadowed his handsome face, but couldn't hide the heat coming off him, or the sound of his breathing. He may be angry, but he cared for her.

"Why do you do it, Fox?"

His scent came to her on a sudden breeze. One of the windows must be open.

"Perpetua."

Her heart leaped. He hadn't asked what she was talking about.

"Perry. Call me Perry, as you've been doing."

She stood and he took a step back.

"You tease me and draw me close, and then you push me away. Why?"

"You need to go home, Lady Perpetua. You should not be here in the home of a single man—and yes, for now it is my home, not yours."

She caught a note of desperation in his voice. "And you're engaged in a dangerous business."

He paused. "Yes."

"Thank you for the truth. You are looking for my mother's murderer."

"Yes."

He'd hesitated again. Finding her mother's killer was not the only reason he was here then. "And you also are a spy."

"I'm not—"

"Yes. I believe you are. But for whom? Nine years ago, our countries were at war. Were you at Cransdall ten years ago spying on the spymaster?"

Fox took a step back. She moved closer.

"A portraitist with well-heeled clients moves in the highest circles. He dabs paint in the corners of rooms and listens to people talking. Did you spy for France, Fox?"

He grasped her arms and locked his to hold her away. "I would never spy for a country of brutes who turn the guillotine on so many of their own."

"England has brutes, so I've heard. Yet here you are. Spying for America then?"

"Perry."

He'd softened that one word into a wheedling tone that made her shiver.

She pressed harder. "Yes, I think that's what you did. You met friends from the embassy for drinks or lunch and passed on the tidbits of what you learned. Charley often operated that way. And then shortly before our countries went back to war, you did that one job for my mother."

"You have it all figured out," he said.

He was trying for his usual bland sarcasm, but she heard it—that note of distraction, a lack of air, a deep pain that called to some still deeper part of her womanhood.

"You did this one job and it almost got you killed." She set her hand over his pulsing heart.

HER PALM PRESSED LIKE A HOT IRON, THE LONG FINGERS trailing lightning into his soul, streaks of white heat beating into him, centering in his groin, inflaming him. She was here. In his room. Could be in his bed in one quick move.

Muscles straining with effort, he pulled her hand away.

"Let me escort you back downstairs. Jenny will have dinner ready." He infused his voice with the type of ennui he'd heard at the hundreds of dinner parties he'd attended as the interesting American artist. His few years of formal education and the pedigree he'd embellished had made the novelty guest acceptable. "You must be famished." He should get her downstairs, fed, and back safely to her chambers. The smugglers might return tonight for their booty. When they found two kegs missing they'd be pounding on his door for answers.

"Oh, I am famished all right. Where is the painting of me you were working on?"

Bollocks. "So you saw that."

"I did." She inched closer. "I will pose for you, should you wish to work from a live model."

Perry the woman, grown into Aphrodite. His arms itched to pull her against him.

He took a step back. At this rate, she'd edge him out of the window.

The tiny brain between his legs shouted, *Why not take her?* She wanted him, and by all the wild Indians in Kentucky, he wanted her. He'd stepped back once from a woman he'd wanted and she'd fallen into another man's arms. His brother's arms.

The memory jumbled his brain. Seducing a virgin was not his way. He'd been honorable with Constance, the wealthy Philadelphia girl who'd abandoned him for his older brother, and he'd looked back many times thanking his stars. Losing Constance had wounded his pride—and been a great blessing. He would never have progressed so far in his painting, or had such adventures, or met *this* magnificent woman.

Who he also could not have.

123

In spite of the dimness, her eyes shone brightly. He should light the surviving lamp.

"You were not the model for that painting."

She twitched. "Was I not?" A deep sigh escaped her. "Why the lies, Fox? Why always the lies? Why push me away?"

He broke from her, found his tinder box, busied himself with lighting the lamp.

Then cursed himself—in the light, she glowed more than ever, beautiful, and with a strength that surprised him.

"You want me, Fox, and I want you."

Without touching, without removing one article of clothing, she was seducing him; artless, gawky, Lady Perpetua. He almost laughed.

He was but a man, dammit, and she a lovely woman.

The daughter of Lord Shaldon, his employer and benefactor. A virgin.

"Look at me, Lady Perpetua. I paint pictures for my living."

"And spy."

He sighed. "That is not a means of support. I paint pictures for my living. Where I go, I rent cheap rooms. I don't host parties. I don't belong to Brooks's or White's. I don't own a horse."

She opened her mouth.

Do not tell me about your fortune.

She closed her mouth and squeezed her lips together.

"You, on the other hand, are the only daughter of one of the great families of England. You're destined for more greatness, Perry." He swallowed. "Lady Perpetua. You're destined for greatness that has nothing to do with your money. With the right husband, you will be a political leader in your own right, influencing bills and elections."

"Ladies have no—"

"Don't tell me ladies have no power." He tapped a finger on her forehead. "This powerful brain understands the workings of politics. You may not be able to serve in your parliament, but you have a father and brothers who do. Political men need political hostesses."

"My brothers have wives."

"Find the right husband and—"

"No." She closed her eyes and took a deep breath. "You're doing it again." She looked around the room and went back to perch on his bed.

He took the chair across the room. "It's the only way for you. And you can't do that if you start out with a scandal, caught alone with an American painter who's nowhere near good enough for you on any scale of measuring. You have to go home, or back to your brother's, and the sooner we get you out of here, the better. The locals think you're a ghost."

"I know. Pip told me."

"Pip."

"The boy I met on the road."

Tension crept through him. He'd heard a mention of Pip that very day.

Confound it. Pip was Davy's son.

"Dammit, Perry. What did you tell him?"

"After he told me my mother was murdered?" she asked archly. "You don't need to curse at me, Fox. I told him my name was Lizzie. I didn't tell him I was staying at Gorse Cottage. And I asked him to keep our encounter secret. He said he would, and I think the children around here are good at secrets."

He had to persuade her to leave. "Pip's father was down at the cove last night. He saw you in the window." His skin prickled. This window. She'd been in his room snooping. "He thought you were a ghost."

Her back stiffened. "The ghost comes when there's a tenant at Gorse Cottage, Pip said." Perry studied the floor and lifted her gaze to him. "I don't believe in ghosts. Who comes here? Are the smugglers sending in ghosts to keep outsiders away?"

"More likely your father sends the tenants and has them tell a good ghost story to keep the smugglers out of his house and your mother's things. Also, your father and his people must have needed this cottage during the war."

"Not much goes on that the locals don't know."

"True. But you can see you need to leave before they realize you're real flesh and blood."

Her gaze drilled into him. Her fingers gripped the edge of the mattress. "I'll not leave before *you* realize I'm real flesh and blood."

Blood pulsed and heated and sent fire through him. He ached with the need for her. "I know you're real flesh and blood. You're also a virgin. High-born or low, doesn't matter to me. I don't despoil virgins."

Perry watched him, as still as a statue, quite unlike the girl who had wriggled and grimaced all through her sitting so many years ago.

"I'll send MacEwen tomorrow for your brother."

She rose from the lumpy mattress like the phoenix, glowing in the light and floating closer until she was standing over his chair. The shadows played at her neck and her throat, inciting visions of her on top of him. He gripped the arms of his chair.

"I'll make you a deal, Fox." She set her hands upon his and leaned closer, filling him with her scent. "Take me to your bed. Take me." She squeezed her eyes a brief moment

126

and when she opened them they glowed, dark and deep. "Make love to me. And then I'll leave on my own. No need to send for my brothers."

Dazzling, she was. His shaft raged at him, wanting him to open his arms, to shout *yes* and take her. He dug his nails into the wood. He could control this. He could think for both of them.

"No, Lady Perpetua. I'll paint you. I'll protect you. I won't ruin you."

She blinked.

Oh, God, the hurt he saw in her eyes flayed his heart.

"Is that how you see making love to me?"

"I'm an American painter with no fortune and no prospects. You're Lady Perpetua."

She traced a finger along his jaw and sucked on her lip, sending fire through him. "Oh, Fox, I'm but a woman. Will you not see me as that?"

He pulled her finger away. "It cannot be."

Her lovely jaw firmed and her lips trembled. "You do not wish it to be."

She jerked away and walked to the window, taking her heat with her, leaving him bereft. So be it.

He released his grip on the chair arms. "Jenny should have the food ready soon, if she hasn't burned everything. Would you like your dinner served in the parlor?"

"I cannot bear to face the life everyone plans for me." She turned an inscrutable gaze at him. "Are you planning formal dress for dinner?" Turning back, she leaned her forehead against the window pane. "The kitchen is fine. I believe Jenny has a tendre for MacEwen."

She sounded distracted, scattered, emotionally dull, like he had finally broken through her willfulness. He needed to get her out of here before the urge to take her into his arms overcame *him.*

Poking her into anger had always worked. "And what good would come of that?"

Her breath frosted the chilly window. He wondered if her eyes were closed.

"A moment of happiness," she whispered into the glass, and then straightened. "I'll see if she needs help in the kitchen."

The door closed quietly behind her.

He leaned back in his chair and put a hand to his cock, and then pulled it back right away, as if he'd been scorched. It had been a close call when she'd touched his beard.

He sighed. His wash water would be cold. Scraping off this scruff, he might take some of the skin with it, which was just what he deserved.

Shedding his shirt and coats, he set about washing and shaving.

She'd walked off despondent, but she'd come around to hating him again. He'd talk to her brother and ask him to keep this from the rest of the family.

He hated seeing her unhappy, but it was the only choice. Between the Scotsman and the maid there was more chance for a moment of happiness than there could ever be for him and Perry.

Tomorrow, he'd send MacEwen for her brother. He'd get the name of her brother's estate over supper, and then he'd go out, for the rest of the night if need be, anything to keep away from the girl. Or he'd go and sleep in the stable with MacEwen. The straw couldn't be any lumpier than this mattress.

* * *

"YOU'RE SURE YOU WON'T JOIN US, MISS?" JENNY SHIFTED THE tray onto the table, sliding the stacked coins out of the way. And why would Lady Perry be counting her coins?

"Are you quite all right, miss? I can just as well cart this back to the kitchen if you'll but join us."

Lady Perry turned away from the window and sent her a thin smile. "I thought to give you more time with your Fergus MacEwen."

Heat flared in her. "He's not *my* Fergus MacEwen."

That brought a real smile from Lady Perry. "Well, he's more likely to flirt and slip up if I'm not around. You must get him to share one of his secrets."

"I'll serve the men when they come down and come back in a bit for this tray."

"No need." Lady Perry shook her head vigorously. "Leave it until morning. And don't worry about helping me into bed. I haven't had a full night's sleep since I don't know when. Use the corridor door to your chamber. I don't wish to be disturbed."

She softened that last with another smile, but Jenny detected a tension around her eyes.

"Whatever you're planning, I can be a help, my lady."

"I'm not...I'm not planning anything."

"You're counting your money."

"I'm thinking to send for more supplies." She let out a great yawn and covered her mouth. "Go then, and don't fret."

"But, miss—"

"Go, Jenny." Lady Perry crossed the room and Jenny felt the soft pressure of her hand on her back. "Go serve the men their supper and talk to your MacEwen."

That afternoon, MacEwen had stripped to his waist to

129

shave, grinning around the blade scraping his jaws. He'd flirted prodigiously, too.

Jenny put aside her unease and pulled the door closed behind her.

She would come back for that tray though, after the men's dinner was cleared.

17

BOLTED

MacEwen lifted the lid on the pot and took a good sniff. "Mmm. Stew's always better the second day, my mam used to say. Smells good, wee Jenny."

Jenny shrugged and looked away. "That's Mr. Fox's cooking."

The girl's earlier cheekiness had gone to indifference. He laughed. A good game, this was. "And where's yours?"

"I'm only boiling up peas and some turnips, and cooking some bacon."

"I'm sure they'll be as lovely as you."

Her lush lips formed a prim line. "And lucky it will be if they don't turn to mash. I'm no cook, MacEwen."

"Your mam didn't teach you?" He watched for her reaction. He'd heard her story. He was shamelessly goading her, and wasn't all fair in love?

She plopped her hands on her hips, right about where he'd like to put his own, and looked at him full on. "And you know I haven't a proper mam, not past the birthing of me. So, don't play the muttonhead with me, Fergus MacEwen."

He chuckled. His mam—or the cook that his mam

usually employed—could teach this girl all she needed to know about boiling, roasting, and stewing, and he could teach her other things.

"Now go and see if the peas are ready, while I set the dishes out."

"Aye, miss." He saluted. "I will."

"It smells good in here." Fox had entered noiselessly, bottle of brandy in hand. "Shall I ring the dinner bell for Lady Perpetua?"

Half-empty bottle, he noted. Fox had been tippling already.

"No, sir. She's taken a tray in her room."

A grimace flashed across Fox's face. He pulled out a chair. On edge, was Fox, and rightly so. The lady must have pushed him with even more determination during their private talk. There was no mistaking her intent. She was comely enough for a Long Meg, and 'twas clear the two had a hankering for each other. But a man could see by the state of that bottle, Fox had held to his honor.

Or perhaps he was just wary of the father. Shaldon had a long memory and a long reach, and didn't this present duty attest to that.

He and his cousin had balked at working with a portrait artist, but after what had happened in Holland, his respect for Fox had risen considerably. Clearly, he'd been at this game for some time, maybe longer than himself. Aye, and there was some story here between Fox and Shaldon that Kincaid had hinted at.

"Is she feeling unwell?" Fox asked.

"She didn't say." Jenny's voice was so carefully neutral, he knew she was lying. Fox looked up. He knew it also.

For sure they'd had a row. Fox had found her out and about riding astride—damn dangerous for the girl. If

Shaldon's enemies got their grubby hands on his only daughter, that leverage would complicate their mission here.

Tomorrow, Fox would send him off with a message to Shaldon to come get his daughter, and then she and Jenny would leave. He'd have to steal all his kisses tonight, providing he could turn the girl's mood from whatever was bothering her.

Jenny set out the food. He snagged a piece of turnip.

"Ah, Jenny, it looks lovely." He pushed a glass over and Fox poured some drink.

The gin tubs sat stopped up nicely on a wooden counter, bait to bring the free traders to heel.

There were two settings only at the table. "Not eating with us, fair Jenny?" he asked.

She cast him a troubled look. "I've nibbled all through the cooking."

He swept a gaze over her. "Don't want you to wither away to nothing."

She turned away, so he couldn't even see if her cheeks had gone pink. Fox spooned his food numbly. All in all, his dining companions were far too somber.

"Have I ever told you, Fox, that some of the MacEwens went off to America?"

"Is that so?"

"Aye. Had to leave, they did."

"Why?" Jenny asked.

"Well, now." He took a bite of stew and chewed, thinking of which story to tell. Her ladyship was safely moping in her room. The free traders wouldn't be out until midnight cracked.

He'd stretch out this evening with the girl as long as he could.

* * *

SCARBOROUGH WAS NOT SO FAR DOWN THE ROAD THAT PERRY couldn't reach it tonight, then perhaps take a room at an inn and check on the sailings. Or perhaps return to Gorse Cottage before Jenny discovered she had decided on more than an evening's ride.

She let Chestnut find her own way down the moorland road heading south. Somewhere along this way she'd cross over the Baronet's property. What she knew of the man could balance on one fingertip. He was older than Father, Jane had said. Sir Richard would be tucked up tight in his bed, no doubt. He would be no threat to her.

What stars there were, were concealed by clouds. Chestnut couldn't do more than a careful pace.

It was good she hadn't told Jenny she was leaving. The girl would have wanted to accompany her, but she needed Jenny at the house, serving the supper, buying Perry time to sneak out of the front door, to saddle the horse, and slip down the road unnoticed.

Fox's rejection rubbed at her pride, but no matter. She'd find a less noble man on the Continent someday. Maybe.

And if not, well, she'd have her freedom, and that counted for something. Because she was not going to be carted off like a prize mare by her brother.

Her precious bit of money and her jewels were jammed into her boots, cramping her feet. The blade comforted her arms, and the pistols nestled in the waistband of her pantaloons.

To her left, the sea pounded and roared, in and out, a rhythm that echoed the beats of Chestnut's jostling gait. The road stretched, twisting and turning through low scrub.

Had there been enough light, she'd be able to see for miles in all directions.

Under her thin coat, she shivered, and the bit of stew she'd managed to swallow stirred in her stomach.

It was foolish to leave, perhaps. Yet, the men made these sorts of rides all the time. Surely she could also?

Her departure would worry Jenny, and Fox would be angry. With any luck, she'd reach Scarborough before MacEwen caught up with her. Unless Fox came after her himself, and then—

Chestnut shied. The brush to the right fluttered and swayed, and ahead in the road was a shadow.

Cold fear swamped her. She clucked, turned the horse around, and broke into a trot, reaching for one of the pistols.

A hand grabbed the bridle, knocked the gun away, and yanked her down by the leg, plopping her on her bottom. This was a large man, as tall as she, but three times her size in bulk. With his free hand he whacked her across the face, knocking her hat off. Another figure ran up and the mare shied and kicked, pulling at the reins.

Perry flew up with a kick to the second man's jewels. He bellowed, let the horse loose, and snatched at her collar.

While she wrestled, the horse danced and whinnied, trying to shake off the villain.

Dear Chestnut. Perry slapped the horse hard on her rump. Chestnut kicked out at the big man, broke free and ran off into the night, back the way that they'd come.

Dear God, she was all alone now.

But Chestnut would save her. Chestnut would find her way to that stable and Fox would notice. He would come.

A foot flew at her and she grabbed it, pulling this slighter man down. All the times as a child when she'd wrestled with

Charley might not help her win, but she'd not go down without a fight.

Fox had just poured another brandy, MacEwen's mouth was still running with stories, and Jenny was scrubbing pots when a knock came at the back door.

They exchanged looks. "Tubs in the pantry," Fox said. "Jenny, you stay in there with them."

MacEwen hurried both tubs into the storeroom and returned.

Fox waited while MacEwen got in place behind the door, then opened it to the two bedraggled sods who'd given up their table to the Squire. The man called Davy cowered behind his friend, who under all his glower looked to be in just as much a quake as Davy.

"Gaz, is it?' Fox asked. "And Davy."

A tremor passed through Gaz's face.

"We met at the inn."

That settled him a bit.

"You've got summat of ours." Gaz said.

He opened the door wider. "Come in. Have a tot of brandy."

Gaz eyed him warily. "We'll just have them tubs and be on our way."

"Two tubs? You'll have to come in and look for them."

Gaz took a step, and Davy pulled him back.

"There's naught for it, Davy." Gaz shook him off. "Stay out if you will. Run if you will. Won't get far either way with the load going from Robin Hood's Bay and the other to Scarborough. His men be out everywhere." Gaz stepped through the door. Davy swayed in behind him.

Fox led them in and turned to face Gaz's pistol. The door snicked closed.

"I'll have them now and be on my way."

Fox raised his hands. "There's no need for pistols."

Davy wheezed. "He's right, cousin."

"Shut up," Gaz said.

Davy gave another sharp gasp.

"Get outside if you can't stomach this," Gaz said. "I'll have those casks."

The man gripped the pistol so firmly his hand was beginning to shake. He'd shake that trigger into firing if they didn't distract him.

Fox sighed. "Do what you must, Mac."

Davy squealed, Gaz turned, and Fox knocked his gun hand away. A shot rang, rattling metal, crashing into masonry, sending a puff of plaster into the air. In moments they had both men disarmed and settled on chairs. Jenny came out of the pantry bearing a hank of rope.

"Want me to tie them, sir?" she asked.

MacEwen rolled his eyes and took the rope. "*Wist*, girl."

"Get two more glasses," Fox said. "If you're finished with trying to kill us, will you have that brandy with us?"

The two cousins shared a look and nodded.

"Or…" he pulled out a chair, "would you prefer a glass of gin?"

Gaz's eyes flashed. "See here—"

MacEwen gripped the man's collar. "You're the ones seein' here. Invited into a man's home and you pull a gun on him?"

"We need the casks sir," Davy said. "Scruggs'll—"

"Shut up," Gaz snapped.

"How do you know I have anything?" Fox poured the brandy and slid the glasses over to them.

Gaz sucked on his lip for a moment. "Yer were seen leavin' the cove with them."

"No." He shook his head. "No, I wasn't."

Davy's hand trembled as he lifted the glass. He drank down the spirits, eyed his cousin, and wiped his mouth with the back of his hand. "Enough with it, Gaz. No, *you* shut up. Sir, we're here 'cause yer the only one could've taken it. No one else would mess with the Dutchman knowin' Scruggs would pay for it."

"The Dutchman?" Fox asked.

They must mean Carvelle.

"Scruggs wouldna' blink much at a bit of nippin', but the Dutchman's as tight as a hangman's noose. And Gaz and me, we were left with the last of them barrels and we didn't take 'em."

Davy was just drunk enough—or may just sober enough —to tell the truth. Fox downed his own glass. "You're out early tonight."

"Gaz 'n' me, we're bringing the rest of that load up. They're runnin' 'em down to Scarborough tonight."

"Scarborough?" Jenny moved closer.

Fox's insides shifted. The hair on his neck rose. Jenny'd been tetchy, jittery, all evening.

Both of the local men ogled her, their gazes frank and approving.

"Beg pardon," she said, "But I've got to go get that tray."

"Come right back," Fox said.

Gaz and Davy watched the sway of her hips as she crossed the room.

"If I had those tubs I'd need a fair exchange for them."

They looked at each other again.

"We got no money," Gaz said.

"Not money. Information."

"Like what?" Davy asked.

"We're no snitches," Gaz said. "No one's being hanged on our account."

"We give a rat's ass about Scruggs and your gang, right, Mac?" Fox said.

MacEwen pulled out the chair next to Davy and sat. "Time and again, smugglers have done me a good turn or two."

"We've got no quarrel with your village's industry," Fox said. "What we're interested in is murder."

Davy licked his lips and slid his glass over. "Murder."

Fox poured.

"Not a word," Gaz said.

"We need them casks." Davy gulped his drink and stared hard at Fox. "Have you seen her then?"

"Hornswallow," Gaz muttered, but he picked up his own glass and drained it.

He nodded. "I have."

Sweat broke on Davy's forehead. His hand trembled so, Fox poured both him and his friend another.

"She wants her revenge," Davy said.

"No, not revenge. Justice."

"Davy, man," Gaz whispered, "We can't be givin' testimony at a trial."

Fox leaned closer. "She doesn't need a trial to get justice."

MacEwen raised an eyebrow. Fox hadn't briefed him. He hadn't a clue what they were talking about, but he was cagey enough to play along while he puzzled things out.

Jenny burst through the door, drawing everyone's attention. Gasping for breath, she clutched her hands in front of her.

18

JOHN BLACK IS COMING

Fox's heart quaked and he pushed back the chair and stood.

MacEwen nodded at him. "If she be rattling chains again, go on." He drew a pistol and laid it on the table, out of their reach. "Try anything, one'll get shot, the other will go up to that cold room. Give us what we want, and you may just leave with what you came for."

Fox took quick strides out of the room and up the stairs, Jenny at his heels.

He crashed through the door of Perry's bedchamber and his heart skidded to a halt. On the table, next to the silver handled brush, lay a long, thick coil of wheat-colored hair.

What that implied crushed him.

Jenny's indrawn breath shattered the silence.

"Where did she go, Jenny?"

"I don't know." The girl went to a clothes press and rummaged around. "She's taken her breeches and coats."

"Where did she go, Jenny?"

"She didn't tell me, sir." She studied the floor and worried her hands. "Nothing. Only, she seemed bothered about something when I took her up dinner." She lifted her gaze, her lips trembling. "She had her coins out on the table and...on the journey here, she asked me how far I'd like to travel. If I'd like to see France. I didn't think she'd leave without me."

Perry, standing at the window in his chamber, observing that Jenny had a tendre for MacEwen. The fool girl had left on her own, and hieing off to the Continent dressed as a man would be just like her. No one, well, not any man with a keen pair of eyes, would mistake her as a boy for long.

Scarborough was closer and the bigger port. He'd have to chance that she'd gone there. "What else do you think she took?"

Jenny went to a case on the floor and searched it, lifting troubled eyes to him. "Her jewelry and all of her money, sir."

"No note?"

She swept her gaze around the room, and went through the door to the dressing room, coming back with a folded paper, squinting at it. She handed it to him. "I'm still learnin' to read."

"Jenny, good luck with MacEwen. Go to one of my brothers' wives if you are in trouble. I'll send word to them when I reach safety and you can join me if you wish. I'll keep my promise to you."

Ice ran through his veins as he handed her back the note. The road to Scarborough would be crawling tonight with free traders, maybe even with dragoons and uncorrupted riding officers.

"You'll stay here, in case she comes back." And then he ran up the stairs to his room, arming himself to the teeth in the dark clothes of the night, and with every weapon he owned.

* * *

IN THE KITCHEN, MACEWEN LOOMED OVER GAZ AND DAVY. He shot Fox a look that took in his change in apparel and grabbed Gaz's throat.

"We don't know who killed her," Gaz said.

"It was Scruggs." The table rattled and Davy winced. "Enough kicking, Gaz, and enough lies. Can't live with this anymore, and you can go on and leave. I've had enough of the man's whippings. Saw a big man stop the coach. It was Scruggs."

Fox went to the storeroom and came out with the casks. "If you need help, you come here. If Pip needs help, you send him here."

The mention of Pip made Davy pale.

"Lord Shaldon will protect you." He nodded to MacEwen. "If on the other hand, Scruggs or the Dutchman shows up at my door on your telling, Lord Shaldon will not forget. Nor will the lady. Are you taking these barrels north or south?"

"We're to take them to the inn," Davy said. "They've cleared out the rest and will be taking them on to Scarborough."

Gaz hissed. Davy glared back at him, looking sober.

"Enough, Gaz. They're not with the revenuers. Rough water or no, the Dutchman's men are offloading something big north of the point later tonight."

"Davy—"

"No. I'm not shuttin' up. You weren't there. Bein' drunk all the time, people think you're gone deaf. Don't like this Dutchman or the way he rattles Scruggs. Ain't like Scruggs to be so shaken."

"Go on then," Fox pushed them out, shut the door on them. MacEwen glared. Jenny hovered, rubbing her arms.

"I wasn't done," MacEwen said.

He needed a moment for the men to clear out to the road.

"Get what you need to go north of the point." His heart pounded. "Before you leave, give Jenny a pistol and show her how to use it. The lady is out there somewhere, on that south road."

MacEwen bit his lip and huffed. "It needs but that."

Fox strode out to the stables, saddled the gelding in no time and led him out into the yard.

A darker shadow loomed, and his hand went to his pistol, and then his heart crashed. A small figure was leading a horse. Chestnut. And Perry was not sitting atop the mare.

The horse stopped. "Don't shoot, sir. I didna' steal her. I found her like this on the road just runnin' and she remembered and came to me."

This was the boy, Pip. Had Perry taken the boy out for a ride tonight? Had she fallen?

"Where's the lady?"

"I don't know."

He didn't have time to doubt the boy.

The kitchen door opened and MacEwen strode over.

"Who's on the south road, Pip is it?" Fox asked.

The boy shifted on his feet.

"Who's taken Lizzie?"

"It must be the men from down south. Scruggs sent me carrying a message."

"What message?"

"Watch out for John Black. He be coming."

John Black, the smuggler who'd been transported the

143

year before. Fox had read about the trial, and the man had held fast to his innocence until the end.

"John Black's gone."

"There be another one. The real one."

Of course there was, and why had none of them thought of it? The crimes of John Black had been worthy of hanging, yet he'd been transported. Someone had paid off the patsy and the judge. "John Black" was a *nom de guerre* for a local free trading chief.

Who he would bet his right painting hand was not Scruggs. "Mac, put Chestnut up."

MacEwen took the reins. "Then I'll follow."

"No." He grabbed the boy, who squirmed. "This one is going with me." Fox plopped the boy on the gelding and climbed on behind.

"Where yer taking me?" His little voice shook with a combination of defiance and fear.

"South. You'll give your report and help me find my lady."

BLACK NIGHT SHIELDED THE THREE MEN, FROM THEIR BOOTS to their black neck cloths and caps, and dirt darkened their cheeks and noses.

One of them pushed Perry, making her stumble in her stuffed boots. Pain shot through her wrists as she caught herself.

A fist hauled her up by her collar, near strangling her. "What ya doin?" She lowered her voice to what she hoped sounded like an East London growl and brushed the gravel off her hands. "There be no need for this."

"Shut it." That was the big man.

They were speeding her along, walking quickly north

toward Clampton, a good thing, she decided. She'd find a way out before they reached the turning for the village, and scoot her way back to Gorse Cottage.

Or... the Baronet's manor was nearby. If she could find out where, she could seek assistance from him.

"This be Sir Richard's land," she muttered, hoping for confirmation.

One of the dark heads snickered. "He'll not help you, boy."

She clenched and unclenched her hands. They'd taken her pistols. They'd found the knife on her arm. They'd not found her breasts. Praise be to God, hers were smaller than most.

They also hadn't taken the time to question her.

She needed a story. If only she knew who these men worked for, or who they knew in the neighborhood. They must certainly know the innkeeper Scruggs. Everyone knew Scruggs, except her, so saying she worked for him would lead to more trouble.

They wouldn't probably know Fox. Or MacEwen. She could say she was one of the servants from Gorse Cottage. Her master was a painter. He'd sent her to Scarborough at night for a particular color of paint. Had to have it by the morrow.

Would Scarborough have a shop that sold paint?

No, not paint. Something else. *Think*, Perry.

If you're going to lie, keep the lies as close to the truth as possible, and simple. Charley had shared that advice with her more than once, bless him.

Coffee, then. Fox had *said* he wanted coffee, so there must be none to be had in the village. Temperamental and spoiled, he was. Had run out and needed it in the morning, and she was making the trip down and back before then.

145

Thus, he'd armed her with pistols and knives in case of trouble. Like this.

She still had the one knife in her boot, along with her jewels and her money, her chance for freedom. She would use that knife on someone before surrendering her freedom, even if it killed her.

I'm a fool, running away like this. Fox is right. I should have gone home.

No. Father and Bakeley would lock her away in the country. They'd send an armed guard when she went riding or into the village to visit the seamstress. Or they'd marry her off to a man who, besides locking her up, might take away her horses, and possibly raise a hand to her also. No, no, and no.

Anyway, she'd have to get away from these men first.

"*Oof.*" She collided into the large villain. "What the—"

A hand clamped over her mouth, smelling of onions and fish.

A boy came round a bend in the road. *Pip.*

Her pulse quickened and her neck prickled. If Pip was here, surely the men from the village would be nearby. Maybe Fox would have followed them. Yes, of course, he would be out and about tonight.

Under the supper odors of the villain's unwashed hand, she could almost sense Fox's presence.

"Be you the Scarborough men?" Pip said. So brave, he sounded. He'd shown more nerves when he'd encountered her ghostly presence.

"What if we are?"

"Might be that you're with the revenuers."

The big man took a step nearer. "And might be I'll throw you over that cliff."

"I come from Scruggs," Pip said indignantly. "Deliverin' a message."

"What message?"

"He says, be on the lookout for John Black."

In a flash, the big man had Pip hauled up by his jacket flaps. "What's this?"

Perry's heart did flips. These were not Scruggs's men. And probably not the Scarborough men, whoever they might be. These men weren't in league with Scruggs.

"What else did Scruggs say?"

"Nothin' ter me. Put me down."

He dropped Pip and the boy staggered back, turning to run. The big man clamped a hand on him.

"I got to get back."

"You're staying with us." He yanked Pip back to where Perry stood.

The smelly hand came off her mouth and all but yanked her arm out of the socket. She sucked in a sharp breath. "No need for roughness. Let me go on my way."

"And where would that be?" The big man handed Pip over. "Tie their hands together."

"I'm for Scarborough," she said.

"Another one of Scruggs's messengers."

"No."

He leaned closer. "With the Dutchman then."

"I dunna know who the Dutchman is."

"Traveling on that fine horse? Who are you?"

"I work at that cottage. That there one about to slide off the cliff."

"With the ghost?" Pip asked.

"Aye." She took quick shallow breaths, inducing her heart to race faster. She dropped her voice to a hoarse whisper. "Seen her last night."

147

A hand cracked across her face and she held back a scream. Pain burned through her cheek, along her neck and into her shoulder.

She gritted her teeth. He would pay for that, first chance she got.

"Bugger your ghosts. What are you doin' here?" he growled. It would be his palm painted on her jaw, and her extra knife in his belly.

"Master ran out of coffee."

The hand came up again and she ducked, heart pounding. It wasn't so hard to pretend to be servile.

"Wanted me back with it by the morrow."

"He sent a servant, at night, to bring back coffee for his breakfast? And you think you'll find an open shop tonight?"

"Or the mornin'. Sleeps half the day, he does. 'E's a painter. Be back in time. 'An if'n I'm gone at night, I don't have to see..." She sucked in a deep breath, ducked, and made herself tremble. "Her. Yer know what I'm sayin', boy," she whispered.

"I heard tell in the village that Mr. Goodfellow up at the cottage is a queer one," Pip said.

Mr. Goodfellow. Fox was using an alias.

"And I heard tell he's got no servants," the big man said. "So I know you're lying."

"I'm not lyin'. Came later we did. Me and the cook."

The third man beckoned the big one. Out at sea, a shadow floated, impossible to make out as more than a black smudge. The two men held a hushed conference, fragments of French floating toward her.

Fragments that sent her stomach roiling, her hair rising, and her head reeling. *Men*, and *assassins*, and *weapons*, and *payment*, and then they were moving again, pushed along by the thin man.

148

"Bloody hell," Perry said. "Quit pokin' me. Can ye not let me go?"

The big man turned and gripped her throat, fingers tightening, cutting off breath. She managed a sucking wail, and her chest seized, her tongue stuck to her palate, making her want to gag. Pain seared her neck where the blood was cut off.

Rocks clattered on the side of the cliff. He let go and turned toward the noise.

She staggered against Pip, sucking in ragged breaths and gagging.

"Eet ees nothing," the third man reported. "The wind."

"The skiff's not far," the thin man said.

He came up close enough to smell and jabbed her hard in the back.

Pain seared her. She choked and staggered against the boy again.

"More of that comin' if you don't shut up." His breath stung her nose, along with the rest of his dinner—onions, many, many onions.

Him, she could find by his odor. Him, she would kill also.

They skittered off onto a narrow path, switching back and forth down the cliff side. Gorse tore at her breeches and coats, the heels of her stout boots skidded on rocks, and she crashed into the boy more times than she'd have liked, trying to keep from falling over the side.

They reached a low promontory overlooking a sheer drop. Damp air penetrated her coats, and she fought her shivers, fought the fear numbing her mind.

It wasn't hard to puzzle out their plan.

Three men stood between her and escape. She glanced back at the sea.

The folly bridge on the lake at Cransdall was just about this high, and she'd jumped off that many times on Charley's dares. Mama had made sure they'd dug the lake deep.

Would the sea bed be deep enough?

"No witnesses. Take care of this," the big man said, and stalked off.

And he'd spoken the words in badly accented French.

Onion Breath passed by, and she pivoted away from his jabbing. The blow glanced off Pip, who shouted and kicked out.

"Enough," the big man bellowed. "I want to get there before them."

Onion Breath skittered back to the path, and both men moved out of sight. They reappeared again at the water's edge, and she saw it then. A skiff was pulled up, another man holding it against the pull of the waves. They got in, took up the oars and rowed away.

Her heart dropped. The surf battered the shore again tonight. She didn't want to have to fight it, not with one hand tied to Pip. She didn't know if she'd be strong enough.

They turned to face two pistols. "You'll kneel down now." This was the Frenchman.

She scanned the darkness behind the man.

"He's back there." Pip breathed out the words.

"You *could* let us go," she yelled. She must stall. Fox must come, and soon.

"*Non.*"

That was definitely French.

"We're not informers," she said in French. Like every accomplished young lady, she'd mastered the language, but not for social reasons. She'd hoped someday to follow her father into the great Game.

But not like this. Fox, Fox, where are you?

"The war is over," she shouted, "and you have no quarrel with us, or us with you. At least let this boy go. You have no reason to harm him."

White teeth flashed as he grinned. "Please to turn around and go to the edge. And then you will kneel."

All her blood pooled in her legs, and she dragged them closer to the cliff edge. Her nerves skittered, her breathing...her breathing tightened again, pain ratcheting through where she'd been punched.

Pip began to tremble. "What did he say?"

She had to be strong for the boy. "Do not worry," she whispered.

The Frenchman leveled his gun.

"He's going to shoot us." Pip shouted, his little-boy voice high and strained. He waved a hand around.

"Shoot me if you will, but you let the boy—"

"No buts, *messieur*. Or should I say, *mademoiselle*?" He laughed. "These English have no subtlety. I knew from the moment I saw such a fine derriere." The white teeth flashed again.

Panic roared through her. "He's going to shoot us," she shouted and waved.

He frowned and glanced over his shoulder. "We are quite alone, *cherie*. No one is coming to rescue you."

19

RESCUED

The coastal path and the fields behind were dark and silent. The only noise was the crashing surf.

Anger reared in her. Bloody Fox—he wasn't coming.

Perry yanked Pip around. The skiff with the other villains had disappeared round a point. They were quite alone with this villain.

And they must save themselves.

"Do as I do, Pip," she whispered, easing him closer to the cliff edge. He planned to shoot and push them over.

"Very good." The Frenchman sounded pleased. "Now you will kneel. I should have liked more time with you, *cherie*, but I must be off. I am good at what I do. You and the boy will feel no pain."

"I can swim," she whispered. "On three." She put a foot back and bent her other knee, pretending to kneel.

"One, two, three."

They catapulted off, and heard both shots before hitting the water.

* * *

BLOODY HELL. HE'D BEEN ALMOST TOO LATE.

Fox ran to the promontory, shifting the hot pistol to his other hand and pulling out a knife. He skirted the dark-clad body and ran to the edge.

His heart all but stopped. The Frenchman had got off one shot. Perry or Pip, he couldn't bear seeing either hit.

One shot wouldn't have pushed them over this cliff. They'd jumped—in time, he hoped.

Perry's head crested the surface, and his heart started again. She gulped air, thrashing, fighting to stay afloat, pulling at the boy who finally surfaced.

Fox bent to the Frenchman and sliced his throat, neat and deep. He dropped pistols, knives and coats, tore off his boots, and jumped.

Bloody hell, the cold.

He'd cannonballed, bounced off the mercifully deep enough bottom and shot up again. Currents grabbed him, pulling fiercely while he fought, and gulped air, and spat water.

There. She and the boy had been pushed further out. He grabbed the force of a retreating wave and shredded through water, every muscle in his arms and chest and legs moving and kicking.

He grabbed for her, and the current pulled her away.

A swell massed behind them. He treaded water, waiting, waiting, and "Kick!" he shouted.

The wave launched them up. He shot toward them and snagged the boy's arm.

"Kick, Pip."

"I am." The boy snorted up water. "It's too far."

"We'll get there. Are you all right, Perry?"

Her teeth chattered. "Y-yes."

The next wave sent them in closer, close enough for him to stand neck high, the rocks cutting into his stockings and feet. He hoisted the boy onto his hip, and braced against the retreating current, until it shifted. They staggered the rest of the way out of the water, Perry dragging along with them by her tether to Pip.

Perry pulled a knife from her boot, hands shaking.

"Let me." He pried the knife from her grip and sawed at their bindings. Dark fluid trickled down her head. That was blood.

"He hit you," he said through clenched teeth.

Perry's shivering kicked up to a frantic pace, shock overtaking her.

God's blood, she'd almost died.

"Who was he, Pip?"

"I don't know," he rattled out quickly, "Some Frenchie." The boy glanced up at the promontory. "He got away."

Fox saw the fear blooming on the boy's face. "No. He didn't."

"You killed 'im?" Pip's eyes went big. "You ain't a real painter?"

"I'm a painter."

The rope gave way and the boy clambered to his feet. "Can you walk?" Fox asked him.

"Aye."

Fox scooted near Perry, pulled out his tucked shirt and pressed the hem to her head. "You're bleeding, my lady."

Her head plopped onto his chest, rattling his breath and his heart.

"Pip, run up there onto the point. Bring my boots, my coats, my pistols and my knives. Make two trips if you have to. Careful with the weapons."

The boy scooted off.

He lifted her chin to gaze into her eyes.

"I h-hear you, th-thinking. *Sh-she shouldn't have left.*"

He wanted to throttle her. Now wasn't the time.

She took a deep breath and steadied herself. "I'll get it right the next time."

"There won't be a next time." He braced an arm around her shoulders and settled his lips against hers, his cheek pressing her nose. She was cold, so cold—her lips, nose, and shoulders. He nipped and teased, trying to get her to open, trying to warm her.

She turned away. "No."

"Yes." He forced her chin around and pressed again, nudging her lips with his tongue. "You could have died," he murmured. *I could have lost you.*

"No," she groaned.

There'd be no next time. It was this time. This time for them. This night, and as many more as he could manage before Shaldon came and killed him.

He pressed and caressed, found his way under her coat to her breast, teasing the nipple, already hard from the cold. She gasped and opened and accepted his kiss. Heat swamped him and he pushed it at her, letting it swirl around them both. He shifted and sat, pulling her onto his lap, into his heat, kissing her.

A loud throat-clearing interrupted. Clutching her tightly, he broke the kiss and looked up.

Pip stood shivering, his arms full of coats. Davy held the knives and the pistols. Gaz had the boots.

Even in the dark, he could see Gaz's glower.

"Buggerin' painter," Gaz muttered.

"Gentlemen." Fox held onto Perry. "Give me that coat. Pip, wrap yourself in the waistcoat."

"No." Davy set down the weapons, shed his own coat and

155

wrapped it around his boy. "You're drippin' too. You take the waistcoat."

Fox draped Perry in both his waistcoat and coat and started pulling on his boots.

"What about 'im?" Gaz jerked his head toward the promontory.

Perry stumbled to her knees. "He's still there?"

"Dead and drained like a pig," Davy said. "Neck flappin'. Dear God, Pip. Scruggs told me about the errand. Said you should've been back. What the hell did you get into? Dear God."

She struggled to her feet and reached for the boy. "You're c-cold."

"No, m-miss."

"Miss?" Gaz peered closer.

"They'll f-find him." She started toward the path.

She was befuddled as hell. "Wait, Perry." He stowed his weapons and followed her.

"G-going up. R-roll him in."

"No, you're not."

Footsteps crunched in the gravel behind them. "He shot at us, Da."

"Wait up, you two," Davy said. "Come on, Gaz. Grab us some big rocks on the way up. We'll give him a proper burial."

"We have to go that way anyway to get back to the road," Fox said. "I need to check his pockets."

"Aye, and that was a damn fine gun," Gaz said.

"We'll go through them pockets and get those guns. Might be some dry powder too," Davy said. "You keep the lady and my boy here out of the wind so you don't catch your death."

Could he trust them?

156

Davy pushed Pip toward him. "We needs do this now. Don't want them spotting a body from the road."

"It will go faster with my help, and we can be on the road," Fox said.

"That road be busy tonight with pack trains coming south."

"Do you know another way back?"

"Scruggs keeps a skiff here and there. Be cold on the water, but we'll get back faster."

"Check pockets, boots, seams. Under his cap. Keep the weapons and money. Bring me the rest."

Davy nodded and pulled Gaz along.

"And, Davy…"

The man turned. Fox swept his arms around the boy and Perry. "Thank you."

THE COLD BREEZE LASHED LIKE THE DEVIL'S OWN BLADE through the tight weave of Fox's wool coat. Just as soon as she'd willed herself to stop quivering, a fresh slap of air would come down the cliff, snake under her wet clothing, and into her scattered brain.

Fox seemed to know these local men who guided them along the coast, through rock beds and craggy mires. The best route was this way, they said. She'd balked—it didn't seem right. Once they reached the end of this narrow bay, there'd be no way out but up a sheer cliff, and she didn't think her frozen legs would bear her.

"Trust my da," Pip had said.

Fox had simply picked her up and carried her. She was lodged now against his chest, feeling the wild pounding of his heart, hearing his labored breath.

"I can walk." She said it, over and over, a mad litany, while she shivered.

They'd almost been murdered.

Tears sprang, and she sniffed mightily and said again, "I can walk."

She'd almost been murdered. She'd have never talked to her father again, or seen Sirena's and Gracie's and Paulette's new babies born, or played with her niece and nephew again, or been held like this in such strong arms.

"I can walk."

"Shush," Fox said.

"I'm too heavy. Lumbering beast."

He stopped and his breath warmed her, his lips searched her cheek, bumped her nose, and found her lips.

"Here it is," one of the men said gruffly.

Fox lifted his head, leaving her quaking for more.

He set her on her feet and clamped an arm around her, like a footman steadying a prized piece of porcelain. Mama used to hold the precious Limoges chocolate pot like that, a gift from father, while her maid wrapped it in cotton wool. It traveled to town with them whenever they went.

She needed to walk. She lifted a foot and felt the squishing. Jewelry, bank notes: all wet.

Fox lifted her into a rough wooden boat and climbed in behind her. Pip clambered in next to her. The boat tipped wildly with the other men boarding, and then they were off, the two local men rowing.

Fox's warmth poured into her back. He shifted, and sharp pain sliced through her, making her gasp.

He quickly adjusted her. "You're injured?"

"A bruise." The ocean sparkled where stars broke through the clouds. "Those men. If we see them—"

"We loaded the pistols, miss."

Pip was clearer-headed than she. She hadn't noticed them loading the weapons. Perhaps she'd fainted for a moment. But if they saw the men, and they had pistols...She rolled her head toward the boy. "The big man is mine."

"Best to not speak much," Fox whispered. "Sound carries."

FOX HELD HER, THOUGHTS BURNING. PERRY WOULDN'T HAVE A chance to shoot either man. He'd tear them limb from limb, and let their weighted bodies land in the water next to their French friend.

The man's pockets and hems had been empty—no letters, no *laissez-passer*, no encrypted instructions. No tobacco, no keys, no money. He'd stayed at a safe house somewhere near Scarborough. He'd worked for someone near Scarborough. Probably the real John Black.

And what the devil was this? If Scruggs was sending messages to his men about John Black, he wasn't in league with the man. And how did Carvelle fit in?

The rhythmic swish of the oars and Perry's regular breathing lulled him. She cradled the boy, and Fox held her, all the dry coats draping them. For now, her trembling had stopped.

They stayed close to the shore in the shallow-hulled boat and the cliffs helped break the force of the wind.

He'd never be a match for her, but he'd give her as much as he could without taking all of her innocence. He'd keep giving until Perry was tired of him, or until Shaldon stepped in and murdered him.

The coronation would take place in mere days. After

that, Shaldon would make haste for Gorse Cottage. Whether or not Fox sent a message, the spy lord would have sources to pass on the news of his daughter's adventure.

He heard a sharp intake of breath, a muffled oath, and the oars stopped. They'd rounded another point, and almost collided with a cutter.

20

A CROSSING POINT

Fox spotted the union jack fluttering astern and his heart started beating again.

A crew member hailed them.

"Shite," Gaz mumbled.

Fox pushed Perry and Pip up. "We'll come alongside," Fox shouted. "Do it," he told Gaz and Davy.

"Out for a row?" The uniformed officer peered down at the boat. "It is a fine evening."

Another man, attired in dark coats, came up beside the officer.

Fox's nerves prickled, and he pulled the coats higher over Perry. He didn't recognize the man, but he knew the look.

And still, the role must be played. "I'm Goodfellow, from Gorse Cottage. Two of my servants were waylaid and robbed on their way back from Scarborough. Villains held them awhile. We found them just in time to fish them out of the water." He shifted again and braced his arms on the sides of the boat. "Three men on their way to the point north of the cottage took them and left them for dead. They were in a great hurry to meet a shipment coming in further north. Didn't want witnesses."

"Your vessel looks like a smuggler's craft to me. What else have you got in that boat?" the officer asked.

"Nought but these two wet bedraggled bodies needing dry clothes and medical attention. Drop a man over to search if you will, but hurry before a fever takes them."

The two men conversed quietly.

"What are they bringing in?" the civilian asked.

"We don't know."

"You two at the oars. What are they bringing?"

Davy looked at Gaz. "Sir, we don't know. My boy's freezing and I'd like to get him home safe and dry him up."

"Can your boys identify the smugglers?"

Perry swayed in her seat and began to gag. Fox steadied her as she leaned her head over the side, hair shielding her face. Nothing came of her dry heaving, and he wondered if it was a ruse.

"No," Pip called. "It were nobody from here, I think."

"What does the other one say?"

"This one was beaten almost senseless. For God's sake, go north and check. Come round to the cottage after, if you will," Fox said. *Shoot at us if you will.* "Gorse Cottage. Oars in, boys."

"*Assassins,*" she whispered.

"Shhh," he breathed into her ear. *Assassins.* She'd pronounced it the French way.

"Wait," she croaked up at the boat. The plainly dressed gentleman took out a spy glass.

Fox pushed her down.

"They were meeting assassins," she whispered.

"What is he saying?" the officer shouted.

"The cargo might be an assassin."

At a word from the gentleman, the Captain turned to give orders.

The gentleman leaned over the decking. "Take care of your *servants*, and get yourself into dry clothes, *Goodfellow*. Your work here is done."

The cutter sailed away, and Davy and Gaz took up their oars.

Perry sat up and rested her face against her cupped hands. "Farnsworth." She moaned.

Farnsworth. He knew the name. Farnsworth worked with Shaldon.

"Lean back," he said. "You might be concussed."

Her head moved side to side. "I am sick from this infernal rocking, is all."

He draped an arm over her. "He couldn't see you."

"He will know. They always know. *You* always know."

As the boat rocked, she gripped the side.

"I don't get seasick," Pip said. The boy seemed completely recovered. Even his teeth had stopped chattering. "Look, we're almost there."

They rounded a point and saw the dark mass of Gorse Cottage in the distance. The dimmest of lights twinkled behind closed kitchen shutters. Except for the departing cutter, the coastline was free of vessels.

Farnsworth might wait until the next day to visit. They still had days until the coronation, and then at the very least one or two more before Shaldon could reach the cottage. Fox could put off Farnsworth by hiding Perry away. There must be a smuggler's hidey hole somewhere in that massive hillside.

They could hole up together until she recovered, and then take a packet over to Holland.

He shook his head at the mad thought. Perry had no

163

place with him, nor he with her. Besides, he would finish this mission. Shaldon had sent him here to find his last spy, Gregory Carvelle, and he'd stay on to solve the mystery of Lady Shaldon's death.

Perry leaned to the side and gulped air. Her cap had come off in the water, and her hair straggled around her collar, the cut uneven. Her hair, curling down to her waist, had been glorious, ephemeral, turning her into the goddess of the picture he'd painted over, the one he still held in his heart. He'd always see that side of her.

But now, with short hair, men's clothing wet and plastered against her curves, the bare determined hands gripping the side of this boat, now he could almost believe she was just a woman, vulnerable, real, and accessible, even to one such as him.

Heat coursed through him and he leaned forward, resting his chin on her shoulder.

He felt the shiver that rippled through her. "We must get those wet clothes off you. We must get you warm."

"Who are they going to kill, Fox?" she whispered.

He saw the slight stiffening in Davy's and Gaz's backs.

"The King probably," she said. "We must send word to my father."

PERRY HUFFED HER WAY UP THE HILLSIDE PATH, CLINGING LIKE a girl to Fox. At the crest, she gulped in breaths that shattered pain through her back, while Fox whispered to Davy and Gaz.

Hunching against the cold, she set out for the cottage. She'd made it this far, she could make it the rest of the way.

Strong arms came around her and before she could utter

a protest, Fox hoisted her up like a babe. Her teeth chattered too fiercely for her to object.

The kitchen door opened and the immediate sensation of warmth sent her shivering out of control. Jenny stood wringing her hands, but when the door slammed, just the three of them remained. The two men and Pip had gone their own way.

"Jenny. Bring wood to the bedchamber, and hot water," he said without pausing, and then she was bouncing against him, his heart pounding, his breath ruffling the hair near her ear.

He kicked open the bedchamber door, and Jenny rustled by. The girl dropped kindling and wood in the grate and knelt before it with the tinderbox, striking sharp flares.

"Let's get these clothes off." Fox tore at the knot on her sopping neckcloth. He finally gave up and pulled out his knife. "Don't move."

She closed her eyes during the delicate slicing and concentrated on not shivering, letting the first delicate spirals of smoke curl into her with promises of warmth. She heard the knife clatter on the table and felt her neck lighten as he unwound her.

He inhaled sharply and muttered a curse. Strong hands cupped her shoulders.

"Oh, miss," Jenny whispered.

They both stared at her neck. "Is it bruised?"

His gaze scorched her. Fox was well and truly angry.

"Jenny, hot water."

Jenny hurried out.

He pressed his lips together and finished unwinding the cloth, tossing it aside. Then he turned her around, pulled off his damp coats and tugged at her soggy ones.

She pulled away from him. "Stop. I'm feeling much better. I can undress myself."

"No." He tugged at her sleeve again.

"You are too rough. Too angry." Sudden tears sprang and she swallowed them back.

She was yanked back against him, into his heat and his trembling, and she remembered. He was soaked also, and freezing. He needed dry clothes.

She covered his hands with hers. "Go and change, Fox. Jenny can help me when she comes back."

"No."

His heat and his anger vibrated through her. "I won't go anywhere."

For the rest of my life. A sob bubbled inside her. Father would lock her up for her foolishness. Her hands curled into fists, and she bit hard on her lip.

She must do the honorable thing and report this threat to the King, even at risk of her freedom. She would not cry. She would somehow survive this and find another way to break free.

He released her and went back to tugging on sleeves, this time more gently, removing her coats.

"Sit down, now." He moved a chair near the growing fire.

The heat made her skin ripple. Fox knelt before her and removed one of her boots. Money spilled out, coins and bank notes. She picked up one of the notes. It was only a little damp. A night drying by the fire and she could still use it.

Fox's eyes narrowed. He collected the coins and notes and set them next to his discarded knife.

He lifted her other foot. "I suppose this one has the jewels."

Her face heated as he poured out her gold chain, the

pink garnet ring she'd received for her eighteenth birthday, a cameo fob, and a slim bracelet dotted with turquoise. It was paltry. All the best of the jewelry was locked in Bakeley's safe. How had she thought to subsist on these items? She watched him gathering them, noticed how he kept his face carefully neutral. He'd slipped from anger to pity.

Jenny entered with a steaming bucket.

"Put it there." He pointed to the hearth.

"I've tea ready also."

He nodded. "Get it. Some biscuits also, or bread if there's any."

As soon as the door slammed, he eased her out of the chair, yanked out her shirttails, and tore the shirt over her head.

She plopped her hands over her breasts. "*Fox.*"

His fingers tore at her trouser buttons. She barred an arm and hand over her breasts and slapped at his busy hands with the other.

Buttons flew. The loose breeches peeled down her hips and pooled at her feet. He swept a gaze over her, his eyes darker than usual, and walked into the dressing room.

She glanced around the chamber. Where had she left her dressing gown? Where had Jenny put it?

In the adjoining room, he was slamming cabinets. As his footsteps neared, she dropped into the chair, drawing her knees up and huddling into them.

She peered up. Her robe hit the bed where he tossed it. A pile of towels fell to the floor next to her chair. She swung her gaze around, her field of vision at the level of his waist. He'd shed his wet shirt and—*holy saints.* His trousers strained with an erection worthy of the Godolphin Barb.

Liquid heat poured through her, pooling at the part of her she was trying so desperately to conceal.

He wanted her, just as franticly as she wanted him.

She heard the door latch turn. A towel floated over her head, covered her, and began to rustle through her tangled damp hair.

"Put it on the table," he said.

Dishes clattered.

"Sir, let me—"

"Out."

Jenny must have paused, the brave little thing.

"Get. Out."

The door *snicked* closed. The towel came off. Lips pressed against hers, hot and demanding, pushing her chin up, breaking the grip she had on her knees. He'd kissed her on the beach, jolting her back to breathing, back to life, but this—this was so much more.

She reached for him and he pulled her up, his hot length burning her, melding her to him. She squirmed closer, fingers tracing wide shoulders, bunched muscles, hard strength. A fresh, pink scar knotted his chest and she lifted her head to look. Before she could ask about it, he kissed her again, a hot demanding press of his lips, his tongue searching and twining with hers.

She slid her hands down to his waist and squeezed her fingers along hot muscles, and lower. She wanted to see more, feel more.

He tugged at her hand, lifted his mouth away, and said "No."

His eye glowed with so much anger, her heart sank.

His gaze dropped to her breasts, plumped against his bare chest. Stepping back, frowning, he stroked her cheek. "You're injured." He traced the length of her arms, picked up

168

her wrist and studied the bruising. "No skin broken," he said, and the words grated as if they pained him.

Lifting her chin, he focused his gaze at her neck. "But this...I'll kill him."

"I've promised myself that reward." Perhaps his anger wasn't directed at her.

Fox's fingers trailed over her breasts, down her sides, to her waist, his gaze stopping a moment at the thatch of hair between her legs before moving on. "Your knee is bleeding."

Indeed it was. "I stumbled. I'm clumsy as ever."

He settled his hands on her shoulders. His eyes still burned darkly, but his lips twitched. "It's hard to walk on pound notes and garnet rings."

Before she could protest, he whipped her around, and a tremor shook both of them.

"Perry, take a breath for me."

He'd assumed the composed tone he'd used earlier that evening to send her away, stirring her anger.

"Why?"

Fingers trailed lightly over her back, the sensation sending ripples of pleasure through her.

"Does that hurt?"

She swallowed. "No."

He probed more closely and she gasped. "The scrawny one punched me there."

"Does it hurt to breathe?"

She inhaled deeply. "Only a little."

He touched her at waist level. "And here? Does this hurt?"

"It feels tender. He hit me there also."

"The scrawny one. He'll die, as soon as I can identify him."

"Yes, and I'll be the one to—*oh*."

His fingers slid over her bottom and fire blasted through her. She gripped the chair back, and he tugged her bottom against him.

Oh, God. She'd seen the outline of his erection earlier tonight and now she could *feel* it.

"*Fox.*" She had no breath to say more. One of his hands, with those artist's long fingers, had curled round her and was threading that warm thatch of hair at her center.

She gasped.

He froze. "Am I hurting you?"

She shook her head.

One arm pulled her to him. He nuzzled her neck, kissing and licking in a flurry of sensation that drowned out any aches. His other hand stayed busy, stroking, sending liquid heat through her. He backed them to the bed, and seated himself, pulling her onto his lap and taking one of her breasts in his mouth.

That busy hand flattened against her sensitive nub and a finger slid into her.

She touched his arms, his shoulder, his back. She raked her fingers along the soft hair of his arm, through the fuzz of his chest, along the prickly stubble covering his jaw.

The tension built higher. She clutched at his shoulders, reaching for something, in an agony of feeling, and—

Pleasure exploded in her and she gripped tightly while it pulsed.

Oh, oh, oh. She squirmed and gasped and settled.

He'd gone still as a statue, his finger still nestled inside her, his forehead pressed to her shoulder.

So this was it.

Now she understood. When women whispered about marital pleasure, *this* was what they meant. Not just the kissing and touching, which were wonderful, but...a woman

170

would do much for this kind of pleasure. And men—no wonder the unhappily married members of the *ton* chased each other shamelessly.

Fox lifted his head, his face in a grimace.

This she'd heard whispered about also—a man engorged for too long was a man in pain.

She couldn't bear to leave Fox in pain.

She slipped to the floor in front of him, ignoring her scraped knee, and reached for his buttons.

He pulled at her hands. "No."

His tone was as hard as his cloth-covered rod.

Tracing a finger down his length, she watched his jaw tighten.

He squeezed her hand. "We'll not go there tonight."

"But you're—"

"I'll not ruin you any more than I have, Perry."

"Ruin me?"

She sat back on her heels. Fox sounded so angry, and he'd averted his eyes, as if she was unpleasant to look at. But minutes ago, he'd had a finger in her most private of parts.

Perhaps the pleasure had addled her brain, and the lack of pleasure had addled his. She reached again for his fall, and he pulled her hand away.

"You don't understand. I don't know if I can—"

"Control this great manly rod?"

He grimaced.

"I see." That was it. She'd seen stallions at work. He was afraid to unleash that wildness, that mad desire.

In her center, miraculously and without any touching, the pleasure had started again. Fox's mouth parted hungrily. His eyes had gone completely black and feral in a way that sent tension spiraling through her.

Whatever tomorrow might bring, she wanted this tonight. She wanted ruination. She wanted Fox.

She reached for his damp boots and yanked off first one and then the other. His wet trousers clung so to his narrow hips and long, muscled limbs, he might have been naked. He was as beautiful as an Italian marble, and in his own way, as vulnerable as she tonight. Except that she was fully naked.

A lock of his unfashionably long hair touched his cheek, and in his eyes, need and hunger flashed while his tight fists bunched the bedclothes.

They had come to a crossing point.

21

AN HONORABLE MAN

The mattress dipped as Perry climbed up, dumping her closer.

Dear God, she was so beautiful. "Perry—"

She kissed him, stopping his words.

He eased her onto his lap again. She slipped a hand round his neck, and let the other trail down his center.

"No." He lifted her hand from his trouser placket.

"I want—"

Flipping her onto the bed, he clamped a leg over hers, kissing her, teasing her, stroking her, making her writhe.

"Please," she said. "Plea—"

She shattered again and went limp.

He rolled her over and pulled her against him, gritting his teeth, willing his cock into submission. She was a dream —willing, responsive, beautiful.

And he couldn't have her. He could never have her that way.

"Fox," she said, and he heard tears in her voice. "Fox, why...why not? I care for you, and I know you care for me."

Why not? She is here. She is willing. You're here at this cottage with only a servant and MacEwen.

A cottage that had belonged to her mother. They were, in fact, in her mother's bed. "And it's because I care for you, I won't dishonor you."

She lifted his hand away and rolled toward him, wincing.

And then there was the matter of her injuries. "You're hurt."

She pressed a hand to his cheek. "This is not dishonor, Fox. This is love."

The lamp cast shadows across her face and chest but the dark of the bruising stood out.

She bit her lip and squeezed her eyes shut.

Oh, hell.

Tears glistened in the light. He swept a finger through them.

"Perry, I have nothing to offer you but this...physical pleasure. Beyond that, it would be a life lived in shabby rooms on the fringe of society, wife to the season's interesting painter. And in the long run it won't be enough."

She raised up on one elbow and her face lit in a smile. "Marriage has crossed your mind also? Oh, Fox. My dowry will come to me, no matter who I marry."

He closed his eyes.

He shouldn't have alluded to marriage. "Turning over your fortune to a husband would never satisfy you."

In his younger days, he had upon occasion, lived off a patroness he might like but didn't love. True, besides the bed sport, he'd produced portraits for his commission, but it had all become loathsome. There was no honor in those arrangements, neither for the woman nor for the man. He'd rather starve.

Over her silence, the open window let in the sound of waves crashing, rhythmically.

He should be listening for other sounds—voices, the soft rustle of a horse's hooves on the gravelly path, movement downstairs.

He smoothed back the hair from her face. She looked pink, breathless, and completely undone. No one could look at her and not know what they'd been doing.

"I might not want to turn my dowry over to a husband, but as I've mentioned, it's my main attraction for suitors. It might as well go to a man I care for, who sometimes cares for me."

"Oh, Perry." Anger swelled in him. She didn't know her own worth. "It's not true. I've told you that. You're beautiful. You deserve everything. You deserve all the best." He lifted her hand and kissed it.

Hurt shimmered in her eyes. She reached for her robe and covered her nakedness.

What a fool he was. This had been a mistake.

"You offer me…everything…and then yank it away. You care, and then push me away." She took in a shaky breath. "Give me this night, Fox. Please. Take me."

"You're a lady. You deserve to marry honorably, with your father's blessing."

Shaldon would never allow them to marry, and she knew it.

Heat bloomed in her cheeks. "A lady wouldn't beg for a man who is not her husband to make love to her."

How wrong she was there.

"Just tell me one truth. Putting aside your honor, my supposed great beauty and my dowry, do you care for me?"

He sat up next to her. "There's nothing supposed about your beauty."

"Stop dodging and answer me."

Dear God. He wanted her, in his bed, in his arms, arguing, bolting, occasionally falling out of trees. Always. He couldn't tell her that.

She fell back onto the bed, frowning. "I don't even know your first name."

He dropped a brotherly kiss on her forehead, unsmiling. "Yes, I care for you. And you may call me Reynard."

She grimaced and choked out a laugh, as he'd wanted her to. He stood and looked for his shirt.

He needed to leave, and now, before she started probing again.

Perry rolled to sitting. "You are not Reynard the Fox. What is your Christian name, Fox?"

He pulled on his stockings. He had stopped using his true name years ago. It had been part of his cover, and then became who he truly was.

"I suppose should you ever marry, one might find your full name in the marriage lines."

He shook out his shirt.

"*Arrgh*," she said. "It's a curse to love a man so honorable."

His gaze jerked to her. She loved him.

Well, of course she did. She had for years. It would pass.

Still, the anger in her voice and in her expression flayed him. And how had he been honorable? He'd just stripped her naked and brought her to pleasure twice. And now she perched on the edge of the bed, hair floating in a wild halo that suited her much better than the Rapunzel locks she'd left on the bedside table.

His heart clinched. A woman well-loved, a goddess ready to issue a command—he would remember this vision and paint it someday. He let his damp shirt fall over his head and cover his desire.

176

"What's honorable, Perry?" He came and helped her into the dressing gown. She shoved her arms through the sleeves, biting her lower lip. He thought of her brother's ball. He'd been drawn to her, pulled by an invisible tether.

He picked up his damp waistcoat. Dry clothes, that's what he needed. He pulled on the waistcoat anyway. "I won't lie to your father. When he shows up, and you know he will, eventually, I'm telling him everything."

She straightened, the fine muscles around her mouth and her eyes barely moving.

"You won't," she said.

"I will. Are you afraid for me, or for yourself?"

Her gaze dropped and she squeezed her lips together. "I hardly know my father. If it doesn't involve the fate of England, I don't believe he'll truly care." She shook her head. "Or he might lock me up and arrange a quick marriage, to some rural squire. I don't know. My brother Bakeley, though, he's more likely to kill one of us."

"Bakeley won't kill his *sister*." Fox sat on the chair and pulled on his boots. They were damp on the inside.

"And he won't kill you. Fox, stay with me tonight. I promise I won't plague you."

He went to her then, armored with boots, coats, and trousers and knelt, bracing his hands on each side of her. "You need to rest and I can't stay. MacEwen will be back soon, in one piece I hope. Gaz and Davy, also. I sent them to retrieve the gelding after they settled Pip. And there's no telling if Farnsworth may be along behind them."

She looked down at her hands twined in her lap. "I shall get dressed and come down." She lifted her chin, mouth dropping open, eyes shining with sudden tears. "Chestnut. Oh dear, I forgot—"

"She's safe. Pip found her and brought her back."

"Oh." She blinked several times. "I'd hoped she would…I sent her off when they captured me. I cannot thank him enough. And you. Thank you for…" She waved a hand.

"I'm going to find some dry clothes, and then I'll send Jenny up." He kissed her knuckles and released her. "Rest. Sleep. Tomorrow will be very busy."

HE FILLED PERRY'S VISION, MOVING AROUND THE ROOM, picking up and stowing the last of his belongings and his weapons. She gathered her robe around her, cinched the belt, and walked with him to the door.

"Fox." She went on tiptoes and kissed him, watching his eyes blaze again.

He wanted her. There was pain in him setting her away. He was denying himself out of some notion about class difference, perhaps that she, being an earl's daughter, was better than him.

She wouldn't be for long. If he wouldn't have her, she'd leave England and build her own life. She'd just go about it more sensibly than she had tonight.

For now, she would dare to be brave.

"When you are finished with MacEwen, will you come back to my bed?" she asked.

Desire lit his face, but he said nothing, nor did he need to.

He kissed her forehead. "Rest, Lady Perry."

He would only marry honorably with Father's approval. He would expect to have banns called.

Her heart quaked at the thought of a lifetime with Fox. Would he really tell her father everything? And if Father demanded Fox marry her, would he do it? Would she make him happy?

What he wanted with his life, she had no idea. Perhaps he would travel back to America. Perhaps he would go to the Continent and paint. Or perhaps he expected to stay in England and eke out commissions among merchants and gentry. Perhaps her father would send him somewhere else to spy, if he didn't first challenge him to a duel and shoot him.

And Fox, if he left, might not want her along.

For just a few moments, he'd made her feel warm and almost powerful. But *he'd* mastered her, not the other way around. Certainly, another man would have lost control and let her seduce him.

Thoughts of other men made her skin crawl. She wouldn't be forced into a loveless marriage. She only wanted Fox.

She closed the door and padded across the carpet to the table. The tea had gone tepid, but she drank some anyway, took a crumble of biscuit, and realized she was starving. She shoved the whole damp mass into her mouth and chewed, groaning.

All of her injuries had come to life when that door closed, and stiffness crept into her shoulders and arms from the fight with the waves.

But between her legs was a satisfying wholeness that echoed in her heart.

"My lady."

She'd not heard Jenny enter. "Has MacEwen returned?"

"Not yet." Jenny picked up her discarded trousers and looked at them. "I'll try to mend this hole in the knee." She examined the neckcloth. "This is done for, I'm afraid." She tossed them aside and lifted the lid on the teapot. "And this has gone cold. Are you all right, miss?"

Jenny did not seem at all scandalized. Well, she was a girl

from the streets. The memory of his warm hands washed over her.

"What happened out there? Mr. Fox rushed in so fast with you in his arms and blood on your shirt, and them bruises…" Jenny took a deep breath.

Jenny wasn't worried a bit about Fox and her almost swiving.

The events on the road came back to her. "I was taken by the worst of smugglers. Oh, Jenny. I shouldn't have gone."

"Not without me, miss."

Fox's stinging rejection earlier came back to her. He'd have MacEwen go for her brother to take her away, he'd said. Even so, she'd been a fool to take off on her own.

"Mr. Fox sent up his brandy." Jenny poured some into an empty teacup. "Drink this while I brush out your hair."

She settled into the chair and felt the first gentle tug.

"A little pink on your jaw is all you'll have, I think," Jenny said. "The bruise on your neck we can cover with a scarf. It's much like the bruise Lady Sirena had."

Nonplussed was Jenny, as if she dealt with that kind of injury quite regularly, and well, hadn't Bakeley's wife, Sirena, been assaulted by a villain also?

And…she recalled a story shared by Bink's wife, Paulette. Jenny had once also faced a violent man intent on harming her.

"For certain, it will be easier to comb out your hair now, miss. I knew as soon as I saw that chopped off plait you'd run off for good."

"I should have burned it."

"No. Mr. Fox and I would have known anyway, though we mightn't have been so certain." She tugged at a knot and clucked when it unsnarled. "And anyway, hair that lovely shouldn't be tossed out."

No one wanted her hair. Her mother might have, but she was dead. Her father and brothers wouldn't want it. And Fox...her heart twisted as doubt crept in. She took a big swallow of brandy, letting the hot liquor burn her, and glanced at the table where she'd left the long plait.

It was gone.

Her heart picked up its pace. "What did you do with the braid?"

Jenny's hands paused. "Me, miss? Nothing."

Heat poured through her, making her heart swell, sending her nerves tapping against her skin. He could have the plait. He could have every strand of hair attached to her head, and her dowry, and this house, and every horse in her stable. The dowry was hers, this house was hers, through her mother. Father wouldn't, and Bakeley couldn't take them away. And if they did, she'd learn how to cook. She'd learn how to clean brushes. And stretch canvas. She'd even live without a horse if need be. She would marry him, somehow, with or without Father's permission.

She clenched and unclenched her hands, itching to find him and touch him. She just had to somehow, get Fox's agreement.

"It's still long enough to put up, miss, and the curls spring up better. There." Jenny set down the brush. "Shall I get your nightgown?"

"I'll put on a dress. When MacEwen returns, I want to hear what he has to say."

Jenny didn't protest. She wanted to hear also. "There's much afoot here, that's for sure, miss."

She returned with the pale green morning dress draped over her arm.

"Not that one." The other two gowns she'd packed were just as flounced and beribboned. If they'd caught the man

181

who'd abducted her, she might have to go out again tonight. "I want something more practical. What about the travel gown?"

"Still damp. I did find some plain kerseymere dresses in the press that might be long enough for you."

Her mother's. She sprang from the chair. "Let's have a look."

22
THE EARL'S ARRIVAL

Fox donned dry clothes, checked the stables, and carried his spyglass out to the cliff edge. Any vessels afloat were hidden in mist.

He should have been out here watching, instead of upstairs fighting with his cock. A man capable of control, he was, but he needed to put that skill to his mission.

In the cove below, nothing stirred. On the hillside to the north, all the shadows stayed put.

He walked the path toward the stables, skirting around them and moving up to the front door of the cottage. The house muffled the waves to a dim roar. Otherwise, all was quiet.

The skin on his neck rippled. If the shadows were moving, he couldn't see it. Yet something was wrong.

Aye, and much had been wrong this entire day. With Perry, he'd gone from harsh rejection to near ruination, in between spurring her into danger that'd almost killed her. He'd sent the boy, Pip into danger also.

He leaned back into the shadows, bracing himself on the door frame, watching.

Nothing skulked on this moor. All of his unease came from inside him. He'd been wrong—wrong to send Pip alone to speak to Perry's captors. Wrong not to step in sooner. Hell, when he'd heard her gasping, he'd slipped on the rocks and damn near fallen right onto the rocky beach.

He tapped his head back on the hard wood. He hadn't been able to see. He'd only heard the big man's grunting voice, her choked response, but the man's voice had been familiar. He'd met him, somewhere. Once Perry was rested, he'd question her about her captors. She'd remember some detail that would help him identify the man.

He should have been questioning her tonight instead of stripping her naked and pleasuring her.

He stood in the shadows for long minutes and watched the darkness shift and weave around him. The hair on his neck settled, but the ominous feeling had only sunk deeper into his bones. He made his way back down to the kitchen door and let himself in.

The scent of toasting bread wafted up, and he spotted it next to the boiling kettle on the hearth stove. A great hunk of cheese had been set out on a plate on the sideboard.

"Jenny?"

Dim lamplight moved in the storeroom.

His nerves went on high alert, and his heart did cartwheels. His cock took that moment to stand at attention again.

The storeroom held the smallest of cots, not much more than a raised pallet really, where a kitchen boy could rest between tending the fire on a long cold night.

He had a fire that needed tending.

A figure appeared in the doorway, and he turned away, resting his spyglass on the table, carefully arranging it so it wouldn't roll off, keeping his hands busy.

"You should be sleeping." *Don't look at her.* That one glance had shown hair brushed into the sparkling halo, and a dress plainer than even the fashions of past years—no laces, no furbelows, no flounces. When he'd gone looking for linens, he'd seen dresses in one of those presses. Perhaps it was her mother's, or her mother's maid's.

He flicked another gaze over her. Lady Shaldon had been shorter, and this dress only hit the top of Perry's slim ankles. And she was wearing no stays to interfere with the shape of her breasts and the curve of her waist.

"I sent Jenny to bed with a promise to wake her when MacEwen returns." She set plates on the table and went to turn the bread. "Oh, excellent. It's not burned. I've seen this done. I had only but to remember. Charley and I used to sneak down to the kitchen at Cransdall for toast and eggs."

She was nervous of him.

"I brought the brandy back for you." She pushed the bottle over and set about making tea. "Did you see anything outside?"

"No. All is quiet."

"Chestnut—"

"Is fine. The gelding is not yet back."

"Is he one of my father's?"

"Yes." He grabbed a plate and carried the toast to the table, standing too close to her. "Are you all right, Perry?"

She turned an open gaze upon him. No bruising marred her cheek or her eye. Perhaps she'd found some paint among her mother's things.

But a scarf loosely covered her neck, making his gut clench.

He reached for her with his free hand, and she looked up.

"I need to be a part of this, Fox."

185

The plate rattled onto the table. He draped an arm around her, unable to stop from touching her. "You already are." And he hated it, hated the danger she was in, hated that he couldn't deny her anything. "But I'm afraid your participation may only last until your father arrives."

"We have some time. He'll stay in London during the coronation." She turned fully into his arms. "We need to talk."

He dropped his arm and stepped back. He wouldn't take her maidenhead and have her go into an arranged marriage facing another man's shaming.

Her shoulders lifted in a big sigh. "We need to talk about who killed my mother. We need to talk about why Gregory Carvelle is here. We need to talk about these assassins."

The corner of her mouth tilted up. "When you left me tonight, all I could think about was you coming back to my bed. And then Jenny reminded me, we have a mystery to solve. Three mysteries."

His heart swelled and pounded. *We.* He liked that.

He loved her.

He was every kind of fool, and so was she if he thought he'd let her chase villains with him. "Tell me what happened on that road."

She stepped back and framed her hips with her hands, her elbows akimbo.

"You first. How did you happen to come after me? And why didn't you rescue us sooner?"

The darkness reared up again slamming him with his guilt and unworthiness. He would never be good enough for her. He drained his brandy glass and poured another.

When he dared to look, her eyes were dark pools.

"Mind you." She cleared her throat. "Mind you, I was every kind of fool for running off like that."

She'd reached into his mind and stolen his words.

"And I'm so very grateful to you for shooting that man and for fishing us out of the water. And for…" she took in a shallow little breath, "and for showing me the…pleasure of love."

Blood raced through his body, pounded in his ears and hurried south. *Take her*, his cock screamed, and his legs yelled, *Run*.

Almost swiving was not love, he wanted to say, condescendingly, the way he'd always kept her at bay.

She stepped back, crossing her arms over her chest, and suddenly she was a girl again, defensive, defiant, drawn-in, as if she'd heard his sarcasm before it left his tongue.

He touched her shoulder. "Wait." The chair was too far for them to reach and sit without having to release her. If he drew her in closer he'd give in to the urge to kiss her. "I was going out to look for you when Pip came walking into the yard with Chestnut. Pip was on that road, delivering a message to Scruggs's men coming up from Scarborough. I assumed they were the ones who'd taken you. So, when we got close, I hid the gelding as far off the road as possible and sent Pip on with the message."

Her gaze flitted over his eyes, looking for lies and omissions.

"I was wrong." He circled his thumb in the hollow next to her shoulder. "Those weren't Scruggs's men."

Her white teeth worried her lower lip for a moment. "What was Pip's message?"

"John Black was coming."

She shook her head slowly. "Yes. I remember now. Pip told the men. John Black. I've heard of him."

"He was a smuggling lord in these parts. Brutal when crossed. He was transported last year."

187

Her eyes went wide. "And he's back?"

"I imagine the real John Black never left England."

A frown creased her brow. "That big man who took me. That was him?" Her jaw firmed. "His speech was distinctive —not of a higher class, but not as broad as the men who rowed us back. If he's here, when I hear him speak, I'll recognize him. Is it Scruggs, do you think?"

"No. I've met Scruggs."

"Are there any other men his size in the area?"

"There were a few at the inn. Likely the man's from farther south, around Scarborough or beyond." He took a step closer and tugged at her neck scarf. "When he did this to you, I was on the slope, listening. When I figured out what I was hearing, I managed to almost fall down the cliff trying to get to you."

"The rock slide."

"Yes."

Her gaze searched his face. "So, you did save me."

"And I was a while righting myself and heading in the wrong direction. I should have—"

"No. No, Fox. Just you and an unarmed woman and child against three hardened men?"

"I could have taken them."

She lifted his hands, kissed the knuckles, and dropped them. "What do we do next?"

The question was matter-of-fact. She shook herself loose, picked up a knife and sliced pieces of cheese.

This was where a sensible man would say, *We pack you up, Lady Perpetua, and send you home.*

A slice of cheese plopped onto his toast. He sat, pulled the plate over, and yanked her down onto his lap. "Now we eat." He took a bite while she squirmed, letting his free hand slide along her waist, seeing the muscles play under her fair skin. Perhaps a barium white pigment, with a faint wash of sepia. He would have to experiment to achieve the shadows and planes of her satiny flesh.

She gripped the edge of the table. "*Fox.*"

"Very well. We eat, and then we wait for MacEwen to report back." He held the toast up to her mouth. She took a bite, chewing slowly, keeping her gaze locked on him.

And he had an idea what they could do after that.

He shook off the images. He wouldn't dishonor her. He should set her off onto another chair, but they were both fully clothed, and feeding her had its own satisfaction. She ate with the same relish she'd displayed up in bed.

He wiped his face and pulled the tray with the tea setup over, pouring, and mixing all with one hand.

"Thank you." She accepted the cup like an earl's daughter taking tea in a Mayfair drawing room.

Reminding him again, she was too far above him.

A smile lit her face and struck a spark of hope within him. By some miracle, might he gain Shaldon's approval? And if he did, could he ever make her happy.

WHEN PERRY'S CHEWING STOPPED, FOX PUSHED MORE FOOD at her. This business of him feeding her was annoying, but also rather endearing. Still, she began taking smaller bites, chewing more slowly, listening to a disconcerting story of frustration and danger.

After Bakeley's wedding ball, her father had set Fox on the scent of Carvelle, a quest that had taken him to Holland, across the Low Countries, and back again to Gorse Cottage. In his time on the Yorkshire coast, Fox had acquainted himself with most of the smuggling paths in the district and many of the players from Clampton, including the corrupt

Riding Officer and the maid from the Red Lion, who Scruggs used to control the officer and other strangers.

Fox had not spared her delicate sensibilities. Her heart swelled with that, and then quickly collapsed under a niggling suspicion.

"Fox. *You* were a stranger here."

His hand flattened along her back and stroked up and down. "I've no interest in her wares, nor did I partake of them."

It was cunningly done, that stroking and distracting. He might be telling the truth. She scrubbed a hand along his jaw, looking deeply. "I've heard that men often lie about such things. But perhaps I'll choose to believe you."

"I'm glad, because it's the truth."

He went on with the story. After Carvelle's embarkation the previous night, they'd lost sight of the man, and MacEwen's eavesdropping on Carvelle's conversation with Scruggs had yielded no news.

Fox had met Davy and Gaz earlier that day at the inn as well as the local squire, Sir Richard Fenwick.

"What was he like?"

Fox hesitated and frowned. "Bluff and hearty, and dim as a sputtering candle. Your local Squire Western."

His frown belied his words. "But he is surely part of the free trade?"

"As a receiver of bribes, yes, most likely. As an organizer..." Fox's frown deepened. "He does throw his weight around."

A muffled knock at the door made him pause. He set her aside and stood.

It was only Davy, bearing a covered basket. "Others are comin'." He yanked off his hat and lifted the basket. "You *are* a real woman," he said.

Her cheeks warmed. "I am."

Davy glanced at Fox and dropped his gaze to the floor. He seemed an innocent sort, truly not old enough to have a child of Pip's age.

"What have you brought in the basket?" she asked.

"Eggs. From my aunt. For savin' Pip. And I thank ye, miss," he added, his voice gravelly.

She took the basket and almost fumbled it. "It's heavy." A faded yellow cloth had been tucked in along the edges and she peeled it back carefully. At least two dozen eggs of assorted sizes and colors nestled there. "Oh, my." As a girl, she'd had occasion to gather eggs at Cransdall, but they'd never had this much variation. "They are lovely. And there are so many."

"Chickens be layin' good. And lucky thing because you and your man be needin' them with more mouths to feed."

She saw Fox's mouth quiver. Davy thought she was Fox's woman.

The warmth flooding her made her giddy.

"Is Pip well?" she asked.

"Dried up and tucked in. One of Gaz's sisters is sitting on him to keep him from coming back out with us."

"Thank goodness."

"Did you find the horse?" Fox prodded.

The man nodded. "Gaz is putting him up in the stable along with your other men and their horses."

"Other men?" Fox asked.

"Aye. Two Scotsmen and an older gent."

Fox's eyes burned into her. Father had sent MacEwen's cousin, or perhaps the cousin had been on that boat with Farnsworth.

She was not going to run away and hide.

"I believe I can manage to cook eggs for..." She did a

191

mental count and smiled at Davy. "For six hungry men. You and Gaz will join us, Davy." She pulled a crockery bowl from the open shelving above the food dresser.

Fox handed Davy a lamp. "On the top floor is my room. You'll work out which one. Bring down two bottles of brandy. Stop on the floor below and knock on the door at the end of the hall. Tell the girl there to get up and come down. She's a real woman, too. There are no ghosts here."

Davy grinned and shuffled off.

She picked up an egg and weighed it in her hand. "He's happy to go exploring."

"And happy for the brandy."

"And the extra woman." She took a deep breath. "I'm not running away again. Nor will I be sent away."

"Like this." He snatched an egg from the basket, cracked it on side of the bowl, and emptied the bright orange yolk and the clear sac surrounding it, using only one hand.

His smoothness made her laugh again.

"It might soon be quite dangerous here," he said.

She cracked an egg and it exploded, the contents sliding along the outside of the bowl. She tried to pick it up with her fingers and punctured the yolk. "I'm hopeless." More giddiness took her and she laughed again.

"Use two hands, Perry." He demonstrated with another egg then watched her try again. "Yes. Like that."

She whooped and giggled, and he laughed with her. Only a tiny piece of shell had slid into the bowl. "I shall master this yet."

She gazed up at him. He was honorable, and kind. "You're a good teacher, Fox."

His eyes went dark.

"Will you truly tell my father everything when he arrives?"

"Perry—"

"And what *if* Father would give his official blessing?"

Cold air touched her cheek.

"His official blessing for what?"

Her heart thudded to a halt. The egg in her hand dropped, bouncing into the bowl, whole and unbroken.

A thundering stag of a man, dressed in dark wool, had belied all of his size and crept through the door while she and Fox fumbled eggs. And she knew him.

Father had not sent minions. He'd come himself.

The Earl of Shaldon crossed the room and tossed his gloves onto the table.

Next to her, Fox froze, and said, "Sir." The silence that followed was as cold as the wind off the water. Fox didn't bow like a toady. Nor call Father *my lord*. Nor shout, *We didn't expect you.*

One could never expect the Earl of Shaldon. Or *not* expect him.

She opened her mouth and words wouldn't come. He was here for her. Somehow, he'd learned of her visit to a friend in the country from one tiny piece of intelligence crossing his desk, and he'd made his way straight to her hiding place.

She might, after all, run, and require Fox to come with her.

Father's face was unreadable, as bland and devoid of expression as ever. "You have egg on your face, my dear."

She rubbed the back of her hand on her cheek and felt the tight pull of the dried membrane. She didn't remember touching herself there. Fox handed her the yellow towel from the basket and she rubbed at her cheek.

Father raised his arms, and behind him, Kincaid

appeared, helping Father out of his coat. All the while, Father's eyes stayed fixed on Fox.

"You'll be hungry, Father. I am making eggs and a bit of ham." She took a breath, trying to keep her voice from quivering. "Good evening, Mr. Kincaid. Was your journey a hurried one?"

"Rather." Kincaid pulled bundled packages out of a saddlebag. "Are you sharing that cheese, my lady?"

She nodded. "Yes, of course. There's a bit of toast also. And some brandy."

Father and Fox stood, eyes still locked. A bottle of whisky appeared on the table, and Kincaid went off and came back with glasses. Only two, she noticed, and wasn't that rude? He should offer some to Fox, the man who had saved her, who'd almost made love to her, who'd taught her to cook, and who wouldn't marry her without Father's blessing.

Her breath caught. "Fox." She touched his sleeve, and made him turn his gaze to her.

An honorable marriage with her Father's blessing. They might have that. It wasn't impossible. "Fox, yes."

He blinked, because, of course, he hadn't asked her to marry him, and what he was thinking she couldn't guess. She couldn't ask, not with Father and Kincaid in the room.

His arm slid around her. "Lord Shaldon, sir, I should like a private word with you."

She let out a breath. It seemed that he didn't hate her.

Father's gaze narrowed on her, sending a shiver through her. "A private word." His lips pressed together. "She shouldn't be here, Fox." Father sat down heavily and tossed back the spirits Kincaid had just poured.

"That is one of the things I would speak to you about."

Not without her. He meant to send her away. She opened her mouth to object, but Fox's look quelled her.

She stiffened her spine, fished the egg out of the bowl and cracked it. Perfectly, this time. "I'm not leaving."

"She's not leaving," Fox echoed, the steel in his voice sending a thrill through her. Not many men stood up to the Earl of Shaldon. "I'll protect her."

Her heart swelled and pounded. She cracked another egg, the yoke plopping whole and intact into the bowl. "I'm getting good at this," she murmured.

MacEwen walked in, saw them, and smirked behind Shaldon's back while he shed his coat. "Night's turning foul," he said. "Business as usual."

Gaz slipped through the door, hat in hand, his gaze wandering the room. Davy rolled through the inner door juggling two bottles of brandy, with Jenny behind him still tucking her hair under a cap.

The maid's sleepy eyes widened at the sight of the crowd in the kitchen, and Perry saw the moment the girl spotted Father. She stopped in her tracks, her mouth dropping as low as her curtsy.

The chill wind that was Father wiped away Davy's grin, and he clutched the two bottles of spirit to him like the two sides of a breastplate. Fox's grip on her shoulder tightened a fraction. A log cracked and spit. The whisky bottle belched as Kincaid poured two more shots.

"For heaven's sake." She smacked an egg loudly, cracking it neatly. "Jenny, lay the table upstairs and then come help me. There'll be one more for breakfast when Lord Farnsworth arrives."

23

PROPOSAL

The breakfast discussion was inconsequential, as if everyone present already knew the details of all of the evening's events. Which was impossible, since only Davy and Gaz knew what had happened and they were confined to the kitchen with Jenny.

Farnsworth, the one of Father's men with more insight, didn't arrive until the dishes were being cleared. His appearance up the backstairs from the kitchen made it clear to Perry that this house—her house—was a regular gathering place for her father's people. It must be a safe house for the spies taking this route to and from the Low Countries. They all knew their way around the stables and kitchens.

While MacEwen, Kincaid and Father made room for Farnsworth, Perry fidgeted, gripping the edge of the chair seat, the urge to jump up and help Jenny, Davy, and Gaz clear the dishes almost overwhelming. All of her many lessons on proper decorum had vanished this night.

Farnsworth addressed the full plate of food with a lack of gentility, as if he were used to eating quickly when food was available. He'd been attached to a revenue cutter for the past several days and looked the worst for it, his hair plastered wet, his dark, well-cut clothing salt-stained. In between bites, he made his report.

Under the veil of the tablecloth, Fox's hand slid around hers. Farnsworth's level gaze moved over her, the tiniest of frowns forming.

She clasped Fox's hand tightly. "Did you catch up with the smugglers, Lord Farnsworth?" she asked.

"We lost the three men in the skiff in a rocky cove." His frown darkened. "We sent men in and found naught but an empty boat. They'd disappeared into those cliffs."

"And the smugglers' ship?" Fox asked.

"We saw it off the coast. The weather turned us all back."

Perry's heart eased. They'd heard as much from MacEwen. They'd have another chance at stopping the assassins.

Farnsworth peered closer. "Are you quite all right, Lady Perpetua?"

She nodded. "I am."

He looked back at the two local men, hovering along the wall. They'd come back up from the kitchen to wait for Farnsworth's dishes and eavesdrop.

"And the boy?" Farnsworth asked.

Davy brushed back a shock of hair. "Tucked into his bed, thanks to the lady and Mr. Goodfellow."

Father's lips pressed together. His dark gaze scooted between her and Fox and the other men, like he was a spectator at a cricket match. She shifted closer to Fox and straightened her spine.

Outside, the wind howled, making the candles flicker. A sliver of light shone through the glass of the doors. Dawn would be upon them soon.

"You're all very tired." Father looked at Davy and Gaz. "You men, when Scruggs asks, as he will, you may tell him I've come." He sent them off to their homes and their beds.

Kincaid looked a question at Father.

"Might as well set events in motion," Father said, "and tomorrow is soon enough to speak to them. Off with you, too, MacEwen."

MacEwen went off to the kitchen, presumably headed for his bed in the stables. And perhaps to spend time with Jenny first.

There were two more bedchambers next to Perry's own. She would take one of them. "I'll just move my things, Father, and you may have—"

"No need."

"But there are only two empty bedchambers. Take Mother's, and Kincaid may have my maid's cot in the dressing room." Jenny could bed with her, and Farnsworth could have the other, assuming he was staying on.

"Fox will yield his chamber for Farnsworth, won't you, Fox?"

That meant him sleeping in the stables.

Or…with her. Could they manage it, right under Father's nose? Would Fox be willing? She squeezed his hand.

Fox nodded curtly. "I'll spell MacEwen on watch," he said, without budging from his chair.

Kincaid tossed back one more gulp of whisky and stood. "Not much to be done now. We can catch a few hours of sleep. I'll ready your chamber, Shaldon." He nodded his goodnights and left. Farnsworth followed him.

Leaving her and Fox alone with Father. A wild thrumming started up in her. Fox would tell him the truth, he'd said, and then what?

Father wouldn't beat her, she didn't think. He might despise her. He might try to marry her off to some lord in his service.

Farnsworth, perhaps. He was a baron, long-ago widowed, but not in a million years would she have him.

"Go to bed, my dear," Father said. "I would speak to Fox privately."

Fox's grip on her hand slackened and she looked at him. He wanted to send her away also.

She pulled her hand away and stood. "I will not. What he has to say concerns me also." She twisted her hands in the kerseymere skirt and paced around the table where she could face both of them. "I'll not be shut out, or sent to bed. I'm not a child any longer."

PERRY'S EYES HELD SO MUCH HURT, IT TORE AT HIS HEART. She'd not been a compliant girl, and she wouldn't be a compliant wife, either. Yet, she must give him his due as a man to talk to her father in his own way and own time, especially since she'd forced the issue. He wouldn't beg Shaldon to bless a marriage between them. Only a blessing freely given would make for a marriage that would endure. If Shaldon begrudged them this marriage, Perry would be unhappy. If they were sent away, she would miss Cransdall, her brothers and their wives, and her nieces and nephews. She'd miss her horses also.

Love wouldn't sustain without the friendship of her family.

But if he took her to America...his brother had written seeking reconciliation, promising his share of their father's lands, if he returned. Land yes, but no guarantee of the friendship of *his* family. More than likely, she would be desperately homesick for England.

She'd forced this hand and he had no choice but to play it.

He reached for her and she came to him. He could feel her quaking.

"Lord Shaldon, I care very much for Perry, and...we've shared this cottage without a proper chaperone. I've compromised her." His throat tightened and took a deep breath. "I would like your blessing to marry your daughter."

"And you've spoken to her before speaking to me, or her brother?"

The ass. He was every bit as condescending as Fox had expected.

"I'm of age, Father." Anger flashed in Perry's eyes. "And Bakeley has no say over me."

"So, I take it, daughter, you are willing to marry Fox?"

Her lips formed an O sending his heart crashing, but she finally nodded. "Yes."

"And if I oppose the match?" His gaze took them both in. Shaldon's shoulders lifted in a sigh. "Come here, Perpetua."

She bit her lip and stalled, what she had said, that she didn't truly know her father, displayed on her face. "Fox has been very honorable. I should greatly appreciate your approval, Father, but I shall be willing to marry him even without it."

Dear, defiant Perry. He opened his mouth to set the record straight, but Shaldon spoke first.

"Yes. I know. Come here."

She glanced at Fox and he nodded.

Her father grasped her hand. "So cold," he murmured. "And there is that bruise on your cheek that you've painted over. I've been wondering about it since I arrived."

He shot Fox a look that sparkled with anger. "Now let me see what else you are hiding under that scarf at your neck."

Perry gasped. "It wasn't Fox's doing—"

"The scarf, Perpetua."

Fox stood and went to help her, his fingers fumbling with the cloth. "It wasn't my doing, but it *was* my fault." It'd been his rejection that'd caused her to take flight.

The scarf slipped away, and Shaldon took in the ugly bruises, his mouth going hard. "His brows drew together and he turned a look on Fox. "She's been wincing and favoring her left side. Is there more?"

"Blows to the back. Above and below the kidney, I'd say. Nothing broken, but badly bruised."

"How did this happen?" Shaldon addressed the question to him.

"She was…" he fumbled for words that would not make her feel foolish. "taken on the road to Scarborough."

"And this was before or after you compromised her?"

"It was after I spent a night alone in this house with a single man." Perry's tone was laced with anger. "And I left because Fox was being so honorable and so determined he was unworthy. He was thinking of your feelings and not mine."

Her eyes glinted with unshed, angry tears. "I'm sorry, Perry." The night's events rushed back upon him and he pulled her close. "She was taken by three men. A big man, who might have been the real John Black, the smuggler, his minion, and a Frenchman."

Shaldon frowned. "The three men in the skiff."

Perry lifted her head. "No. Two of them went off and left the Frenchman. Fox shot him before he could shoot me and Pip."

"Pip." Shaldon rubbed his forehead. "Pip is the boy Farnsworth mentioned?"

"Yes," Fox said.

"I see. Or rather, I don't see. You'll start at the beginning and leave out nothing. Er, except for the part about compromising my daughter. I don't care to know those details."

"Will you give your blessing, Father?" she asked.

He pressed his lips together. "You should not have come here, Perpetua. This is a dangerous business. Fox must keep you alive before any talk of marriage."

Fox helped her into a chair and seated himself next to her, his stomach roiling. They would chase down these villains, find Carvelle, and puzzle out Lady Shaldon's murder, before any talk of marriage. Shaldon would give her a chance to come to her senses and cry off from a promise they'd never made.

He'd never felt less honorable in all his days.

THE SUN WAS ON THE HORIZON WHEN FATHER ROSE FROM THE table. Perry lingered, gathering the remaining glasses and cups, stalling until Father was out of sight.

"Leave them," Fox said. "Jenny can get them later."

Jenny had already gone up to bed.

"I have a new spirit of republicanism." She joked but her heart was quaking. The old Fox, the one who kept his thoughts hidden, was back. "And I'm not sure I can sleep. Are you angry with me, Fox?"

"For forcing my hand?" He dropped a kiss on her forehead and reached for the tray. "We'll talk later. You go to bed." He headed down the stairs to the kitchen.

She followed him.

He set the dishes to soak and gathered her into his arms.

"You don't have to sleep in the stables, Fox. You can come upstairs—"

"With your father in the next room?" He pressed his lips to hers lightly and then broke away, taking her elbow. "Come on. I'll escort you upstairs."

Reluctantly, she let him lead her, dragging her tired limbs. They'd got to the parlor floor when the sound of a carriage reached them.

"Wait here." Fox went to the door and peered out.

Perry ducked around him to look. A traveling chaise was coming up the drive, with black-clad outriders in front and behind.

MacEwen came up the drive from the stable and greeted one of the outriders.

"That's MacEwen's cousin," Perry whispered.

"Did I not tell you to wait?" Fox said.

Indignation mixed with apprehension, and she clutched his arm. "And that is one of my father's unmarked chaises. Charley would not take a chaise. Or Bink. Nor would Bink come after me. That had better not be Bakeley."

"In a chaise? Your brother?" Fox opened the door and went down the steps.

The chaise door opened to a display of a wine-colored traveling dress. Perry hurried after Fox.

24

THE CHAPERONE

Fergus MacEwen handed Lady Jane Montfort down and Perry hastened to greet her.

She hugged the older woman, relieved that it wasn't Bakeley appearing at her door. "Why are you here?" she asked. "Oh, never mind, you are meant to be my chaperone, no doubt."

Lady Jane held her at arm's length and looked her over, frowning. "What has happened here?" She turned the scowl on Fox. "You. You're Mr. Fox. The American painter."

He bowed. "At your service, ma'am."

"Fox, this is Lady Jane Montfort, a dear friend of Sirena's, and my friend as well. Lady Jane, Mr. Fox and I are affianced." She crossed her fingers. "Father has just given his approval."

Jane's scowl deepened and she waved a hand at Perry. "You are not the one who caused this, are you?"

"No," Perry and Fox said at the same time.

He sent her a look that had shame roaring through her. Because of her foolishness, he was destined to be misunderstood.

And trapped in a marriage he didn't want.

"You must be very tired," he said, "and Lady Perry is exhausted."

Perry nodded. Making peace with Fox would have to wait. "Come then," she said woodenly. "I'll take you up."

HOURS LATER, PERRY WOKE TO THE SOUND OF MOVEMENT below stairs.

"We have visitors?" The sleep-slurred voice next to her broke the room's silence.

Perry sat up. "I believe so." She glanced at her bed companion.

"I know I'm not the sleeping companion you wished for, my dear, but your reputation will be safer with me," Lady Jane had said while she'd climbed into bed earlier.

Lady Jane was a spinster poor relation of Lord Cheswick making do on a small inheritance while rescuing young ladies' reputations. Since she'd moved into Shaldon House, Father also had apparently found a use for her.

Perry rubbed her eyes and smiled. Lady Jane's bed cap had slipped, and the lacing on her nightrail had come undone, revealing a plump freckled shoulder. She looked like a wanton tavern wench and not at all like a lady of middling years. Straggling across the feather stuffed pillow was a long wheaten plait, the color not much different than Perry's own, except for some fine lacings of white shot through it.

Perry threw back the covers and went to the window. The morning had gone to gray with a heavy cloud cover, but it was bright enough to be afternoon. A single horse was tied up in front.

Not a Cransdall horse, she decided, unless one of her

brothers had arrived on one of the plodders that worked the fields.

She crossed to the dressing room and peeked in. Jenny was up and gone. She would just have to dress herself.

"Come," Jane said next to her. "We'll help each other." She ducked into the dressing room where her trunk had been lodged.

Perry blinked back sudden tears. Her three brothers' marriages had brought three sisters and this kind, wise woman into their family. Jane hadn't chided or lectured her about Fox.

She would hate to be cut off from these new friendships.

Fox must keep her alive, Father had said. How hard could that be now, with Father and so many of his men here? This was Yorkshire, after all, and not some Peninsular battleground.

She peeled her nightrail up and caught her breath, a sharp pain stabbing her. She'd almost forgotten.

Well, perhaps there were dangers here, but she'd be safe if she stayed close to Fox. The need to see him, to touch him, swamped her, and she hurried to dress.

FOX GROUND THE BEANS HIMSELF AND CARRIED UP THE coffee tray to the dining table where Shaldon, Kincaid, and Farnsworth sat.

Lady Jane's chaise had accommodated more provisions, and this one—coffee—they all needed. The faces around the table were haggard from years of such fast travel and long nights and worries.

"I'll need to leave soon to meet the Lieutenant," Farnsworth said. "Seas will be calmer. They'll try again to land tonight."

"Sit down and join us." Shaldon motioned Fox to a chair. "Farnsworth has just been talking about his encounter with you in the boat last night."

Fox's fingers tensed around the china cup, the warmth of the liquid unable to drive out the chill that went through him.

"Lady Perpetua is a brave girl," Farnsworth said. "I was relieved to find her so well-recovered."

Shaldon's harrumph sent anger sparking through Fox. The man didn't appreciate his daughter enough.

"Tell Kincaid and Farnsworth what you and Perpetua learned last night."

As Fox opened his mouth to speak, a loud knocking at the hall door drew everyone's attention. The others exchanged a knowing glance.

"Excellent. Things are moving along," Shaldon said. "Coming to the main door instead of the kitchen, this will be someone of interest."

Fox set the cup down. "Perhaps it's Scruggs. Davy and Gaz—"

"No," Kincaid cut in, shaking his head. "Scruggs would be at the kitchen door, as usual. This won't be Scruggs."

"I wonder if Scruggs can still be trusted." Farnsworth drummed his fingers on the table. "John Black and Carvelle. Perhaps the screws are turning on him and there's naught to be done but play it out."

More loud knocking, this time more insistent.

"Well then, let's find out who is this someone of interest." Kincaid rose.

"Stay," Fox said. "Mr. Goodfellow can answer his own door."

His boot heels clacking along the tiled floor, Fox checked his weapons.

207

Bang, bang, bang. Only the stoutest of hands could make the thick oaken door rattle thus on its hinges.

Beneath the dark worsted of his unfashionably loose coats, his knives were in place, as was his pistol, all hidden away, and if this was the man who'd harmed Perry…he took a deep breath. He couldn't kill the man just yet. Shaldon would want to question him.

He pulled open the door. The bright, sweating face of Sir Richard beamed at him.

"Goodfellow," he said, "good day to you. A fine day to pay a call on a neighbor."

SIR RICHARD'S HORSE, A STOUT FELLOW TO CARRY SUCH A weight, nibbled at the bush where it was tied. Otherwise, it seemed the Baronet had come alone.

"Sir Richard." He beckoned the man and led him to the dining room, his back prickling. The Baronet was big, like the man who'd taken Perry, but that man'd had none of the bumbling softness of Sir Richard. Nor had he heard, in all of his travels, any hint that the Baronet did more than receive bribes from free traders. He'd not even been involved in the case of John Black. That had been another judge, a man from further south.

Kincaid looked up with interest, but Shaldon's face betrayed nothing. No reaction. Farnsworth sat up. None of the men rose.

"Why, you have guests, Goodfellow," Sir Richard exclaimed.

Fox looked at Shaldon, who nodded.

"Not exactly guests," Fox said. "This is my landlord, Lord Shaldon."

Sir Richard's eyes brightened. "Lord Shaldon?" He

bowed deeply. "Indeed, indeed. Pleased to finally make your acquaintance."

"Join us," Kincaid said, introducing himself and Farnsworth.

Fox pulled out a chair at the foot of the table for the man.

"Well, well." Sir Richard squirmed and blustered. "Such a pleasure."

"Indeed," Shaldon said.

"Fancy me paying a call on old Goodfellow and finding you here. What brings you to these wild parts, eh? A bit of shooting, I suppose. Or, are you here to check on this good young fellow?" He laughed heartily. "I assure you, he's been a quiet one in the neighborhood. No complaints. No complaints a't'all."

Shaldon sat as still as death.

Sir Richard played the buffoon heartily—perhaps the man really was a person of interest.

The Baronet accepted coffee and chattered on about the weather, fishing, the coronation, accepting a few nods and grunts as encouragement.

Fox's head ached with it and his thoughts went to Perry, glad she was in the capable hands of Lady Jane. For all he knew, that lady might be one of the many who'd served Shaldon during the war years. She had that look of quiet intelligence about her.

Jenny appeared with a fresh pot, and Sir Richard's eyes flashed, a look then quickly veiled. He glanced from her to Fox and back again.

"That will be all," Fox said in his best lord-of-the-manor tones. Jenny bobbed a curtsy and he heard her footsteps retreating, and then a few minutes later, growing louder.

His chest tightened. The steps and the rustle of skirts were not Jenny's.

Lady Jane stepped into the room in a swirl of rosewater scent, clad in a blue day dress, a fichu tied high at her neck, just like the one Perry, who entered behind her, wore over the simple gown that must be another of her mother's. They'd both dispensed with caps, their hair twisted into simple knots, even Perry's shortened locks.

Sir Richard jumped to his feet, bumping his cup and splattering coffee. "Well," he murmured. "Well, well, well."

"Good morning, or perhaps I should say, good afternoon," Lady Jane said.

"I trust that you both slept well?" Shaldon signaled, and the ladies took seats down the table from Sir Richard, Perry shielded by Kincaid, and Lady Jane by Farnsworth.

"Yes, indeed," Lady Jane said. "After such a journey, rest is just the thing." Her gaze traveled around the table and landed on Sir Richard.

But the man didn't return the lady's nod.

A pounding started up in Fox's ears. Sir Richard's eyes were riveted on Perry.

25
SIR RICHARD VISITS

Shaldon had seated his daughter so that the painted over bruise on her face was away from the Baronet's eye. Fox saw all of that, along with the man's intense interest in Perry. The creeping feeling that slithered along his spine could not be ignored.

Perry sat taller and shared one long glance at Fox, and then her gaze returned to her father, as if she were studiously avoiding Sir Richard.

Shaldon patted her hand and squeezed it. "Will you go down to the kitchen, my dear? Have the maid bring up a tray so you ladies may break your fast."

Color flooded her cheeks and she rose. "Certainly, Father."

Sir Richard's gaze trailed her as she left and he exhaled loudly. "That is your daughter, Shaldon? Spitting image of Felici…er, her mother."

Shaldon didn't so much as blink, but Fox sensed a prickling in the man at hearing his dead wife's Christian name trip off the oaf's tongue.

Lady Jane cleared her throat and glanced at Shaldon, who seemed disinclined to take any hints, and then to Fox.

Well, he was the lowest in their noble pecking order, wasn't he, even lower than the silent Kincaid, but he *was* the resident tenant here. He made introductions.

"Sir Richard," Lady Jane said. "We met, many years ago, though I'm sure you do not remember."

The man studied her. "I beg your pardon, my lady, but I don't. Though beauty such as yours should not—"

"Don't be silly," she waved a small hand at him.

Not inclined to accept flattery was the lady, though Sir Richard was right—there was beauty in the contours of her face. The shallow crinkles around her eyes and mouth looked to be the marks of a truly gentle woman who smiled often and looked kindly on many. In her younger days, she wouldn't have been a fashionable beauty perhaps, but she would have turned some heads.

An interesting face. He would have to sketch her, if she would allow it.

"It was a ball many years ago." She pinned a clear gaze on Sir Richard. "As I recall, you left early."

Sir Richard shifted in his chair.

Ah, so, Lady Jane was perhaps not always kind. She could also wield the velvet-clad blade of a society lady, and the fact that she'd parry and thrust with Sir Richard meant Fox's instinct about the man was correct.

If Sir Richard but laid another long look on Perry...

"I dare say, I don't remember," Sir Richard said. "May I inquire how long you will grace the neighborhood with your presence, Shaldon?"

"Our plans are not certain."

"Surely you must be back in London for the coronation.

The King cannot do without you, eh?" He chuckled and sipped at his coffee.

Shaldon did not answer.

Perry and Jenny entered, both setting trays on the sideboard. Perry seated herself and Jenny served the two ladies.

"Bring a plate for Sir Richard, girl," Lady Jane said.

Jenny ducked and bowed with proper servility—another clever woman—and did as asked.

Sir Richard ignored her, his attention thoroughly fixed on Perry. He wanted an introduction, and damn him if Fox would oblige him when it came to Perry.

"I'm hosting a bit of a fête for the local society to celebrate the coronation, for those of us who cannot attend, and I'd thought to invite Mr. Goodfellow here. But imagine the stir if the great Lord Shaldon would deign to appear?"

Was that sarcasm under that hearty bluffness?

"You are the highest-ranking neighbor around, sir, and one so frequently absent the neighbors would love to meet you, and of course, your guests, and your lovely daughter."

"When is this event?" Lady Jane asked.

Sir Richard took a bite of toast, chewed, and sipped his coffee. "Next week. 'Twill be a small affair, I fear. Dinner and, er, perhaps a bit of dancing."

"I fear we cannot promise you next week," Shaldon said.

"Well, then. You and the ladies must come for dinner. Tomorrow night. I'll not take no for an answer."

Shaldon leveled a steady gaze on him. "We shall be honored."

"Excellent." Sir Richard caught Perry's eye. "And I shall particularly like to make your acquaintance, my dear."

Perry's eyes narrowed. She set down her fork.

"Your mother was a childhood friend. Used to gallop across my land whenever the notion took her. Always a horsewoman, wasn't she? Do you share her interest in horses, my lady?"

Perry washed down a bite of toast and glanced at her father before answering. "My brother runs the equine operations."

"Well," Sir Richard said. "Of course. No doubt finer than my own, though I dare say there are a few fine mounts in my stable. I should like you to feel welcome to come over any time to ride, and, er, Lord Shaldon, I'd be happy to have you ride any of my mounts." He stood. "Well then, tomorrow night. Though I am but a widower, I dare say I have one of the best cooks in the county and can spread a fine table. I shall be happy to see you then."

Fox walked out with him. At the door, Sir Richard turned on him. "Bit of a surprise, eh, his lordship showing up?"

The skin on his neck prickled again. Shadows hid Sir Richard's expression, but he'd lowered his shoulders in a threatening stance. A tall man he was, about Fox's height, and the flabbiness around him was, Fox realized, merely an excess of linens and coats crowned with a mask of stupidity. Strip him down to a dark jumper and one would find muscle and brawn and a keen intelligence.

The man tilted his head, the rabbit waiting to see what the fox would do.

Only, who was the rabbit and who was the fox here?

Fox nodded. "And good day, Sir Richard." He held the door until the man passed, and then snicked it quietly shut, turning the lock.

Perry would not be going to that dinner, at least, not

without him, not without Kincaid and Farnsworth, though none of them had been expressly invited.

Well, Sir Richard's cook would just have to stretch the fare a little further.

26

UNTANGLING THE PLOT

*P*erry's skin had been crawling for the last several minutes, like she had landed in a pile of maggots. Not that she'd ever done such a thing, but this surely must be the feeling.

Her father's hand rested on hers for the second time that morning.

"Are you quite all right?" he asked.

She glanced up at him, and then Fox returned, drawing her attention. His look of concern must mirror her own.

"I am," she said. "But I am not sure I should have dinner at Sir Richard's until after my injuries have healed."

"I'm not sure any of us should," Farnsworth said, "but especially not the ladies."

"That is a dangerous road for an evening excursion," Fox said.

"He did not mention the assault on your servants last night, Fox," Farnsworth said. "Does he call on you often, Goodfellow?"

"Never," Fox said.

"Interesting. Fancy him paying his first call just after we've arrived."

"Lady Perpetua," Kincaid asked, "have you met him before?"

"No," she wheezed, a pain in her injured rib sharpening the pronouncement, another uncontrollable wriggle making her back spasm. Sir Richard might've picked her up from the chair and carried her off, his interest had been that palpable. Without the men here, she would have run for a knife in the kitchen. Father's dislike had been clear.

Which, she reminded herself, didn't mean he wouldn't try to use the man's interest for one of his schemes.

"If you need my help, Father, then I shall determine to go to dinner. I can work out a way to cover this." She touched the scarf at her neck.

A necklace of wide ribbon and a brooch would work—it had for Sirena. There would be something among her mother's things she could use. And if Fox would come with her…

But the invitation had gone to her father and the ladies, had it not? She strained to remember.

"Will you remove your scarf, Perpetua?" Father said. The question was a gentle command, but there was kindness in his eyes. "I should like the others to see what we are dealing with."

Heat shot through her. She must be a bright shade of crimson.

"Sir." Fox pushed back his chair and opened his mouth to say more.

"It's all right, Fox." She unwound the scarf she'd found in her mother's things, sending the lilac scent rising. The damp sea air touched the skin above the dress's deep neckline. It should have cooled the flush racing through her but it only made it worse.

She'd been so foolish. She dropped her gaze and hitched in a breath.

Kincaid cleared his throat. "Who did this, my lady?"

Jane leaned in. Despite her promise to Jane, she had put off explaining her injuries. She'd not shared the story with anyone but Father. Nor had Fox, apparently.

She repeated the story about being taken on the road.

"A big man," Kincaid said. "Might it've been this Sir Richard? He seemed taken with you."

"I was dressed as a boy."

Kincaid and Farnsworth shared a look.

"She was," Farnsworth said.

Could it have been the Baronet? The voice was different, gruffer, surer, the body more solidly muscular. Sir Richard looked like a stuffed hog swathed in quality worsted.

She shook her head. "It couldn't have been him. He left me to be killed by one of his men. Sir Richard would have held me for ransom or…"

Or worse. Her heart pounded wildly. The previous night's villain wouldn't have hesitated to take her virtue. The thought sent her mind reeling.

"He didn't know he'd captured an earl's daughter," Kincaid mused. "How did you escape?"

All eyes turned on her and she finally found her voice. "Fox saved us," she whispered.

"Us?" Kincaid asked, showing no surprise at Fox's heroics.

He'd worked with Fox before. Fox was indeed part of their circle, respected by Father and his men. She glanced at her lover down the table. His eyes burned through her, but she couldn't decipher his emotion.

"Us, Lady Perpetua?" Kincaid asked again.

"Yes. Davy's young son, Pip, had joined me."

Fox crossed his arms. "I sent Pip in." He told them about the message Pip was supposed to deliver warning about the very men who captured Perry and him. "It was a grievous mistake."

"So, Scruggs and this John Black are not working together?" Farnsworth said.

"I'd say Scruggs is afraid of the man," Kincaid said. "Lady Perpetua, how did Fox rescue you?"

"I didn't." Fox shook his head. "Lady Perry and Pip rescued themselves. They jumped off the cliff into the water."

All eyes turned on her, and the room grew warmer again.

"That's why you were soaked." Farnsworth's gaze held sympathy and interest. And perhaps, respect. "Were there other injuries?"

She waved a hand. "Another bruise."

"A very large one out of sight on her back," Jane said, pursing her lips and frowning at Fox. "She should see a surgeon. She might have broken a rib."

Jane could not know Fox had seen it. Or perhaps she was frowning because she thought Fox should have done more.

Perry lifted her chin and looked at a spot on the wall. "Fox examined my injuries. Nothing is broken, is it, Fox? And he truly did save us. He shot the Frenchman, just as the man was firing at us."

"A Frenchman?" Farnsworth sat up.

He'd been completely distracted from the notion of Fox examining her. She hoped Father was as well.

"Is the man dead?" Farnsworth asked.

Perry glanced at Fox.

"He's dead," Fox said.

"No name?" Farnsworth asked.

Fox shook his head. "He was checked thoroughly. There was nothing on him."

"What did you do with the body?" Kincaid asked.

"Weighted it down and tossed it in the sea," Fox said.

"With luck, the tides will wait until after we've settled this matter to wash him up," Farnsworth said.

"And by then the fishes will have eaten around the bullet hole." Kincaid took a piece of buttered toast. "I take it Davy and Gaz rowed them back here?" He addressed the question to Farnsworth.

Farnsworth nodded. "Those two will have reported to Scruggs." He looked up from his plate. "Where is Carvelle?"

Fox took a deep breath. "MacEwen saw him last at the inn with Scruggs, night before last."

Farnsworth stood. "I'll just go check with Mac."

WHEN FARNSWORTH LEFT, FOX MOVED UP NEXT TO JANE.

The quiet around the table chilled her. She'd set something in motion with her foolhardy escape. She'd endangered a child, and Fox, as well as herself.

"I'm sorry, Father," she said.

His look was long and indecipherable. "I do not like to see you injured. Though we do know more today than we did yesterday."

She dropped her gaze to the uneaten toast on her plate, then looked up. "What, Father?"

He blinked.

Of course she would have to draw it out of him. "The assassin," she said. "Are they bringing him in to kill the King?"

Her father exchanged a look with Kincaid.

"Carvelle arrives," Kincaid said speculatively, "Carvelle working with Scruggs. Or is Carvelle working with John Black to bring in a French assassin? Scruggs is a mere smuggler, not a traitor to England. Done us more than enough good turns through the years."

His arm brushed hers as he turned to her, this man who had always been a strong, shadowy presence in her father's life. It was no wonder Father kept him around. His loyalty was unshakable.

"Can you remember anything about this Frenchman, Lady Perpetua? Any words he spoke to you?"

"He…" She inhaled and the sharp pain bit at her. "He said he knew I was a woman. Yet…he didn't mention it to the others. He was not the one who did this." She touched her neck. "That was the big man. A smaller man with horrible breath punched me in the back." She closed her eyes and thought of that moment on the cliff. "The Frenchman said, *I am good at what I do. You will feel no pain.*"

Kincaid and Father exchanged looks, the air vibrating with their silent communication. Lady Jane frowned down at her plate. Fox's mouth had firmed, but she read anguish in his features.

"Did you recognize him?" She directed the question to Fox. He looked at Father.

Fox shrugged. "He could have been any number of French torturers."

"But the French have been defeated," Perry said.

"Maybe they're settling old scores, also," Fox said.

His face went pale. His gaze lifted to Father. He took a deep breath and turned back to her. "But most likely this was not personal for him. Most likely he'd hired himself out to do what he was so good at."

He knew more than he'd told her. Like always.

"Hired by whom? To assassinate whom?" She looked around at the inscrutable faces.

Lady Jane rested her elbows on the table and steepled her fingers. "Perry, I fear you are mistaken about Sir Richard."

Lady Jane's clear blue eyes held hers, her mouth firmed in an angry line.

27

A COMPANY OF SPIES

*W*as Lady Jane Montfort also a member of Father's network?

Father frowned, and Lady Jane glared back at him.

"If you could but see the bruise on Perry's back…" She inhaled sharply and turned a hot look on Fox. "And you. I don't even want to ask why she was out on that road last night."

"We've been over this before. It wasn't his fault."

"I take full responsibility," he said.

Perry pushed back her chair and hurried around the table, gripping his shoulders. "It was *my* own foolishness."

She swallowed hard. Fox didn't reach up to touch her. Father had shown her more affection this morning than Fox.

Maybe he hated her.

Lady Jane shook her head. "Look at them, Shaldon. Would you keep them apart? She has been mooning over him since the wedding ball. Enough to run away and come to him."

Perry gasped. "I didn't know Fox was here."

She thought back to the day she found the papers about this house. She'd been snooping, as usual, when Father was out, and that time he'd left his study unlocked, the documents relating to this property on his desk. It had been during the turmoil of Charley's and Gracie's problems, and she'd thought it had been an uncharacteristic, and for her, fortuitous, moment of carelessness on Father's part.

Father's face was unreadable, as usual. She wobbled, and Fox pulled out the chair next to him, helping her onto it.

His warm strength enveloped her. Perhaps he *didn't* hate her. If only they could be alone and she could talk to him instead of in this room with Father, Kincaid and Jane looking on with disapproval.

And yet, and yet...had Father manipulated her into this reunion with Fox? If Lady Jane had seen her interest in Fox, then Father had seen it also. Perhaps Father was throwing them together, not keeping them apart.

And perhaps, he'd seen that Fox had some interest in *her*.

Heat shivered through her. Well, of course. Even if he didn't wish to wed her, the drawings, the painting, those were proof Fox had at least been thinking about her. Perhaps Father had seen them.

Where her brothers were concerned, Father had been making up for the many years of his absences, the lost time he could never recapture. He had been watching them, and manipulating them.

Into the matches of *his* choice.

She reached for Fox's hand. Surely, they already had Father's blessing. He might have expected her to behave better, but *he* himself hadn't, had he? Not when her eldest brother Bink, Father's by-blow, had been conceived.

Lady Jane's gaze bore into her. She certainly expected

better from Perry. And...what had she said about Sir Richard?

Blast it, she'd been distracted again.

"What's this about Sir Richard, Lady Jane?" Perry asked.

Lady Jane's frown only deepened. "You are the very image of your mother at your age. Is she not, Kincaid?"

"Yes, you are very like your mother, Lady Perpetua," Kincaid said. "She also was not averse to a gamble and would occasionally get a hair up and—"

"Kincaid." Lady Jane tapped the table.

Kincaid nodded and leaned back.

"I'd first met Sir Richard many years before that ball I mentioned, when I was a child. I'd been brought along to a house party where your mother, Felicity's, engagement to Lord Shaldon became known." She turned to Father. "That was Lord Shaldon, your brother. You were still in Ireland."

Father did not so much as nod.

"Sir Richard hadn't yet succeeded his uncle as baronet. He was simply Richard Fenwick. It was clear, he'd set his sights on your mother, and especially her lands and her dowry." She leaned across Perry for a long look.

Her mother had been sole heir to a great fortune amassed in trade and banking.

"Sir Richard followed her around for days, trying to lure her out alone." She shook her head. "She did go eventually, but not alone," Jane said, glancing at Perry. "I was there."

"You were friends with my mother?" Perry asked.

"No. I was but a child, as I said, following the older girls around. Your mother was kind to me, and as it turned out, I was useful to her."

"Did you intervene directly?" Fox asked, his voice laced with concern. "Will he remember you?"

Perry's mind skipped back and forth. If Jane had

225

interfered...surely Sir Richard would not pull up a memory of her as a little girl.

"I ran for some grooms. Her grandfather bribed them soundly to keep silent and dealt with Sir Richard. I don't know how, but the villain departed within the hour."

"What exactly did Sir Richard do to my mother?" Perry asked.

Jane blinked and glanced at Father, who was staring intently, his face still without expression, but with a tightness around his mouth that hadn't been there previously.

Father, who knew almost everything, hadn't known about this.

"He had a carriage waiting. He planned to force a marriage."

"What did he *do*?" Father asked.

"She was struggling in his arms, fighting him while he tried to carry her off to a waiting chaise. The grooms arrived in time and her grandfather soon after." She looked around the table. "He is not a mere bumbling baronet. He is a brute, I daresay quite capable of assaulting a boy and a young woman dressed as a boy on a dark road."

"He wanted Mother's money."

"Yes. But I believe he also wanted *her*."

Perry shivered. She didn't have her mother's fortune, but she had her looks.

Fox's arm slipped around her. "He'll not lay a hand on you," he murmured.

Father's gaze had gone somewhere else. Had he cared for their mother? She'd always wondered. When his brother died, he'd claimed the title and the fiancée. After the marriage, Father had been away more than he'd been home. She'd always thought it a marriage arranged for money, on his part, and status on her mother's. She'd always imagined the love of his life had been Bink's mother. Perhaps she'd been wrong.

Lady Jane's gaze went to Father. Sirena had hinted that the lady had once had a beau, so many years ago. And she'd also met Father, a long time ago.

And Sir Richard had wanted her mother. All the ancient romances, the ancient discords and plots, swirled around them, reaching from the past, confusing the present.

Fox's hand dropped from her shoulder, making her heart plummet. Perhaps love was always a muddle.

Farnsworth swept in from the kitchen, silently, glancing around at the change in seating and taking the chair at the foot of the table. "Mac will check at the inn on the whereabouts of Carvelle. And I've sent word to the cutter that I'll stay on land tonight. They'll patrol to the north."

"And if they land further south?" Fox asked.

"We'll bring the dragoons up at dark," Farnsworth said. "Every moment we delay the landing is to our good." He leaned back in his chair. "And I've set men to follow Sir Richard."

"We'll join him for dinner tomorrow night," Father said, "and see what is what."

"I shall go," Perry said. "Perhaps my presence will unsettle him."

"Let us get through tonight first." Father stood and looked from Kincaid to Farnsworth. "Join me in the study. Fox, you have learned the terrain around here. We'll need your services tonight. In the meantime, I should like sketches of Lady Perry's captors. She will help you, and we can have the boy brought over also."

They left, and Fox's hand rested on hers. "You will be safer here tomorrow night than at Sir Richard's."

"That is true," Lady Jane said.

Perry took a deep breath and put his hand aside. "I thought we could announce our engagement and see how he reacts."

"I don't believe I was invited," Fox said. "Only you, your father, and Lady Jane."

"All the more likely to bring about a reaction from Sir Richard, if, in fact, he is a villain." A shiver went through her and she frowned. "*The* villain." If he was the man who'd attacked her, she could take her revenge. But she must visit his house to do that.

"Let's start with those sketches," Fox said. "The light is better in the parlor. I'll get a sketchbook."

28

SETTING THE TRAP

"*I*t was so very dark, and the faces were blackened. You cannot possibly expect me to remember." Perry stood and walked to the fireplace, away from the distracting ripple of Fox's muscles as his hand flew across paper.

He'd removed his coat and peeled back his sleeves, refusing to meet her eyes. All she wanted was to make better use of these moments alone, before Father, or one of his henchmen returned.

"Perry."

When she looked, that muscled forearm and wide hand were extended.

She went.

He smoothed those hands, with their sprinkling of dark hair, up her arms, slipped them around her waist, and pulled her to him.

She would surely melt. She had certainly died and gone to heaven. They should run off now, to Scotland, to the Lowlands, to France, anywhere. To hell with Prinny and his coronation, and the men who wanted to kill him.

"Your father is right—a sketch may help. The others may recognize the men. Perhaps we'll even be a step closer to learning what really happened to your mother."

Her chest tightened. *Yes, of course.*

"And we'll certainly be a step closer to punishing them for what they did to you."

He pulled out a chair for her, quickly turning back to business.

It was all so confusing. "Shall we really solve the mystery of Mama's death?" she mused.

Fox's mouth firmed. "We shall try."

While she gazed over his shoulder, his pencil flew again over the paper, sketching a hulking black figure, as if he'd dipped into her brain and funneled out her only impression. The skin on her neck crawled, tension constricting her spine. The form was exactly right, the posture heavy, as if the man's shoulders and head were too much to prop up straight.

"That's it," she whispered. "How do you do that?"

"It's what I do," he said, without stopping. Perspiration glimmered on his forehead.

Another figure began to emerge, slimmer, shorter, slighter, taking the shape of her other tormentor. She clutched the edge of the table and tried to breathe.

The pencil dropped. Fox's arms came around her again and she buried her face in his neck, taking deep gulps of his comforting musk. His hand slid along her back, easing her breath.

"I'm sorry," he said.

He growled the words, as if he couldn't breathe either. She touched her lips to the smooth spot of his neck below the place where his stubble started. A shiver went through him, and her body answered with a wave of pleasure.

He shared this with her, the bad and the good. They were partners in the events of the previous night. Well, up to a point.

She squeezed her eyes together, sat up, and mustered the courage to look at the partially disguised figures. It was her job to add eyes and brows. She passed a hand over her face and looked hard again at the picture that reared up in her mind.

Eyes that burned coldly and bushy brows bowed like the horns of a devil. Her imagination added lips contorted with the foul taste of malice, nostrils flared with evil intent.

All in shadows, like they'd been spit forth by the moor's demons.

He'd brought down a clutch of pencils. She reached for one. "Let me try."

FOX WATCHED AS SHE SKETCHED, HIS HEART SWELLING. SHE was a brave one, her hand with the pencil clutched too tightly for her to be wholly competent, her teeth clamped over her lower lip with the effort. As a girl, she'd not been fond of drawing, he recalled, not because she had no skill, but because her competitiveness got in the way. He'd apprenticed with Peale in Philadelphia, and Copley in England; hell, he'd even studied for a brief time in France, and he had the added motivation of needing to draw well enough to eat. Of course, his work would be more competent than hers.

She closed her eyes a moment to let her mind's eye see for her and took a breath, hitching it around what must be the pain in her back.

Anger overwhelmed him. He shoved it down, trying to concentrate on her breasts under the gray cotton. She was alive. Her wounds would heal, and he'd do whatever it took to make up for his failures the night before, to avenge her, and to keep her safe. And after that...

He wouldn't think about what might come later.

She added a few more strokes and dropped the pencil, frowning. "I doubt myself, Fox."

He pulled the paper over and stared at it a long moment, his gut clenching. The mind's eye could be nearsighted, could even be blind, the memory mistaken. It was how some artists got away with the lies they painted to accommodate the vanity of patrons.

She tapped her fingers on the table. "It was very dark. And I was frightened out of my wits."

"Let us try something. Close your eyes. I promise I will not hurt you."

She did as he asked, so quickly that it humbled him.

"Keep your eyes shut and see." He put his hands to her throat so gently he was barely touching. Still she froze, squeezing her lips and eyes in a grimace.

When he dropped his hands, her eyes shot open, shining with tears.

"Oh, Fox."

He pulled her against him and stared down at the paper where the face of Sir Richard stared back.

Perry's head settled on his shoulder again, the soft plumpness of her breasts on his chest sending his blood churning. It was a miracle the men on the road had not unmasked her. And if she but touched her lips to his neck again—

"Fox."

The whisper into his neck cloth sent him from half-staff to full erection. His hands slipped down to her buttocks and carved handfuls of softness.

232

"Oh, Fox," she said, tilting her head to touch his lips.

He matched her demand and guided her off the chair and onto his lap. His hands were busy, inching her skirts up, while she clutched his head at an awkward angle and plundered his mouth.

The sound of footsteps and men's voices floated in the hall and stilled them. Jane had left the door ajar when she'd walked out. Perry sighed and rested her cheek on his shoulder.

Fox groaned. "He can move more stealthily than that. He's giving us fair warning." And thank God for it.

A tremor went through her and she sat up, her eyes searching his. "I believe Father arranged for us to meet here." She sat up, her eyes searching his. "Did you expect me?"

"No. In fact, your brother warned me away from you."

She looked away a moment. "Bakeley?"

"Yes."

"Bakeley was upset that we danced twice at his ball."

"It was before the ball, when he visited my rooms with your father."

She sat up.

Perhaps she hadn't known about the visit that preceded Bakeley's wedding ball. There had been undercurrents then between the Earl and his heir, frustrations that Bakeley took out on the drunken artist. He *was* drunk that day, as he'd been most days when he wasn't working.

Fox had considered not attending the ball, though he'd designed the chalk art for the ballroom floor and was curious to see its execution. When he'd stepped into the ballroom, Perry had drawn him a like a moth to a flame, and all of the threats and warnings had been nothing to him.

A rumbling throat-clearing came from the doorway. Perry sighed, but he was grateful for the interruption.

"I see I've come just in time." The voice was Kincaid's, not the Earl's, after all. "Leave off comforting the lass, will you now, Fox? His lordship wants you to join us."

Perry's chin went up.

"Lady Perry is coming also." Fox patted her bottom and moved her off him.

She looked up, a world of love in her eyes. "Thank you," she said.

"Well, you *are* part of this."

"Of course, she is," Kincaid muttered. "Stop your mooning and come on. And," he called over his shoulder, "bring along the sketches."

IN THE STUDY, DAVY STOOD FINGERING THE BRIM OF HIS HAT, while Pip gawked at the wall of books. Fox hadn't spent much time in this room, tucked under a stairwell and poorly lit by the tall slender window that squinted north. It had no use for a painter, but it was the perfect sort of cave for Shaldon's plotting.

He and Farnsworth had arranged themselves around the desk.

Perry gaped at the bookshelves—apparently, she'd not yet seen this room—and then spotted Pip. She went to the boy and turned him around by the shoulders. He dropped his cap, and she picked it up. "Are you quite all right?"

His face scrunched in a freckled frown, and he stared at her neck.

"Pip," Davy said, "her ladyship asked you a question."

So, Davy had been apprised of the rankings and pecking order.

234

"Aye, miss," Pip said. "That's a right big bruise you have."

She nodded. "It will go away." She set her hand to his forehead and the boy visibly flinched. "I feared you would have a fever after that dunking last night, but you feel all right."

Shaldon cleared his throat. Fox handed him the drawings. The room went still, as it always did when the spy lord was thinking.

The man's face revealed nothing. He'd mastered the art of concealment needed to survive the veiled knives of his class. His work for the government had required him to firm up that mask even more.

But Fox saw the grimness forming as Shaldon lifted each sheet and examined it.

He silently slid the sketches to Farnsworth, seated across the desk from him. Farnsworth looked and passed them to Kincaid.

"Come here, lad." Kincaid took an empty chair and beckoned the boy. "Tell me what you think." He laid the sketches out on the desk.

Pip scrunched his face over them, leaning in close. The boy was, quite possibly, nearsighted, which made for questionable testimony.

Though they didn't need his testimony. Perry's was enough.

Davy stood stock straight and unmoving near the bookshelf. Pip cast him a quick look, and Fox realized it wasn't nearsightedness driving him, it was fear.

Pip had known the big man all along. In the way of the children within any criminal enterprise, he had kept his mouth shut.

Davy nodded.

"Aye," Pip said. "That be them."

Heat pounded through him. He'd recognized the man who assaulted Perry, and yet neither he nor his father had said anything. What the hell was afoot here?

"Who is the short man?" Fox asked, trying to keep his tone even.

Another look was exchanged between father and son.

Davy let out a long breath. "The Squire's groom, Harv. I don't know the last name. Not from these parts. I'll need to get going soon, sirs. Scruggs is calling all to the inn."

Shaldon nodded. "Take the boy to the kitchen. The ladies will look after him."

"I want to go, Da," Pip said.

Perry took a step toward the boy, but Fox touched her arm and shook his head.

"You'll stay here like I told you." Davy's voice was firm, and surprisingly gentle. For once, Davy appeared totally sober.

"And your women?" Kincaid asked.

"Gaz isn't here today, is he? Scruggs won't finger him as a traitor so my aunt and the girls will be fine. And I'd best get myself to the inn before he notices I'm missing. You'll stay here, Pip."

"Go with Davy, Perpetua," Shaldon said.

"She'll go in a moment," Fox said, putting steel into his voice. If he and Perry were to marry, he must begin as he planned to go on, else Shaldon would have both of them jumping through hoops. "For now, she is part of this discussion."

Shaldon's jaw tightened and he gave a cursory nod. "Very well."

. . .

236

"THE INFORMANT SAID THEY WILL LAND FURTHER SOUTH, IN this cove." Farnsworth's finger settled upon the map laid out on the desk, and Perry moved closer to peer around his shoulder. On Farnsworth's other side, Fox was frowning down at his lordship's fingertip.

"You have an informant?" Perry glanced at Fox who was staring hard at Father.

"Do you know the area, Fox?" Father asked.

Fox took an audible breath.

"Mayhap they will find that Frenchman's body when they land," Kincaid said. "Is that what you're thinking?"

Her heart began to race and she leaned closer. How could anyone tell one craggy inlet from another? And last night, she'd not been paying attention. She'd not thought of anything except trying to survive the trip in her wet clothing in the breezy skiff.

And who was this informant?

Father slid the map her way and settled a fingertip on one rocky point down the coast from where Farnsworth had indicated. "Here is Gorse Cottage," he said. He stretched his arm further and a bit inland. "And here is Sir Richard's."

Her pulse rattled. The night's landing place was closer to the Baronet's estate than to Gorse Cottage. "Will you take him tonight then?" she asked. She must get her chance at him. She *must*.

The three older men exchanged looks.

"Tonight, it is Carvelle and his cargo we are after," Father said.

Anger spiked in her. "Why?"

Father's face hardened and he lifted his gaze to her, his eyes a dark agate, his look binding up her tongue. She was here at his allowance, his gaze was telling her. They would carry on according to his schedule, not hers.

237

"Are they working together, then?" she asked. "I should at least like to go with you when you go after Sir Richard. I should like to assist you."

Father reached for her hand, his touch warm and firm, sparking moisture behind her eyes. "Revenge will endure, Perpetua," he said, "until the time is right."

She blinked several times and swallowed hard. Agents of the Crown did not cry, nor would she.

And Father knew quite a bit about pursuing revenge.

"Yes, Father," she said.

Just as quickly, he dropped her hand and went back to the map. "Now. Our source points us at this cove, but Davy says Scruggs has his men going here." He pointed at a spot to the north of Gorse Cottage. "What say you, Perpetua? You wish to be involved—what do you advise? Go north, or south?"

Davy was not their informant. Was it perhaps Scruggs misdirecting them? "They are both claiming the same cargo?" she asked.

Father blinked once, no doubt with the effort of deciding how much information to share. "Davy does not know what the cargo is, only that Scruggs has been seen working with Carvelle."

"And thus, he thinks Carvelle will be at the north point?"

He didn't nod or shake his head.

"And thus, *you* are guessing Carvelle will land to the south," she said. "As your informant said."

His lips quirked ever so slightly, and she leaned over the map again. Smells swirled around her—damp wool, leather, horses, shaving soap. The smell of men; not the dandified men of the ballroom, but honorable men working at something important and washing whenever they could.

238

And she was part of this important work. Her blood raced just a little faster.

The point south was a further distance away, close to Sir Richard who was a villain…and likely a smuggler. She stood up and rubbed her forehead. A source had pointed to this cove.

"Who provided the information?" she asked.

"I'd rather not say, just now," Father said.

Of course, he wouldn't. She wondered if Fox knew. She would ask him later. "Do you trust this person?"

The only noise in the room was a scant rustle of wool as Farnsworth uncrossed his leg.

"His intelligence has been reliable so far," Father said.

Well, that was nicely parsed. "But Davy is more trustworthy since we have his son below in our kitchen." Did they have enough men to split up and go to both locations?

No, belay that. They were four here, plus the MacEwens and two more men. Eight split two ways—she would not want to risk Fox in either fight. She'd seen how dangerous these men could be.

"Well?" Father asked. "Your advice?"

"The north, so close to Gorse Cottage, might be merely barrels of gin or crates of dry goods. The south may be a feint, or a trap." She leaned on the edge of the table. How would Father think? "I would rather go south and see what that is about. Have your cutter keep them away from the north or force them to go south."

He nodded. It was as much approval as she would ever get, and it emboldened her. "I should like to go with you, Father."

"I know, my daughter. Another time. I thank you for

your thoughtful counsel. Tonight, I need you here to prime your pistols and protect Lady Jane, your maid, and the boy."

With the men all away, they *could* be in danger.

She nodded. "Very well."

Farnsworth cleared his throat and the men began talking about dragoons and the coastal patrol cutter. When she lifted her eyes, Fox was watching her. She went to stand next to him, and Father's momentary pause was gratifying.

She had withstood Father's test regarding the landing spots. She would protect Gorse Cottage and defer her revenge, but she would have her reckoning with Sir Richard and his groom. Perhaps, if she was very, very lucky, Father would capture them and it would be tonight.

"We should all rest now," Father said. "It's likely to be a long night."

He nodded to her. He meant for her to leave, but no one else was stepping away.

Next to her Fox, stirred. "I'll be in the stables." He glanced her way and held her gaze for a moment.

She followed him out.

Fox TUGGED HER UP THE STAIRS TO THE DOOR OF HER bedchamber and turned her to face him. Dark smudges hollowed his eyes.

"We need to talk," he said.

"You didn't sleep at all after Lady Jane's arrival." He was dead on his feet and she'd only just now noticed.

Selfish, spoiled aristocrat.

"I'll be fine."

"I know you will." She opened the bedroom door and pulled him in.

"Your father—"

"Won't find us in this comfortable bed together. Much as I'd like that. I'm going to help Jenny and Jane in the kitchen."

"Perry."

She dropped a kiss on his chin. "We can't talk sensibly when you're exhausted and going into battle. Take my bed and sleep."

She hurried out and leaned back against the closed door, trying to still her hammering heart, blinking back tears.

Boots clacked on the stairs and she hurried down, greeting her father and Kincaid as she passed.

"ARE THEY ALL RIGHT, DO YOU THINK?" JENNY ASKED. THE girl glanced at the case clock for the hundredth time, sending Perry's nerves skittering. It was well after midnight in the short summer darkness, but not one of them would sleep.

"Do pay attention to the game," Perry said, trying to keep the crossness from her voice. She was as much on edge as Jenny. She dealt another card in their game of hearts.

"Do be patient, girls," Lady Jane echoed, pulling a needle through the fabric of Perry's trousers as peacefully as if she were embroidering a chair cushion in the morning room at Shaldon House. The window rattled and Lady Jane jerked her head up frowning.

So perhaps her calm was a deception. She certainly had seemed a bit restive when she'd yanked the mending from Jenny's hands and ordered both of them to play cards. And the expression on Lady Jane's face when she'd seen his lordship in his black jumper and trousers had inspired a great deal of speculation and questions that Perry had put aside until now—now when the time wore at her nerves like the waves wearing away the cliffs.

241

Like, for example, why had *Jane* followed Father here? Father could have ordered Charley and Graciela here, or Bink and Paulette.

"It is kind of you to stitch my trousers, Lady Jane," Perry said.

"Well, I ply a good needle, if I do say so," Lady Jane said, "I can repair anything from fine lawn to stiff leather."

"But I must say, Jenny is far better at hearts than you," Perry teased.

"Then it is a fair exchange. Jenny, if you are to be a sought-after lady's maid, you are going to have some sewing lessons with my maid."

"Your former maid," Perry said. Lady Jane's maid, Barton, had left to go into trade with a French modiste, Madame La Fanelle. "And if you engage Barton to train Jenny, Barton will want an investment to start a school for ladies' maids."

Jane laughed. "To be sure. She has an excellent mind for business. I shall be seeking employment from her someday."

The wistfulness in her voice caught Perry up again. Lady Jane had very little income. She was living on charity and she hated it.

Perry had not fully realized that until now.

A soft rumbling snore came from the sofa, and Jenny giggled. "My brother used to snore like that when we could find a bed to sleep in."

Perry looked over to where Pip lay, the huge black shawl cocooning him, and she thought about their interview earlier. Pip had recognized Sir Richard and kept silent.

Like her brothers had kept silent about Father's business, or what they'd known of his business. It was an art she must learn if she wanted Father's trust.

She sighed. Father's trust was hard-earned. Likely he'd

obliged Davy to leave Pip with them, because he didn't trust Davy entirely. For his part, Davy had seen that Pip, who was inclined to run about on his own, would be safer with them.

Pip had settled in well, eating his way through two plates of a very acceptable dinner Jenny had prepared herself from provisions brought in by the new arrivals. She'd hinted that MacEwen had been teaching her more skills in the kitchen.

Perry smiled. And perhaps on the kitchen cot, as well. Jenny seemed happy. She'd brought up their tea and they'd compelled her to join them. They'd built a fire in this parlor against the evening chill, and Jenny had listened closely as Perry read Pip to sleep from a book of fairy tales she'd found in the study.

Jenny pressed her hand against a yawn.

"None of that." Perry tapped the table. "Wake up now. It's your draw."

She would not sleep until the men returned.

29
TAKEN

*T*he south had been Shaldon's destination all along, that questioning of Perry only a test. The man was a pain in the arse.

Fox crept up next to the Earl. Before they'd left for the cove, he'd pulled the man aside and asked him to stay behind.

Carvelle's traitorous cousin, Lady Kingsley, had been arrested some weeks ago, before she could escape on the yacht of the Duque de San Sebastian. And Sir Richard bore Shaldon a grudge. The assassins might well be targeting Shaldon and not King George.

The stubborn man wouldn't listen.

The stars backlit a soft mist that had settled over the beach, high enough that they could still see the vessel coasting along on the water, turning toward shore, and low enough for the damp to settle into a man's pores and drip down his nose.

They'd stationed a lookout, and spread out in pairs, he and Shaldon, Farnsworth and Kincaid, along with four dragoons brought up from Norfolk.

Another group of dragoons had gone north with the MacEwens. Whether they could trust these outsiders was anyone's guess, but Scruggs's guest at the inn, the local Riding Officer, had not been included in any of the plans.

The soldiers had orders to arrest only one man, should they encounter him. Shaldon wanted Carvelle alive.

They'd not issued orders about Sir Richard. Shaldon was keeping those suspicions close to the vest.

Carvelle was somehow tied to the Spaniard and that damn painting. The Spaniard's lust for the return of his family's artwork made no sense to Fox, but then, none of the power-lust stirred among men by Napoleon did either.

Shaldon's need for revenge? That he understood, and he'd help him take it.

Soreness seared his chest where Carvelle's man had, a month ago, sliced him.

Hell, it was his revenge, also. He signaled the Earl an *all ready*.

As they watched, a boat lowered, three men aboard. He slid his glass from his pocket, looked through it, and handed it to Shaldon. They watched the oars churn, silent against the louder noise of the surf, and waited. The clear path to the beach was before them, but so far, a greeting committee hadn't arrived.

Whilst a second boat with more figures in it launched from the ship out at sea, one man fought the surf to climb out of the first one, waves lashing at his boots. Carvelle.

With only himself and MacEwen to keep a watch on the inn, the man had slipped away back to his ship.

He'd been distracted by Perry, and, oh hell, if she was correct, her father had known that would happen, just as he probably knew of the Scot's interest in the little maid. Which meant, he'd been willing to risk Carvelle's escape.

Did that mean that, all along, Carvelle had not been the real target? And would this bastard of a spy lord have let them know so Fox could have done more to keep his daughter out of danger?

Hell, he might have seduced her the very first night and kept her close to home, and didn't that notion send heat through him? The only thing keeping his prick limp was this miserable dampness.

A rock fell behind him.

That wasn't right. The others were arrayed elsewhere.

Before he could turn, a voice came out of the dimness. "So, you chose the path I set for you."

Rougher, deeper, surer, the voice was, but he knew the speaker. Fox turned slowly. Two men stood there, one big man and a smaller shadow.

"Good evening to you," Lord Shaldon said, sounding bored. His hands brushed, pulling a knife. A practiced move, unseen from the two men's point of view.

Fox slid a blade from his own sleeve and got to his feet, the steel at his side.

"Ah, Goodfellow. Put the blade away. My man here has a very fine pistol he took off your manservant. Was it only last night? Whatever happened to that fellow? You didn't mention he'd gone missing." He chuckled. "Harv's not a crack shot, but this close he's bound to hit something."

"Harv has a gun?" Fox said. "Is that so? I can't see it."

Harv's hand came up. "Loaded and primed." He pointed it at Fox's chest. "Want proof?"

This was the weasel who'd punched Perry. A bigger man would have broken a rib or shredded her kidney. Harv would die tonight.

Steel flashed and Fox dropped. Powder exploded above him and his own blade clattered.

He lunged at Harv. A knife had stuck in the man's shoulder and the pistol was gone. Fox grabbed the man's flopping arm, just as Harv yanked the Earl's knife from his shoulder and slashed with it. He ducked, spotting Shaldon atop Sir Richard, rolling over and over down the rocky hillside. Behind them, men shouted, and more shots rang out, powder swirling in the air.

Fox ducked again, pulled Harv off balance and laid a punch on his wound. Harv howled and lunged drunkenly. Fox took the opening to lock the wrist of Harv's knife hand, and the man charged again, teeth flashing in a stench of onion.

Perry had smelled this.

He dodged a bite from those putrid teeth and whipped Harv around by the wrist. Bone cracked. The knife went in clean to Harv's back with a *pop*.

Like a damn Christmas pudding being poked.

Fox slid Harv to the ground. Shaldon was gone, as was Sir Richard. The fighting on the other side of the path had settled. The second skiff had turned back, the first one drifted out empty. Bodies littered the rocks, some of them starting to pick themselves up. He hurried down to the beach.

30
AN INVITATION TO DINNER

A keening cry made Perry look up from the game of Patience spread before her and pull her shawl closer.

It was only the wind, soughing through the fireplace where the wood had ceased its spitting, the fire having long died down. Outside, the waves still crashed ceaselessly.

Jenny raised her head from the table where she'd fallen fast asleep. Lady Jane put aside the book she had been staring at for long minutes.

And then she heard another sound—men's voices, growing louder.

Whoever they were, they were not being at all subtle. The tones were choppy, urgent. And soon enough they were right outside the oak paneled main door.

She glanced at the pistol on the mantel. Speaking so loudly, these surely must be their men.

"Wait." Lady Jane ran right behind her to the door, pulling her back from the latch.

On the other side, a key rattled into the slot. Perry yanked the door open.

Alarm raced through her. Fox juggled a big body between himself and Farnsworth, the head drooping and swinging, the dark hair spraying droplets of dampness.

"Put me down now, you bluidy sods." That voice was Kincaid's.

"Save your breath," Fox said. He moved a hand up to bolster his grip on Kincaid.

Fox's hands were crusted with blood. The wet coming from Kincaid's head dripped red too.

"Clear the sofa," Perry called.

"No," Fox said. "He needs a bed. Let's get him upstairs."

Perry caught a glimpse of other men, crowding in behind. "Have you sent for a surgeon?"

"No bluidy surgeon," Kincaid said.

"Mac can sew him." Farnsworth said. "Send him up, when he comes. You there," he called to a man, "Help the maid fetch hot water and towels."

"I'll get my sewing kit," Lady Jane said. "Sewing up Kincaid can't be any tougher than stitching a hide."

"We'll put him in my bedchamber," Perry said. "It's the biggest."

"No," Farnsworth said. "Take him to the chamber Shaldon was using."

Perry's heart seized. *Was* using, Farnsworth had said.

"Where is Shaldon?" Lady Jane whispered.

"Missing," Farnsworth hissed.

"Taken," Kincaid croaked. "He's alive. I set men to follow them. We'll find him."

"Aye," Farnsworth said, "and let's get you upstairs before you bleed all over the carpet."

. . .

249

Fox watched Perry fussing over Kincaid as he lay in the small bedchamber, his back propped on a pillow, his bandaged chest carefully draped by a clean sheet.

The last hour had been a flurry of stripping, washing, and stitching the Scotsman. Fox's own wounds, and those of the others, had been no more than scrapes and bruises.

He'd not had a chance to tell her about Harv. Face frozen in a frown, she'd insisted on washing the big man's wounds, demanded to thread the needle for Lady Jane, and not flinched a bit as the stitching began.

His heart ached with pride in her, and relief that she'd stayed behind. He must find a way to get her father back.

Downstairs in the kitchen, the dragoons drank coffee, waiting for orders and guarding the guest Fox had shoved into the pantry.

The door opened and the MacEwens slid in with Davy, taking the last bit of breathing room. Fergus carried over a steaming cup. "A tisane." He handed it to Kincaid who sniffed it suspiciously.

"'Tis whisky and summat for the pain. Drink up."

Perry's mouth firmed grimly. "Before you drink that and pass out, first tell us what happened, Kincaid."

"Let him sip at it. He's hurting." Fox reached for her hand.

She let him take it, her face screwed up in a frown. "He'll be woozy. He won't remember details. And we need to get Father back."

Kincaid stared into the cup. "I'll not drink it if it puts me to sleep."

"Wheesh, there's not but the tiniest drop of laudanum," Fergus said. "I made it myself." He grabbed the cup, swallowed a sip, and wiped his mouth. "There."

Kincaid grunted and accepted the drink.

"You'd best not be flat on your back after that." Perry glared at Fergus. "My father has been taken, and I may need every one of you to help me." She squeezed his hand. "To help us."

She thought she was going with them.

Not in a blue moon. Not the way Sir Richard had drooled over her yesterday afternoon. "Here's what happened, Perry: we *did* go south. Carvelle *did* disembark there, and another boat was headed in and turned back. We'd set a watch for the greeters on land, but they found us first."

He told her about the attack, but not his killing of Harv. Not yet.

"We should've been with you," the second MacEwen said.

"Aye." Kincaid wiped his mouth and handed the empty cup to Jane, seated on a chair next to the bed. "Couple of the dragoons set to watch ran off."

Fergus swore softly. "That lot downstairs—"

"No," Farnsworth studied the carpet. "They didn't run off."

Perry went still.

He shook his head at Farnsworth. More details to share with her later, privately. They'd found the two men with their throats nicely sliced.

"Carvelle is dead also," Farnsworth said. "Shot through the heart during the fighting."

Kincaid muttered an oath. "'Twas Sir Richard who wanted him dead then. Our men had orders to take him alive."

Perry's thumb swept over the back of his hand. "Was he

working with Sir Richard then? Was Carvelle bringing in the assassins for him? And why would Sir Richard wish to kill the King?"

She glanced all around. She still believed the King was the target.

And he himself no longer had any doubts.

Kincaid cleared his throat. "I saw them carry the Earl off."

Perry's breath came in small audible puffs. Her hand in his started to tremble. "Was he…was Sir Richard your informant?"

Farnsworth glanced at Kincaid and then paced to the window. "Sir Richard must have wanted him alive."

"Alive," Perry said. "But for how long?" Perry looked from Farnsworth to Kincaid, and then at Fox. "What is going on, Fox? What are they not telling me?"

Farnsworth exchanged a look with Kincaid. The MacEwens slouched, looking bored.

Fox didn't know, and he'd warrant the cousins didn't either. Lady Jane frowned at Farnsworth. Only Davy looked on with frank curiosity.

"It's a fair question," Fox said. "One I'd like the answer to, also. If we're to get Shaldon back, we'll need to know what you know, Kincaid, Farnsworth."

"Who was Sir Richard to Father?" Perry shook loose his hand and stalked to the bed. "Tell me, Kincaid."

"Let him rest, Lady Perpetua," Farnsworth said. "I'll explain. Sir Richard came to us a few months ago offering information on Carvelle. Said he'd heard we were looking for him. Which we were. I know you knew that much."

She opened her mouth, closed it. Nodded. Took a deep breath. "He *was* your source. And why would you doubt *him*? He's a justice of the peace."

252

"We considered that." Farnsworth paced again. "A justice of the peace. A baronet. A country man with no debts and no known enemies. There didn't seem a reason for him to lie. Quite the opposite. He's privy to rumors about the free trade in these parts and might be inclined to enforce the law."

Farnsworth turned to Fox, his gaze boring into him. The skin around his fresh scar prickled.

"And then," Farnsworth said, "one of our agents following up on a lead that Sir Richard provided was almost killed."

Perry's gaze followed Farnsworth's and her eyes widened. "The fresh scar on your chest."

The muscles in his back tightened like a death grip. Fox shrugged, trying to loosen them. Shaldon and his games—there was always more than one. "And you sent me here to recover, right under the man's nose."

"He never knew the identity of our man."

Anger flashed through him. If Sir Richard hadn't learned it, it was because Fox had killed the man who'd attacked him in Belgium. "So you say."

Perry pulled her hand away and began to pace. "Sir Richard plays a double game. He's a squire passing on information on a smuggler. And as John Black he runs a smuggling enterprise. Which might have stumbled last year when a substitute was tried and transported."

"Why?" Perry asked. "Why would Sir Richard do this?"

"It may be he's trying to take out the competition," Fergus said.

Perry stopped in front of him and drew herself up into a tight determined line. "But why bring in an assassin? Why take Father?"

"I know why." Lady Jane's skirts rustled as she rose from

253

the room's only chair. "We talked about it earlier. Sir Richard *wants* the man who stole the woman he thought should be his bride. He wanted Felicity Landers, enough to try to wrestle her into a carriage and make off with her. He's been stewing in anger for decades. He wants revenge."

Perry went still. He moved his hand to her waist and felt anger trembling through her.

Kincaid grunted and Farnsworth shrugged.

The logic of women, those shrugs said. A man, educated, propertied, with a position in the community and a business to run—albeit an illegal one—wouldn't stew thirty years about a bride who was lost, would he? Not even a brute like the Baronet.

His chest tightened. What had he done for many years about his brother's bride? What had Shaldon been doing about the murder of his wife?

"Revenge?" Farnsworth said, sighing. "Not greed. Could it be that simple?"

Perry's breath caught. "It's that simple for Father."

Farnsworth shared another glance with the other old plotter, Kincaid.

Was it truly that simple for Shaldon? Was it that simple for him?

Fox shook his head. He'd stewed in revenge, as had Shaldon, but neither had turned to villainy. Shaldon had his spying, not always honest, but always honorable, at least where his country was concerned. Fox had his painting— and Perry.

Could he truly have her honorably, with her family's blessing? He *would* stew for decades if he were to lose this chance with her. He had to find a time and a place to tell her.

"Your father wants more than revenge," Fox said. "He wants to know how your mother really died. He wants to know who killed her."

Davy's thin voice came from the place near the door. "It's him."

The eyes turned his way made Davy squirm. He cleared his throat. "I allus thought it was Scruggs what did it."

Tension knotted Fox's brain, right behind his eyes, and Perry's face had gone stiff as a bad portrait. What the hell else had this little man kept hidden all these years behind tankards of ale and flasks of gin? Fox took Davy by the collar. "Tell the lady what you know."

Davy's fingers twisted, crushing his hat and he wobbled. "I saw it. I saw the lady's…" he glanced at Perry and ducked his head. "Your mother's killing."

Perry eyed him up and down, as grave and contained as her father would ever be. "Lady Jane," she said, with a softness that the old man would never have shown, "let us have that chair."

Fox pulled the chair over.

Perry gave Davy a nod. "Now sit."

"Oh, miss—"

"Before you fall. Please."

Davy looked around and took the chair, sitting poker straight, like a man bracing for a beating.

"Go on," Perry said.

"I saw the carriage on the road. Saw the accident." He gulped for air.

"What happened?" Fox moved round to stand by Perry.

"I don't know. Well, it may be the wheel slipped off. Or the driver swerved right off the edge of the cliff. I don't know. I was below, in the cove, and couldn't see all. I'd gone to—well, Scruggs had some barrels sunk in the water there." He tucked his chin down and squeezed his eyes shut a moment. "I *did* start up the hillside to help. The carriage was tipping, the horses going wild, the driver trying to hold them." He paused and gulped more air. "Then a man comes down the road from the house, all in black, he is, and I'm thinking, it's Scruggs, and I says to myself, if he sees me tippling his tubs I'll take a beating. I says to myself, no need to go up—he'll help 'em."

Davy's face had gone ashen, the light from the lanterns and candles not finding a trace of pink in his flesh, the memory of that day draining the blood from him.

Shame did that to a man, drained the life out of him, made him walk through life like a cadaver.

"He goes behind the carriage and next thing I sees, he's got the lady, and she was fighting him, and I'm thinking, *slow down, stop hitting her*, she's panicked, is all. 'Tother lady came up, waving a pistol. Fired it, she did. Didn't hit nothing before he slapped it away."

The room had gone stuffy with exhaled breaths and the flames of the lights. Davy wiped a hand over his face and shuddered. "Coachman was off by then, horses going wild. Knew what was happening, they did. Gave a good fight the man did, but the big man beat him until he stopped." His breath came, short and shallow. "Picked both ladies up and threw them over the cliff, he did. Dragged the man to the edge and rolled him."

Davy's eyes shone. "Looked, straight my way, he did. Scruggs'd know me, even at that distance. I pulled back, I stayed down, heard the carriage topple. Then I ran. Went around the point. Went home. Pretended I was there all day." He gulped and shook his head. "I should've helped. I should've done something."

. . .

PERRY SWALLOWED BACK TEARS AND TOUCHED DAVY'S shoulder. It was too late for her mother, too late for doubts, too late for recriminations. Davy couldn't have been much more than a boy when her mother was killed, a slight boy against Sir Richard's bulk. She couldn't blame him.

And they needed him. "Help us *now*, Davy. You know these parts. Where would Sir Richard take my father?"

He screwed up his face with the effort of thinking and set his gaze on Fox. "Scruggs might know. He knows more."

Fox's mouth firmed in that obstinate, secretive way of his.

"Scruggs?" she asked.

"We had him brought in," Fox said.

That had been when she and Lady Jane were wrestling Kincaid into submission.

"And?" Perry asked, wanting to throttle him. It was time for these men to talk to her, and to Lady Jane.

"We didn't get much out of him," Fox shifted. "We left off the questioning to come up here. He's locked in the pantry."

"MacEwen," Kincaid said, "you and your cousin go talk to him. Send the soldiers outside."

They didn't know who to trust.

"Don't beat him," Perry said. "Not until after I have a chance to talk to him."

Fox sent her a cryptic look. "Davy, go and wait in the parlor with Pip. Mac, have one of the soldiers stay with him to make it look like Davy's a prisoner too. Don't you dare leave."

Or I'll kill you myself, his tone said.

"No, don't leave," Kincaid said. "You'll stay and help us, too."

257

Davy frowned. "I'll stay."

He'd heard the *or else* in Kincaid's tone. Honestly, these men could be brutes also.

Perry touched Davy's shoulder. "If you must leave Clampton, we'll find you work, and no matter what happens, we'll look after Pip."

Davy nodded, and followed the MacEwens out.

"The man's been wallowing in drink for ten years to cover that shame," Kincaid said. "Had enough of it he has. We can use him. Now, I've no more dignity left here—can one of your ladyships fetch one of the Earl's shirts from that satchel?"

"You're not getting up yet." Lady Jane pressed him back. "You'll lie there a bit longer and let that flesh knit."

"She's right," Farnsworth said.

While Kincaid glowered and the others bickered, Fox settled an arm around her, and she curled into his warmth.

"You should sit," he said.

She shook her head. "No." While Father was suffering, she'd take no comfort.

How would Sir Richard torture him? A man that cruel might have many means.

"We need to plan how to get Father out."

"We need to know where he is." Lady Jane plopped on the narrow bed, abandoning all etiquette. "One of your men should have reported by now."

"Aye," Kincaid said. "It's possible they can't get away themselves."

Lady Jane's mouth firmed. "Or it's possible they've been taken, or killed."

Through this east-facing window, Perry could see the sun on the horizon.

She sighed into Fox's shoulder. "A new day. A totally

258

different day." She lifted her chin and searched his eyes. "We have an invitation to dinner."

Sir Richard had invited them to dinner even while plotting to take her father. Or maybe, he'd planned to take Father at the dinner and instead had availed himself of the earlier opportunity.

The silence in the room fairly buzzed, though no one uttered a word, and her attention was on Fox, so she couldn't see whether brows were working into furrows as the two old spies and Lady Jane turned the idea around in their collective heads.

Fox was doing his own brow furrowing. "No," he said. "And anyway, the invitation was for you, Lady Jane, and your father."

"And Father is already there."

"Maybe not. Maybe he has him stashed in some smuggler's tunnel somewhere. We need to hear what Scruggs has to say."

"And how will you get him to talk?"

His mouth firmed. "We'll charge him with murder. Davy saw a big man do the deed. It could have been him."

"We're wasting time." She turned in his arms. "Farnsworth, you and Kincaid. if you're able, will come along tonight."

"I'll be able," Kincaid said.

"And Fox, you'll come as my fiancé." Her nerves rattled and she took in a breath. She could do this. She *would* do this. "That should draw a reaction."

"Sir Richard saw me at the cove," Fox said. "And you want me to just come along to dinner?"

Outside, the first ray of sun stabbed through the haze. Dinner—even a dinner by country hours—would be hours and hours away. Between now and then, anything could happen to Father. Bad, cruel, horrible things.

"On second thought, we're not going to dinner," she said. "We'll join Sir Richard for breakfast."

"*No.*" The cry came from all the men, but the loudest voice was the one in her ear.

31

THE PLAN FORMS

Talk, talk, talk.

Perry set to grinding coffee, the beans as hard as Fox's stubborn refusal to allow—*allow*—her to drop in on Sir Richard that morning. She wrestled the crank, letting the aroma fill her senses, willing it to chase away this sluggish resentment.

Running off on her own hadn't worked out well. That was a truth that poked at the sore spot in her back with every downward crank.

She closed her eyes and swallowed hard. Papa was a hard, strong man, a wily man. Old, but not decrepit. If any man could survive a physical challenge, it was the Earl of Shaldon.

"He won't come." Kincaid spoke around a bite of bread.

Lady Jane pounded her fist on the kitchen table. "He might, and then we'll have drawn him out, and some of you can go in. And if he doesn't, well, then we'll know."

Lady Jane wanted to send a message calling Sir Richard to a crime, a normal duty for a country justice of the peace.

"And then he'll know," Farnsworth said.

"Oh, hell, Farnsworth," Kincaid said. "We know he knows. The time for subtlety is past."

They argued on. Fox caught her eye and came up behind her, enveloping her in his arms.

All of her nerves tingled, warmth rippling from the top of her head to her toes. He'd best not be playing with her.

She leaned into him. "I should go to his manor," she said. "Make a big splash. Stop at the inn and tell the world where I'm going. He won't kill me then."

"He's tried once already." His breath tickled her ear.

"But I was alone. And that was in secret. This will be different. Perhaps I can bring Scruggs along."

The innkeeper had been, finally, talkative after they'd told him someone was bringing in assassins just in time for King George's coronation. MacEwen had twisted his arm with the mention of the hanging and beheading the previous year of the treasonous Cato Street conspirators.

However, if Scruggs thought Sir Richard was the famous John Black, he wasn't letting on.

Father might be in a cave down the coast, said Scruggs, now housed in an unused stable box, and the innkeeper could lead them to it.

Or, Father might be at Sir Richard's manor, the man had said.

Fox's arms tightened and two large hands cradled her hips on opposite sides. She flexed against him. And...he was aroused.

Desire shot through her, sudden, demanding.

What was he doing? Did he want her or not?

She watched her hand gripping the crank, turning, churning, chopping the beans to tiny bits.

"I don't want you hurt." Fox's quiet murmur stopped her hand's motion. The *drub, drub, drub,* of her heart, the muffled roar of waves breaking, those were the only sounds. Behind them, the room had gone quiet.

She set her hands atop his. "It's too late for that," she whispered.

She craned her neck and looked around him. The others studied a paper spread before them on the table, a crude map, and another man, dirty and disheveled, had joined them.

And she'd not heard a thing. Some spy she would make.

And then Davy entered, towing along a young woman dressed in worn cambric. She had Davy's same coloring but an air more watchful.

"This is my cousin, Edie," he said.

The girl curtseyed in the awkward, bobbling way of someone with an ailment, or perhaps someone much older, or someone not used to giving such deference. The brown eye she raised to Perry held curiosity and a touch of apprehension.

Perry swallowed a chuckle. One didn't see a ghost every day.

"Edie will help us." This was the most assurance Perry had ever heard in Davy's voice.

"How?"

Kincaid's blunt question set the girl to frowning.

These locals were not obsequious towards their so-called betters. Oh, they might be cowed by people like Scruggs and Sir Richard, but that was the practical consideration of physical intimidation. But merely being born to a higher rank didn't rate the kind of deference Perry had always received from the tenants of Cransdall.

Free trading gave them freedom.

Plus, Perry thought, they'd seen the colonies revolt, and a revolution in France that had sent people of her own class to the guillotine, and had others fleeing to England, perhaps arriving on these very shores.

Edie raised a pugnacious chin. "I was in service with Sir Richard."

In service. The girl had probably been a housemaid, one who flicked dust from every piece of furniture, in every nook and cranny. She would know about secret doors and hidden passageways and where they led. If there were stories of treasures hidden in a priest hole or some such, she would have heard them. She would know Sir Richard's ways. She would have learned early when to steer clear, when to be one of the invisible girls with a broom and a duster. She would know how many servants there were and where they would be.

Jenny crossed the room. "I'll finish that, my lady," she said.

Edie's eyes widened, taking in Perry's plain dress, the frowzy hair, and her necklace of purple bruises. And the big, handsome man with his hand on her.

Perry's man. Well, he would be for a few hours more, and then his damned honor would take him away. And she couldn't think about that now.

"Please sit, Edie," Perry said. "Make room for her at the table."

32

BREAKFAST WITH THE BARONET

They'd involved Scruggs and his village in this rescue, but only one villager was crowded onto Perry's borrowed cart sitting up in the cargo box, while her three companions there lay low and rolled out, one by one, as the cart crawled up Sir Richard's long drive.

Perry's skirt flapped along, soaking up the moist drizzle. She pulled it in tight around her legs and gripped the seat edge.

They came to a narrow part of the road, densely thicketed and deeply rutted. Sir Richard must have few visitors. If he truly was John Black the smuggler, his merchandise wasn't traveling down this path. This jarring ride would pop open half the tubs.

"Use that pistol." The low voice came from the back and the cart jumped again, dispensing the last of the muscled cargo.

Her heart flipped with it, but she dared not turn to look. "I will. You use that knife."

I love you, Fox. I shouldn't but I do.

All around her the air seemed to thicken and she struggled to breathe.

Fear. This was fear.

"Steady now." Lady Jane's hand came down atop hers and squeezed.

She turned her hand over and squeezed back.

Lady Jane had sensed the panic rising in her. Thank God, it had been this sensible woman following Father to Gorse Cottage to chaperone Perry.

Along with Fox, Farnsworth and Fergus MacEwen had slipped off the back, leaving Edie propped up against the side gripping a basket. The three men would steal through the woods on their way to the house. The other MacEwen, Fergus' cousin, was leading the dragoons and some of Scruggs's men up the steep hill at the back side of the estate.

All of them would be, please God, mopping up Sir Richard's watchers and henchmen, if there were any.

"Kincaid," Lady Jane said, "must you hit every rut and hole? You'll burst that wound open, and then where will we be?"

"Hang on." Kincaid pulled the reins and finessed the cart around a particularly watery rut. Bottomless, it might be, fathomless perhaps, and filled with illusions, like everything surrounding Sir Richard.

Edie had shed a great deal of light upon Sir Richard's dwelling and his personal habits. She'd served as a maid until two years past.

Under MacEwen's, and later Farnsworth and Fox's questioning, Scruggs had enlightened them more about the man's business enterprises, bit by excruciating bit, the questioning sweetened with promises that the Crown would look kindly upon a man who gave evidence against a traitor.

266

Clouds had gathered again, thickening the late morning sky to a purple as mottled as the bruise at her throat. The rain was like a slick exhalation of those heavy clouds, and it would soon come heavier, God's tears or perhaps a demon's spit.

She shook off the fanciful thoughts.

The blouse she'd donned under the stark, servile gray dress helped soak up the wet. The square of Indian cotton she'd borrowed from Jane added another layer against the dampness. As well, it concealed the damage he'd already done and was too bulky for a garrote, should Sir Richard decide to come at her again.

If he uses his hands, stab him. If he comes from behind, claw his eyes out. If you're a distance away, shoot him.

Watch the trigger. Don't shoot yourself in the leg. Don't fire too soon.

As she ran through the lessons Fox and Kincaid had rushed her and Lady Jane through, the manor house came into view. She was traveling gloveless, a blade up her sleeve, a pistol in her pocket, and a bellyful of anger needing revenge.

And this *bloody* house looked deserted. No lights in the windows, no smoke in the chimney, though the day was dim enough and chill enough for candles and fire.

Sir Richard's manor was a gothic lair. Restoration, perhaps, with chinks in the bricks where the mortar had given up, and windows that held onto thick grime for the extra layer of secrecy. Over the years, Sir Richard had driven off most of his staff, Edie said. The young maids—if they wished to remain maidens—wouldn't stay. Those left were a collection of the willing and the old.

A fine dinner party Sir Richard had planned for them— Father as the main course and herself as dessert. And poor

Lady Jane. What plans would he have had for a fine-looking woman of her age?

Kincaid took them through the likeliest archway into a back courtyard. A decrepit brick building—stables or carriage house, it was hard to tell which—stood, its doors closed securely. Broken barrels and rusted farm tools littered the fringes among waist high summer weeds, and not so much as a chicken wandered the mud-puddled yard.

Bakeley would never allow a Shaldon property to be in this state. The villagers would find plenty of work here once Sir Richard's heir, whoever that may be, came into possession of this property.

Which, if she had any say, would be very soon. This very afternoon.

While Kincaid grunted himself down from his perch favoring the tear in his chest and saw to their horse, Perry slid off, helped Jane and Edie down, and hefted a laden basket from the cart bed.

Her boots squished in the mud leading up to the kitchen door.

"Ever so foul," Lady Jane muttered. "Steward and 'ousekeeper ort to be sacked."

"Aye," Edie said.

Now they were here, Perry's insides tingled. She smiled at Lady Jane. In her plain gown and white cap, she could pass for an upper story servant. And what accent was that?

She reached the door first but waited for Kincaid, as they'd agreed. He tried the latch. It didn't budge.

"What the divil," he said, and winked at them. "No key under a brick somewhere, Edie?"

"Nay. Never."

"Well, then, I've a key." Perry pulled her set of picks from a pocket.

Kincaid snorted. He surely had his own set hidden somewhere, but he took her basket with his good arm and stepped aside to let her to do the honors.

As poorly kept as everything else on this manor, the mechanism gave way quickly, flaking off rust when the picks came out.

Kincaid set his hand over hers on the latch and fixed her with a firm stare. "Allow me."

She stepped out of the way and watched the door creak open.

Kincaid slid a hand under the cloth in the basket for the extra pistol lying there.

AT THE BACK OF THE PROPERTY, FOX SLIPPED THROUGH THE brush as quietly as when he was a young man hunting game in the backwoods of New England. Farnsworth and MacEwen had fanned out, moving with just as much stealth. It seemed that a peer, a Scotsman, and a humble colonial could work together. He hoped so, for Perry's sake.

Leaving her to go in alone with the others...his heart stuttered. He'd given into the plan, reluctantly, but he'd make his way through these blasted woods and catch up and—

A twig cracked, an arm raised, and he ducked just in time, a knife slashing down into the empty air where he'd been standing. He lunged and slapped his hand over a mouth, plunging his own blade into that same spongy place that he'd hit on Harv. This man groaned and writhed and finally stilled.

Fox turned the assailant over, his stomach rolling with this bundle of bones and sinew. The boy's chin was pimply and practically hairless. A search turned up no other weapons but the knife, and Fox tucked that away.

The air rustled and Farnsworth appeared at his side. Two more, he signaled and pointed.

Fox took one, Farnsworth, the other. These two were older. He and Farnsworth made quick work of them and plunged on.

Perry needed him. Every moment she stayed on this property, she was in danger.

He forced himself to focus. She wasn't alone—Kincaid was crafty, Lady Jane was no ninny hammer, and Perry had weapons. Add to all that, Sir Richard would want to keep her alive, at least for a while.

They skirted the overgrown green surrounding the manor and cleared the stable buildings, prepared for the worst, but they only encountered several horses and an elderly stable hand who quickly raised his arms in surrender.

Fox went to work tying him up. "Where are the rest of the hands?"

A stream of spittle flew past Farnsworth, and Fox paused. It hadn't been aimed at Farnsworth, he decided. Nor did his lordship look offended. No need to clock this old fellow.

"Ain't never enough hands," the old man grumbled. "And that Harv didna' bother to come home last night."

The words teased a stray thread in Fox's brain. "Nor will he. Cocked up his boots, he has. And if you'll be a gentleman, we'll see you cut loose later, and you won't wind up like Harv." He nicked the tie in the old man's kerchief and pulled the cloth from his neck.

"How many are in the house?" Farnsworth asked.

A low, unintelligible grumble rolled out.

Farnsworth leaned in with enough menace to prevent any more flying spit. "How many?"

"I don't know. The squire's there. And he brought a man with him, and some of his other men from down south. I don't ask."

"How many?"

"In the house, I don't know. There be three, out there." He jerked his head toward the way they'd come and squinted at a spot mottling Farnsworth's coat. "I reckon you've met them already."

Farnsworth nodded, and Fox finished gagging the old man with his neck cloth.

They went out the back way, and came round, sliding along the stable wall, keeping low in the thick weeds.

Farnsworth signaled and slipped off, heading toward the backside of the house where he'd meet up with both MacEwens.

Fox inched his way toward the inner court. Across the courtyard, he saw hired servants unloading the cart. Three of them huddled near the door. Another was on her knees in front of it.

Picking the lock. Fox pulled his hat down, and crept below the first story windows to join them.

PERRY FOLLOWED KINCAID INTO THE HOUSE, HER HAND IN her pocket. A short, ill-kept vestibule led into the kitchen where a low fire burned, and a pot swung from an iron chimney crane.

Her skin rippled and a touch on her back made her startle, sending her into a panic.

When she turned her heart calmed. *Fox.* He'd made it safely through the woods.

She swept a gaze over him and all of the nerves in her arms and her legs tingled. Blood spotted his neck cloth and her gaze raced over him again. He wasn't injured. Someone had shed blood on him though. He'd had to fight.

"You're here then." A servant looked up from her place in the corner, mob cap pulled low and fat jowls drooping to join the layers at her neck. She must be the cook Edie had spoken of.

"Old Rose," Edie said in a breathy tone.

The servant leaned on a tall central worktable, edging around it.

Edie was frightened too, though she'd insisted on coming, because, she'd said, Old Rose would need saving.

"We're to help with the dinner tonight," Lady Jane said.

"Edie," the cook whispered. "You shouldna be here. He said they be coming. You be taken up with him, the old fool, and then what's to become of your mam. You shouldna be part of this."

"I'm not. I'm here for you." Edie set her basket on the table and went to the old woman, hugging her. "I'm taking you home for good." She patted the old woman's plump arm. "Yes, and I am. He's gone too far."

Fox and Kincaid moved around the perimeter of the room, listening at doors and opening them to peer into corridors and pantries. Fox came out of one closet gripping the collar of a tiny kitchen boy. Rose swept the shaking child up in her arms.

And she did it noiselessly, Perry noted. The boy was equally silent and the conversations were whispered. The only sound was the creak of the wind hitting the windows. This was a house living in fear deeper than what she was feeling this moment.

"Where is the Squire, Rose?" Fox asked.

She slid her eyes toward one of the doors. "I don't know."

"What room did he tell you to stay out of?"

"I'm the cook. I stay out of all of the rooms."

"Your master will hang as a traitor," Kincaid said. "Those protecting him will, too."

Her eyes widened.

"A traitor?" Rose said. "What's that? To hear tell, any smuggler is a traitor to the King."

"True," Fox said, "but besides the King, he betrayed the people of Clampton. Scruggs is locked up. Dragoons are rounding up everyone in the village."

It was the lie they'd agreed on.

"But not me," Edie said, "And not you if you'll but come with me."

Rose wrapped the boy closer in her plump arms. "It has naught to do with us."

Kincaid nodded to Fox. "Tie her up then. We'll have her charged as an accessory to the murder."

"Come then, Rose." Edie put an arm around her. "Come with Edie. We'll bring your grandson out of here. We'll take him home where he can chase chickens and play with my cousin's boy."

Fox pulled out a length of rope.

"Wait." Perry edged closer. Old Rose smelled of bacon and bread. "Rose, Sir Richard murdered my mother, and my fa-father. Or, perhaps…does he have him upstairs, Rose?"

The old woman's face went impossibly pale. She looked like a mound of poked flour ready to crumble.

Perry touched an arm as soft as bread dough. "Does he, Rose? He'll murder him soon. And you're helping him."

"Has he killed him already, Rose?" Edie asked.

A chill rolled down Perry's back at the matter-of-fact tone. Was murder so common for these people?

Rose let out a breath. "If 'twere him, he was still alive when I took up the Squire's breakfast a bit ago. Had a man tied to a chair in the front parlor, the Squire did."

"Who else is in the house?" Fox asked.

"The Squire and some boys he has up from Scarborough."

"How many?"

"I don't know. None that I needed to feed."

"Take them and leave, Edie," Fox said.

"We'll wait in the storeroom," Edie said.

"No." Perry shook her head. "If things don't go right, he'll search there first."

Fox gave her shoulder a squeeze. "There's a man in the stable, tied up. If you trust him, take him along, also. Go through the copse and stay off the road."

OUTSIDE THE CLOSED PARLOR DOOR, THEY HEARD FAINT voices, one man talking, another croaking a response. Perry reached for the door latch, but Fox pulled her into his arms, keeping one eye on the deserted hall.

Kincaid's proposal to clear the upstairs first until the others joined them had been overruled, the ladies voting for urgency.

"Not yet," Fox whispered. Kincaid and Lady Jane needed time to get down the servant's corridor skirting the other side of the room and deal with anyone lurking there.

She frowned up at him, and he squeezed her shoulder. Fear and determination quaked in her. She wanted to get on with this and fight, and he needed just one more moment with her.

He cradled her head and pressed his lips to hers, trying to convey in as short a time as possible, as much love as possible. He kissed her until she stopped trembling, until a thread of annoyance crept into her gaze, and then he stepped back and nudged her away from the door.

Be damned if she was going to die today.

He turned the latch on the door.

Locked. Hell.

Perry went to her knees and began working. She was good at this task, much better than he was. Picking locks had never been a necessity for his kind of spying.

A shot rang out, muffled, and someone screamed. Perry's fingers slipped, the picks clanging as they fell. On the other side, a key scraped and the latch turned.

PERRY SNATCHED THE FALLEN PICKS AS SHE ROLLED AWAY AND shoved them back into her pocket, her skirts tangling. Air whooshed over her and the door crashed into something solid.

Fox had gone over her. She scrambled to her feet, pulling her pistol.

Inside, a melee had erupted. Fox rolled on the floor with a man, knives flashing as they held each other off, and Kincaid struggled with Sir Richard. A body lay stretched on the floor.

Panic rising, she finally spotted Lady Jane bent over an overturned chair with a man tied to it.

She ran to help.

"Stop wriggling, Shaldon," Lady Jane said.

"We'll get you out, Papa." Perry knelt and set the pistol down on a corner of worn carpet.

Father's arms came loose and he yanked at the rope

275

tying his ankles. The front of his shirt was sodden and dripping. "Go and lock the door, Perry," he wheezed. "Two more in the house. Cut these ties, Jane dear."

As she ran to the door, Fox took one valiant slash, his man falling and almost tripping her. Kincaid had Sir Richard against the wall, but the big Scotsman was injured, one of his arms a limp wing. Fox ran to help.

She threw all of her weight against the door, *snicking* it to, but the keyhole was empty. She scanned the surrounding floor.

There. By an overturned urn.

Perry scrambled for it and shoved the key in the lock. Lady Jane clutched Father with one hand and Kincaid with the other, the three of them stumbling toward the servant's door. Fox had Sir Richard by the scruff.

"We want him alive," Father called.

"Go," Fox called. "We're right behind you. Perry, go with them."

"In a minute." Before she could turn the key, the door opened, smacking her back, her head cracking against the wall. Stars flashed in her vision and she slid to the floor.

33

SIR RICHARD'S DRAWING ROOM

A dull ache drummed in the back of her head, rolling down to her neck. Perry opened her eyes and blinked, clearing her vision.

Her stomach rolled and bile rose. This dark chamber was Sir Richard's drawing room and...she looked down... she was seated in the same worn chair her father had vacated.

She wiggled her hands and her toes. Still working, and she wasn't bound.

A loud thwack pulled her attention across the room and her blood roared.

"Stop that," she yelled.

Sir Richard turned.

The loud drumming in her head picked up, making her shake. Fox slumped in another chair, tied and gagged. Sir Richard stood by him, his shirt and hands bloodied.

"Awake are you, mishy?"

She remembered. She'd been about to lock the door when it slapped open and knocked her back.

He waved a hand and a short barrel of a man limped

from the corner. Only two bodies littered the floor and she recognized neither. Fox must have felled one of the new intruders, and this one was the only one to survive. Father and Jane and Kincaid must have escaped.

They would send help. She and Fox must stay alive.

Sir Richard approached and she stumbled to her feet, reaching into her pockets. Her pistols were gone. Her knife also. She'd left the pistol on the floor but she'd seen it in Father's hand when he left.

"Looking for the pishtol?" Sir Richard's eyes glittered. His mouth was twisted, his jaw swollen, and one eye blackened. Either Fox or Kincaid had done that damage, bless them. "Bringing pistols and knives into my home, Felicity?"

Her skin slithered and crawled. It wasn't pain making his eyes glitter, it was insanity.

Little bolts of panic sparked through her and her chest tightened. Battered or not, nothing was stronger than a madman, and the henchman looked hale. He'd escaped any knife, or bullet, or fist aimed at him.

And Fox couldn't help her, tied up as he was.

Perhaps they hadn't found the daggers in her boots. She wiggled her ankles. The warm steel still crowded them. She shoved her hand deeper into her pocket.

And she still had the picks she had scrabbled from the floor.

She opened her mouth and said "Perpetua," but it came out like a squawk.

"Frightened, are you?" Sir Richard's smile revealed bloody gums where a tooth had gone missing. "Cat got your tongue?"

Fox or Kincaid had done that. A laugh bubbled up in her, bringing bravado with it.

She cleared her throat. "I said, Perpetua."

His gaze traveled the walls behind her. "Oh, aye, Felicity and Perpetua."

"Yours is quite an unrestful manor, Sir Richard."

His eyes focused in on her, widened, darkened. A hand shot out to her neck. "Unrestful."

She leaned back, trying to contain the fear, mind reeling. Fox roared through his gag, and one of Sir Richard's eyes ticked.

She must distract him before he turned back on Fox. "Unhand me," she said calmly.

The muscles around his eyes worked. He was confused. He thought she was her mother, whom he had wanted. Perhaps she should use that against him.

She summoned the memory of her mother's calm tone. "Unhand me, please, Richard."

He took his hand away, looked at it, looked at her neck. "Felicity." There was disgust in his tone. "I've left blood on your fichu." He reached for the scrap of cloth.

"No." She tried to hang onto the scarf but he snatched it away and let it drop.

"What the devil?" He peered closer. "Who did this to you?"

You did. But I can't remind you of who I am now. "I…I bruise easily," she said.

His brows drew together. "No. Barely touched you. That's old. He did it. Who is he to you, Felicity?"

Her mind raced. Could she get to one of her blades in time? Or a pick?

The henchman pulled Fox's head up by his hair and she saw the fierce gleam in his eye. He still had fight in him.

"Unrestful," she said again, sternly. "How could you expect a woman to want to live in a house—"

"A lover." Sir Richard paced in front of Fox, who followed the Squire's movements with his eyes.

Perry slumped forward in the chair, and none of the men noticed. She moved a hand under her skirt and slipped out the razor sharp *sgian dubh*.

She slid it into her pocket, praying it wouldn't cut through the stitching or cloth before she could use it on one of these villains.

"Leave that man alone," she said.

He jerked around to look at her, mouth firmed. "Well, it doesn't matter. Untie his feet. We'll settle this."

Prickles raced down her arms and legs. "Just let that man go. He's nothing to me, and he's no bother to you."

"No bother, eh? Killed two of my men, here. And you coming in with him. And..." He drew his brows together again and shook his head. "Shaldon."

He leveled a steady gaze at her and she could see the moment the fog in his head cleared. A laugh rumbled up inside him. She eased herself up, flexing her hands and stiffening her back. Alone, she would run. But she wouldn't leave Fox. She had to delay whatever Sir Richard planned. The others would come for them.

Keep him talking. "What is your quarrel with Lord Shaldon?" she asked.

"He took what was mine."

She saw Fox's head move in the smallest of shakes.

"Gorse Cottage?" she asked.

The Squire's laugh was nasty. "Not even a fare-thee-well. Didn't even waltz in for a courtship. Brother died, and he swooped her up with the title. Bloody greedy bastard. All arranged by letters until the wedding itself. Busy saving the country, the great man."

"Why did...why did you hurt Felicity?"

"Hurt her?" He smashed a fist on the table. "Left her alone, I did, her and her spawn. Never wanted to hurt Felicity. She just wouldn't...she just wouldn't come. Wanted the title, she did. But John Black had ways."

"Ways? What ways?"

He glanced at the door to the servants' exit. "I've a whole army outside, enough for a beaten ox, an old woman, and a jackanapes who'll collapse any moment from the tea I fed him."

Her heart raced. "He spat it out."

"There'll be enough to sicken him and make it easy for my men." He strolled closer, lifted her chin, studying her neck, and grunted. "Never send a Frenchie to do an Englishman's work." He nodded to his henchman.

The man raised his hand, steel glinting.

"Wait," Perry screamed. "*Fox*."

"Hold there."

The henchman stepped away at Sir Richard's command.

"Fox, you said?" He went back to study Fox's face.

Perry gripped the hilt of the dagger.

"Fox." Sir Richard laughed. "Well, well. I knew Goodfellow was not your real name, but I had no idea..." His head jerked up and he eyed Perry. "Alone at the cottage, were you? Aye." He jabbed a thumb at his man. "His feet. I said untie them."

The bloody hand clamped on her upper arm. There'd be another bruise there that Sir Richard would pay for.

281

34
A SOMBER TRUTH

*P*erry.

Her stifled *oof* on the stair behind him made his gut clench, and her name had come out muffled. Dear God, he couldn't even reach to help her. He couldn't strike out at Sir Richard. He had a foot free to kick but he might hit Perry by mistake.

His captor wrenched his arm, and all but dragged him down a corridor. Mildew and dust clogged his nose, and between that and his rage, and the damned gag, he struggled for breath. He'd settle up with this lump when he was done with the one grasping Perry.

Shaldon might want Sir Richard alive so he could pick through the schemes that tied the two men together. Shaldon might want to fight on, but maybe this score should be Shaldon's last. For Perry's sake.

Let this be done. He'd find his chance—a shard of broken glass, a razor laid out. He'd get out of these cords. He'd got out of worse before in bloody France.

Up one flight. Past one, two, three doors to a massive door on their right, this one oiled and dusted. Sweat crawled over his skin, and his jaw locked around the filth of the rag gagging him.

Being taken to the master's bedchamber could not be a good omen for Perry.

His captor stood only as high as Fox's shoulder, and walked with a rolling, side-to-side gait. He was thin-necked but thick in the chest. A sailor, Fox guessed, from the tail of an inking that curled up his neck, and a scar that reached under his chin. He'd have taken the lash, this one. A hired hand, and not a local free-trader either, unless he'd run off to sea for a spell.

His tongue stuck on the gag. Hell, he couldn't even gobble the words to offer the man better wages to turn him before the rest of their company came.

They shuffled into a dingy room smelling of brandy and piss, and something worse. Mostly something worse, because Harv wasn't here anymore to lick the Squire's chamber pot.

Sir Richard closed the door and a lock *snicked*. He left Perry and went to the window, pulling back drapes. The sun had come out, and the midday light streaming in sparkled with dust motes.

Perry sidled closer, her jaw clamped tight, her hands buried in her skirts. The weapons were gone, they'd said, but she still had the ones he'd slipped into her boots. Maybe.

He caught her eye and nodded. If not, he'd think of something. That tumbler there would shatter just fine into sharp shards.

Sir Richard turned away from the window, his square face molded into a dour frown and punctuated by bruises and blotches of blood. The Baronet had found the injury in Kincaid's left side and pushed that advantage. But even stung by his injury the night before, Kincaid was a master of the right hook, on or off balance.

Fox followed Perry's line of sight and his hands curled into fists inside their bindings. The great four-poster bed was heaped with mangled linens.

"Light that brace," Sir Richard barked to his man.

Fox's captor growled low and went to the mantel.

Fox shuffled closer to Perry. She leaned her head onto his shoulder and angled her breast into his arm.

A fine, smooth, object slipped awkwardly into his palm. He fumbled, almost dropped it, and she steadied his grip.

"Don't worry," she breathed and her hands went to work untying his gag, tossing the foul thing to the floor.

"That's right," Sir Richard said. "Let him shpeak. We'll hear what he hash to shay." He shrugged out of his coat, barely wincing, Fox noted. The man was as much of an ox as Kincaid. No doubt Kincaid had landed a few blows to that chest, but there was no sign he'd cracked a rib.

Perry poked at him and turned around standing directly in front of him. She'd positioned him in a dark corner. He leaned his shoulders against the wall and began to saw at his bindings.

"Take off your gown," Sir Richard said.

"What?" Perry squeaked. "What are you talking about?"

"Take off your gown. You're going to give me what Felicity wouldn't. And then you'll marry me and give me Gorse Cottage and your ten thousand pounds a year."

"Ten thousand pounds?" she croaked. "How could you possibly know—"

"Oh, come. Everyone knows. Take off your gown."

"I'll not do it. My father will kill you first."

"I'll kill you first," Fox said.

"Your father will be dead. And so will you be, *Mr.* Fox." He advanced on Perry, and she backed away.

Fox sawed frantically. She was leading the Squire away from him.

His man was still struggling with the tinderbox, finally catching a spark.

"Have you forgotten?" Fox asked. "She has three brothers, Fenwick."

"Yesh, three brothers. A puffed up bashtard, an heir with his head up every horse's ash, and another chasing skirts. Won't matter once we are married. They'll do the right thing to keep up appearances."

"You don't know my brothers," Perry said.

Blood rose in him. Her voice was strong. That was something. He sawed furiously, felt a line loosen and then nicked himself. *Shit.*

"Three brothers," he said. "One for each squirely ball and the squirely prick."

A snigger came from the servant. Sir Richard advanced on Perry and grabbed the shoulders of her gown, ripping them. The gown pulled apart and he tore at her shift, revealing her breasts.

The lamplighter stopped to stare, and the Squire laughed.

"Look away. Mayhap I'll let you have her too." He swung a glare to Fox. "And you can watch."

Fox pushed himself straight and wrestled his shoulders, holding on to the fragments of rope. Almost there, but not far enough along to risk giving himself away.

Fenwick pushed her onto the bed, and she flopped back and then sat up, clutching the sides of her shift with one hand. Her other hand jabbed into her skirts.

She had something else hidden away. If he could see her move, Fenwick would also.

Blast this rope. He turned the knife and worked it. This sailor had tied a fine knot.

"There'll be blood," she said. "I'm having my courses."

The squire paused. "You're lying. Ladies lie about and moan when they're bleeding."

"Nonsense," she said. "You don't know any true ladies."

"Well, it won't matter. Never been scared of a lady's blood. "He waved his minion over and grabbed the brace of candles. "Took you long enough, you fool. Here now, *Mr. Fox*, I've something of interest to show you." He skirted past Perry and lifted the light.

Fox's heart almost stopped.

The painting, Felicity and Perpetua, hung over Fenwick's bed. He almost dropped the knife, but made himself keep going, sawing as if he were carving through the heaviest wood.

Perry hopped off the bed, rearranged her dress, and backed toward Fox. "You stole it," she said. "You killed my mother for the painting."

The sharp blade broke through the last binding. He flexed his arms. He was free, but he could feel the slick of blood on his arms.

"No," Sir Richard shook his head, and then threw back his head and laughed. "Offered it to me, she did. 'Here, take this', she said, 'and let us go.' A masterpiece it was. She'd sent a copy made by Mr. Fox to ransom her husband."

"Mother wouldn't have done that," Perry said.

"Aye. That duke wants him and so do I. Send a Frenchie. No blame to Sir Richard." He frowned. "Fucking frogs don't know how to finish anything, but I do. I killed your mother

286

because she betrayed me. To own a masterpiece like this was just a perk of the free trade."

"It's not a masterpiece," Fox said. "It's the copy I painted. I know the markings."

He laughed. "I know what's what."

Fenwick plopped the candelabra on the bedside table and swooped like lightning on Perry, throwing her down on the bed.

The fool of a henchman turned to watch. Fox sliced through the tat and the scar cleanly, and the man's garbled cry brought Fenwick round.

"Fenwick!" Perry shouted. She landed a kick squarely on the man's injured jaw. "Lord Shaldon lives," she shouted.

He grabbed her foot and wrenched it, and Fox drove the dagger into thick sinew.

Sir Richard writhed and threw Fox back, injured but not beaten. Perry landed another solid boot jab into his face and he howled. She spun off the bed, fumbling with her boot and another dagger flashed into view.

Fenwick raised his head, bleeding from one eye, cornered between the two blades.

"You failed, Fenwick," she shouted hoarsely. "Shaldon lives. You'll die."

"Do you want to do the honors, my love, or shall I?" Fox asked.

Voices outside drew their attention.

"Father wants you alive," she said, "and then you will hang."

Fenwick threw back his head and laughed. "Shaldon is dead. I've an army out there."

"Those are our men," Fox said.

He hoped.

287

Sir Richard's lip curled up. "Your dragoons are no match for hardened smugglers."

Doors slammed below, and footsteps pounded through the house.

"Maybe," Fox said. "And maybe we have some hardened smugglers on our side."

The bedchamber latch rattled and a fist hammered the door.

"We're in here," Perry yelled. She waggled her blade at the villain. "Care to wager, Sir Richard?"

There was no reply from the corridor, but Farnsworth would be too cagey to speak. Better to keep the villain nervous and guessing. Fox edged toward the door. The key was not in the lock.

"You bitch. I'd get away from the door if I were you, Goodfellow," Fenwick said. "Bound to catch splinters."

"We'll see." Fox nodded to Perry.

A connecting door hidden in the grimy wainscoting opened. Farnsworth and the MacEwens strolled in.

The MacEwens' stunned gazes glanced over Perry's nakedness and quickly away. Farnsworth had a rifle trained on the Squire.

Perry's knife hand trembled. Fox saw it, Farnsworth saw it. Fenwick would see it also.

The squire's lunge was his last-ditch attempt at survival. Perry tossed the knife and scrambled up higher on the bed.

And Farnsworth fired.

IN THE DRAWING ROOM OF GORSE COTTAGE, PERRY PULLED her dressing gown closed and took another sip of tea, watching the military surgeon the dragoon captain had brought in bind the cuts on Fox's arms.

The late summer day had slipped away behind rolling pillows of fog, casting shadows over this gathering.

Father lolled in an armchair, Lady Jane fussing over him, shushing his slurred interjections. Kinkaid was trussed up in a sling, but his free hand flew across a paper, and Farnsworth worked at another one. She and Fox would write their statements soon.

His gaze met hers and he smiled, and hope bloomed in her. After all that had happened, they still hadn't had time to talk about marriage.

"That should do it," the surgeon said. He was a brusque young fellow, quite handsome enough to give MacEwen a run for his money. Jenny had been very solicitous.

And Fox had insisted on being in the room when the surgeon had examined her injuries. Another incident that gave her hope.

She stood and went to Fox, turning his hands over to examine the bandages at his wrists. "Excellent work."

"You should rest, my lady," the surgeon said. "Let that bruise to your ribs heal."

She smiled at the young man. "Yes. Fox also needs rest, doesn't he?"

"Aye, my lady." The surgeon averted his eyes and began putting away his instruments.

Kincaid and Farnsworth set down their plumes. "Take your bed back, Fox," Farnsworth said. "We'll be in the stables with the MacEwens."

"Alive," Father said.

Father meant Sir Richard, who was locked in the stables in Scruggs's vacated quarters under a heavy guard.

A wave of nausea hit Father, and Lady Jane held a pan for him.

"Fenwick is next for the good bones's attention," Kincaid

said. "We've given him a large dose of his own laudanum. It'll keep him quiet until we decide what to do with him."

"There now," Farnsworth said, blotting his paper. "You'll all write your reports for us next."

"Shaldon will not be writing reports tonight," Jane said. "Farnsworth, help me get him to his bed, and then bring in an armchair from Lady Perry's room. I'll keep watch over him tonight."

"Will you, then, Jane?" Father's voice oozed a sensuality that drew everyone's attention.

Lady Jane colored deeply and clamped her lips tight.

The surgeon cleared his throat. "The effects should wear off by morning. If one of you will take me to the prisoner?"

"That will be me." Kincaid stood.

"You'll want to sleep, Lady Jane," Fox said. "I'll move Jenny's cot for you."

"Write those reports." Farnsworth hooked a hand under Shaldon's shoulder. "Come, Shaldon. Grab his other side, Jane."

When they were gone, Perry pulled a chair near to Fox's.

"It was a near thing, wasn't it?" she said, "But we're all alive."

"You should have let me kill the squire."

"The bullet will fester and kill him probably, not before Father has a chance at him. I hope his man with the bad breath was swept up by the dragoons."

Fox shook his head. "I killed him last night."

The gravity in his voice, the serious expression in his eyes, told her much. "Do I want to know the details?"

He flinched.

"I know I said I wanted to take my own revenge, but I don't think I have the stomach for killing."

She turned her head to the mantel where the painting

rested between a china shepherdess and a porcelain vase. The two figures, Perpetua and Felicity, gazed imploringly into eternity, two victims of a repression as horrifying as the Terror. "Which one is it truly, Fox? Mama surely would have lied to Sir Richard."

Fox went and took down the painting.

"Let's find out."

He tucked the painting under his arm, grasped her hand, and led her all the way upstairs to his bedchamber.

"Light that lamp and bring it here," he said.

While she managed the lamp, he grabbed for his tools, flipped the painting over, and carefully worked the canvas free of the framing. "I left a mark. The tiniest of marks."

"Because you were that good," she teased.

He grinned up at her.

"How confident of you."

He studied the edges, talking. He'd mimicked the colors and brush strokes. He knew Lopez de Arteaga's work, knew the Seville school. He'd seen it once in Mexico, before coming to England. The patina was worn, but the painting had suffered rough handling, so it might still be his.

Finally, he set the painting down and shook his head. "It's not my work."

"It never was your work, Fox. Your work has far more—"

"It's the real painting. It's the original."

Her heart fell. "She swapped them." Perry swallowed hard. *Oh, Mama.*

She reached for the painting. The canvas felt heavy in her hands.

Perpetua, the glowing noblewoman, knelt looking heavenward, while her darker-skinned maid, Felicity, joined her in prayer from her place in the shadows. In the ultimate sacrifice, saintly, loyal, Felicity had refused freedom, had surrendered herself to the Roman persecution.

Mama couldn't even give up this dark somber painting to save Father.

Or Fox.

She squeezed her eyes against the tears that welled. Fox had been trapped by his loyalty, by his love for her mother. He'd been used and almost killed by the French so many years ago, by Carvelle the month before, by Sir Richard today.

The painting slipped from her grip and his arms came around her.

HER HEART POUNDED SO FIERCELY, FOX COULD FEEL EACH beat, and her silent sobs rattled against him.

He'd accepted the likelihood of Lady Shaldon's betrayal years ago. It was all too fresh for Perry, but she would sooner or later, forgive her mother.

Perry pushed away from him and wiped her eyes. "I'm so very sorry, Fox." She sniffed and swiped at her nose. "How you must hate us."

"No. Never."

She sucked in a deep breath and winced.

"You need rest." He glanced at the bed. Farnsworth had at least made it up.

He led her to the bed but she stopped, digging in her heels.

"Fox." She took his hand and looked up at him. "I release you from any promises. I'm ashamed that I forced your hand after the comfort you gave me. It was wrong of me." She shook her head. "You don't want to marry. I won't be that selfish."

"You don't want to marry me?"

"Oh." She gasped. "More than anything." She blinked out tears. "You're right though. I don't care about the *ton*, but I also want Father's blessing."

He dropped to his knees and her eyes widened. "Then, Perpetua Everly, will you marry me? I'm confident your father has already come to terms with the idea."

"Oh," she said again. "May we live here? Or...do you want to return to America?"

She would miss her family if they did. And, he...well, he'd been gone from his home almost half his life.

"Home will be where you are, Perry." He got up, led her to the bed, and seated her there, then he pulled the knot loose on her belt. "Now are you going to say yes?"

"Oh." She pushed him back and climbed upon him, and he was lost.

EPILOGUE

ST. GEORGE'S CHURCH, TEN DAYS LATER

On this warm July morning, Perry stepped out of a carriage on the hand of her eldest brother, Bink Gibson.

"You've still time to escape," Bink whispered.

"She's getting married." Bakeley greeted them, dusting off his sleeve.

Since she and Fox had arrived in town, Bakeley had taken every opportunity to lecture her without mercy until Sirena took to following him around and tugging him away. Bakeley's coronation duties, helping to lug around the King's heavy train, had drained him, Sirena said, and Father's escapade had raised new fear in him. He was in no hurry to become the Earl of Shaldon.

Father climbed out of another carriage, and Bink went to gather his brood.

"Lady Perpetua." Father extended his arm. "You look lovely, my dear."

They'd barely had a chance to speak after the events at Gorse Cottage. Father had left as soon as he could sit a horse to return for the coronation, and Perry and Fox had followed a couple of days later.

Sirena said the laudanum had scrambled Father's brains a bit, for he was warmer, kinder. Or perhaps finally learning what happened to Mama—and what Mama had done—had changed him.

Or maybe he'd known all along about her switching the paintings. Betrayal was so common in his world.

"Bink," she called. "Go and make sure Fox is there."

He grinned and she turned back to the man at her side.

"Father, I want to know…everything."

"Everything?"

"Yes. I mean, these last few years, the man after Paulina, then Sirena's villainous cousin, and Gracie's cousin, Lady Kingsley…was Sir Richard involved with all of them?"

"Perry—"

"Was he?"

He sighed. "I don't know. He ran secrets, spies, back and forth, but much of what happens is compartmentalized. And these traitors worked each for his or her own personal gain."

"Are there more, Father?"

He opened his mouth and then closed it.

"There are always more, aren't there? But the war is over. Can you not step back and let someone else go after them?" She squeezed his arm. "I want to see you happy. And I want you to know my children."

"And I suppose the first one will be coming along soon."

"*Father.*" Heat bloomed in her cheeks. "I am marrying by license. It's been only two weeks since I arrived at Gorse Cottage."

"The groom says to hurry up," Bink called.

"Very well," Father said, "I shall think about stepping back, as you call it."

He led her up the steps too quickly and through the door. Fox stood at the altar wearing new coats, making her smile. He looked magnificent and ridiculous, and wonderful.

The walk down the aisle went far too slowly, and the rest was a blur, but afterward, the vicar took them back to the register. Fox signed first, and she paused over the page.

Joseph Adams Dudley

Good heavens. The Dudleys she didn't know about, but the Adams family included one American President and an ambassador to the Court of St. James.

And she wouldn't be Perpetua Fox at all. She laughed out loud.

Fox raised an eyebrow at her.

"You couldn't tell me this before?" she asked.

The Vicar cleared his throat. "My lady?"

Perry signed and walked out on the arm of her husband to rousing applause and a shower of grain.

"Where shall we go now, wife?" he asked.

"Home, husband. Wherever that may be."

She raised her chin and let him kiss her, for all of the world to see.

KINCAID MET SHALDON ON THE STEPS OF THE CHURCH AND watched the newly married couple climb into their carriage and pull away.

"Well, then," Shaldon said. "What news?"

Kincaid rubbed his jaw. "The painting is missing. And so is Lady Jane."

. . .

The End

IF YOU ENJOYED THIS STORY, PLEASE CONSIDER LEAVING A REVIEW *at Amazon or Goodreads*

A NOTE FROM THE AUTHOR

Though Lady Perry isn't a "son" of the Spy Lord, I thought she deserved her own story. I hope you've enjoyed it!

Writing this gave me the delightful opportunity to research smuggling during the era. There's quite a bit of interesting information on the topic to be found in books and the internet. One good site to look into, if you're interested, is "Smugglers' Britain" (www.smuggling.co.uk).

I also had a great deal of fun researching American painters of the era, especially those who traveled abroad, and how to proof gin. As usual, my characters and story are entirely fictional, and any historical errors are mine alone.

Many thanks go to editor Tessa Shapcott, and a special shout-out to Frankie Reviews, a Yorkshire lass and Facebook friend who suggested the name "Gaz" for one of the characters.

As ever, I'm grateful to my husband for his unfailing support and enduring patience.

I love hearing from readers! You can contact and follow me on Facebook, Twitter, Pinterest, and Goodreads, and at my website, https://AlinaKField.com. For special notices about sales and other news, please consider signing up for my newsletter at my website. I promise I won't spam you or sell your email address!

Best regards and happy reading!

ALSO BY ALINA K. FIELD

Sons of the Spy Lord Series

Marrying Mr. Gibson

Previously titled *The Bastard's Iberian Bride*

Paulette Heardwyn rushes to visit her dying guardian, set on learning the truth about her father. But the only man with answers takes his secrets to the grave, leaving her penniless—unless she marries his illegitimate son.

https://alinakfield.com/book/marrying-mr-gibson/

The Viscount's Seduction

Lady Sirena Hollister has lost everything, even her fey abilities. But when the fairies hand her a chance at a London Season, her schemes for revenge stir up an unknown enemy, and spark danger of a different sort, in the person of a handsome Viscount.

https://alinakfield.com/book/the-viscounts-seduction/

The Rogue's Last Scandal

Falling—literally—into the arms of the *ton*'s most outrageous rogue seems a risky path of escape, but Maria Graciela Kingsley y Romero has no other choice. Only England's greatest spy lord can help her, and he is not to be found—so his son will have to do!

https://alinakfield.com/book/rogues-last-scandal/

The Counterfeit Lady

Vowing she'll never submit to an arranged marriage, an earl's daughter bolts for the seaside cottage that will someday be hers. But she finds her quiet refuge occupied by the last man she ever wants to see—an American artist, who's also a thief. And quite possibly one of her father's spies.

https://alinakfield.com/book/the-counterfeit-lady/

Avenging the Earl's Lady

The long war is over, but honor requires vanquishing one last enemy, and the Earl of Shaldon has no time for romance. But when the lady he longs for interferes in his plot, and his enemy strikes at her, nothing else matters but avenging his lady.

https://alinakfield.com/book/avenging-the-earls-lady/

Novellas and Holiday Stories

The Marquess and the Midwife

Finalist, 2016 National Reader's Choice Award

Uncovering a lie drives a new marquess back from a self-imposed exile at Christmas to find the only woman he's ever loved. Finding her turns out to be easy, uncovering her stunning secrets, a bit harder. But winning her back will be the greatest challenge of all.

https://alinakfield.com/book/the-marquess-and-the-midwife/

A Leap Into Love

Can a gentleman be too charming?

The ladies of Upper Upton think so.

When the single ladies of the village conspire to teach their charmer a lesson that might bankrupt him, the town's loveliest young widow—who's sworn off marriage forever—steps up to warn him.

https://alinakfield.com/book/a-leap-into-love/

Liliana's Letter

The Matchmaker Meets the Matchbreaker

Liliana Ashford's future as a professional chaperone depends on her wealthy charge's successful marriage, but her own close encounter with a scoundrel years ago makes her determined to save the girl from the same kind of rogue.

https://alinakfield.com/book/lilianas-letter/

The Ghost of Deplored Hall

A sweet Halloween short story

It's her mother's last All Hallows' Eve.

When family, friends, and tenants gather, goblins, ghouls, and ghosts are banned from this All Hallows' Eve party.

Only, no one told the Ghost of Depford Hall!

https://alinakfield.com/book/ghost-depford-hall/

Courted by the Earl

previously titled *Bella's Band*

A 2015 RONE Award Finalist

Saddled with his brother's title and debts, nothing about this new life makes the Earl of Hackwell want to stay—until he meets a lady with a secret that can change everything.

https://alinakfield.com/book/courted-by-the-earl/

Rosalyn's Ring

2014 Book Buyer's Best Winner, Novella Category

Done with grieving her losses, a late nobleman's daughter has fallen into a tidy spinster's life in London. But when one snowy Christmas Eve, a young woman needs rescue, she seizes the chance to do good—and to recover a family heirloom that ought to be hers.

https://alinakfield.com/book/rosalyns-ring/

Haunting Miss Fenwick

Thrilled to finally have a permanent home, a Squire's daughter won't let a supernatural creature scare her away. While hunting the ghost she doesn't believe in, she stumbles upon a mysterious flesh and blood man who might be the key to all of her problems.

https://alinakfield.com/book/haunting-miss-fenwick/

Lady Twisden's Picture Perfect Match

Promised York's marriage mart and the hospitality of his cousin's doddering stepmother, Major August Kellborn is shocked to find that his fetching hostess is the one woman who stirs his heart.

https://alinakfield.com/book/lady-twisdens-picture-perfect-match/

Flowers for His Lady

Eleanor Gurnwood has only one goal in sight: to make this year's Christmas service beautiful for the parishioners of St. Tancred's—until the Christmas eve when a man from her past rides in on a white horse. https://alinakfield.com/book/flowers-for-his-lady/

Under the Champagne Moon

Homeless and living on the charity of her former guardian, Fleur Hardouin's heart longs for Captain Gareth Ardleigh, whose kindness to her as a child she's never forgotten, but she needs an advantageous marriage.

Gareth has promised to find Fleur—on behalf of another man. Now he must choose between honoring a promise and trying to win the hand of the woman he loves.

https://alinakfield.com/book/under-the-champagne-moon/

The Upstart Christmas Brides Series

The Duke She Despised

Hiding her true identity, a young vicar's widow takes a position as housekeeper in a remote Scottish castle at Christmas for a new duke who years ago sabotaged her chance for happiness. She quickly falls for the duke's charming but not very competent factor, not knowing that he's hiding something also—he's the duke she despised!

https://alinakfield.com/book/the-duke-she-despised/

Convincing the Countess

A penniless widowed countess with trade in her blood descends upon the country manor of her sons' negligent guardian, intent on confronting him about her boys' futures. Instead, she finds his younger brother, a business-minded aristocrat with a penchant for widows and a distaste for emotional entanglements. A man who once witnessed her greatest humiliation. A man offering enticing distractions that threaten to derail all her plans.

https://alinakfield.com/book/convincing-the-countess/

The Impetuous Heiress

Before dashing Lord Loughton can make amends with his neglected fiancée, the lady's meddling cousin delivers her to his doorstep. He soon realizes more is amiss than his carelessness. Can he uncover her secrets and win her back before he loses her altogether?

https://alinakfield.com/book/the-impetuous-heiress/

The Nabob's Designing Daughter

Ripped from his prestigious London practice to deliver a Highland duke's heir, a young doctor finds there are more snares awaiting than a risky birth, including a surprise—and worthless—bequest. There's also his best friend's cousin, who's blossomed from mousey to heart-stirringly beautiful, with enough wiles to convince an ambitious man that his heart belongs in the Highlands.

https://alinakfield.com/book/the-nabobs-designing-daughter/

The Earl's Scottish Hoyden

Coerced by her brother to spend an English Christmas at the country estate of the handsome but cold earl who all but jilted her a year earlier, Edme Beecham is determined to do no more than assist her brother in his business negotiations with the earl, and by all means, to protect her heart.

https://alinakfield.com/book/the-earls-scottish-hoyden/

The Macbeth Series

Fated Hearts

A Love After All Retelling of the Scottish Play

A Scottish Baron returning from two decades at war meets the wife he divorced and the daughter he disavowed before she was born, only to learn that everything he'd believed was a lie. Determined to win back the only woman he's ever loved he must first face the viper who drove them apart.

https://alinakfield.com/book/fated-hearts/

The Comtesse of Midnight

A Scottish Earl on a quest for the elusive Comtesse de Fontenay, rescues a French lady smuggler during a devastating storm, taking shelter with her. As the stormy night drags on, he suspects she knows the lady he's seeking, the lady who holds the secret to his identity.

https://alinakfield.com/book/the-comtesse-of-midnight/

Claims of the Heart

Since a perilous fall, Lucie Macbeth has been seeing more than a settled future as the heiress to a Scottish barony. The visions plaguing her include a man—one far above her class and breeding, and English to boot. He's engaged to a duke's granddaughter as well, and thus wholly inappropriate. Though she can't marry him, and she won't become any man's leman, when the Sight warns her of danger to him, her conscience, and her heart tell her she can't walk away.

https://alinakfield.com/book/claims-of-the-heart/